THE CIVILIZATION OF NATURE:

ALTERATIONS

AND MUTATIONS

Book 3 of the Starlight Series

I0684891

By: SCOTT NEALE

Word Widget

Copyright © 2017 Scott Neale
All Rights Reserved

A Word Widget Press publication

Print edition: 2017

ISBN: 978-0-9914033-5-6

For information regarding upcoming books in this series, author information, and blog, visit http://www.scottneale.com

1

"I am standing at the site where an exciting new construction program has begun. This is a program that will help to maintain the power our wonderful Alliance has in outer space.

For some time, the Alliance Star Fleet and Star Patrol has been for the most part, self-sufficient... producing everything it needs from salvaging materials from the moon and converting them on the huge star base orbiting our planet. Our glorious leader, the Supreme Commander has wanted to send more materials, troop replacements, and equipment to our brave space crews up there...but to date, with only limited launch capabilities, there was only a small amount of help that could be sent at any one time. As you may know, with the ionization of the atmosphere, it has become impossible for us to launch or fly any of our ion based star ships in the atmosphere...and our mighty space battle fleet uses ion based engines to provide lift and speed. So, because of this, we could not use our modern ships on roundtrips between earth and outer space. The only ships that could make the journey are chemical propelled rocket craft...thus, because of the prep time required for chemical rockets, trips have been limited.

This week, the project to change that begins, as construction has started on a new space port. I am standing here at the site of this new facility, in sector 15, the former site of Denver Colorado. Today, we will witness the groundbreaking events of this exciting new project. When completed, this space port will have over a hundred new underground launch bays. With this new base, we will once again be able to equip our brave space forces by using hybrid fusion-chemical booster rockets. This will allow us to send our brave men and women into space once again, to protect our motherland and the skies above us.

Yes, this is an exciting time in our history and we will be there to show you all of the exciting construction highlights. For Alliance News Network, I am Connie Dahlia."

He had been lied to, and had taught those lies to others. But now he was going to expose the lies and discredit the people who fabricated them. He was going to change history – that is, if only he can find the evidence. Simon Piccolo felt that he had reached the end of the treasure hunt. He had been chasing hints and leads for two years while roaming in the shifting sands of the death zones, and now he felt the end was near.

It was a hot day out in the death zone, but then everyday was hot outside the city domes. He looked at the heads-up display in his protective suit – temperature 189 degrees, and radiation at 280 REMs *"Wow, this is a particularly nasty area!"*

Simon stood at what remained of a military site. He was here to find historical documents – the documents that would give him the missing piece of history he had been searching for. He lied when he told the security agents that he thought there was valuable information supporting the decision to launch the bombs all those many years ago. Simon knew that had he told the truth, they would have stopped him, and removed the evidence themselves. A secret was out in this wasteland that would expose the lies and deceits. Deceptions that nearly caused the destruction of the planet, and that had almost lead to the end of the civilization of man.

Now he felt he was at the end of the trail. He knew today he was going to find the reason for his search. This desolate burning place was going to grant him his triumph. It was only a week ago, that he discovered the location of this ruined structure buried under the burning sands of this former military base. Inside the structure, still buried under the hot sand, his sensors detected a large metal box which he hoped was a safe. Based on his research, he had learned that if he could find this one safe, it would reveal the true intent of the bombings. He also hoped that it would reveal the events leading up to the rise to power of the Supreme Commander and of the Council.

Now, the answer was just minutes away from being discovered – at least he hoped. If he did not find what he was looking for, then the secret would forever be missing from the annals of history. This site was being torn apart to be rebuilt as a new space port. Launch ports were already being dug into the ground. Towers and blockhouses were in various phases of being constructed, and the last of the old ruins were scheduled for demolition. If he didn't find it today, then the secret would be destroyed with this old base.

Simon and his research assistant Malcolm Miter were working to get the protective tent set up around the ruin. This tent would give them a little more time in the harsh radioactive environment as it would provide their survival suits with extended operational time. He also hoped it would help to shield their activities from prying, Alliance eyes.

After the large silver tent had been erected, Simon walked around the structure. He looked down at the ground while he walked. He stopped, and looked down to find a small black box in the sand. He stared at the small box with a puzzled look. He then looked around, and picked up a nearby rock. He bounced the rock up and down in his hand, as he judged its weight. He then gently placed the rock on the top of the small box.

"Launcher?" Malcolm asked.

Simon nodded. "Yep, launcher. They're as curious as we are..."

Simon walked around the tent for a few more minutes and found three other launcher boxes. He in similar manner, placed a rock on the top of each one. He hoped this would prevent the units from performing their assigned tasks.

When he deemed it safe, the pair entered the tent. Inside the protective tent, the temperature was much lower – 154 degrees, and radiation levels were half. Now armed with small hand shovels, they began to gently dig to uncover their treasure – the safe. It took them a bit to dig down deep enough, but they finally found it – it was square, only about two feet each direction. It had a single combination dial and a handle. On the top was written "Top Secret -- Property of the United States of America – To be opened only by Authorized Personnel."

"Keep your eyes behind us – just in case..." Simon quietly instructed.

"Right..."

Malcolm turned on a small display in his helmet to view a camera mounted at a hidden spot on the back of his protective suit. He slowly turned in every direction. "Not seeing anything..." he whispered over his intercom.

"Right..." Simon replied as he quietly attached a lock-pick device to the safe. He then activated the unit and allowed it to begin the process of unlocking the safe. The unit clicked and hummed as it unlatched the tumblers with magnetic pulses. Then the safe clicked – he turned the handle and slowly opened the door. He smiled when he peered inside the small safe to find a large stack of documents, all printed on metallic paper. Also inside the safe was a data disc. He looked at the papers then picked up and looked at the data disc. "Eureka!" he whispered "We hit the jackpot."

Interrupting Simon's moment of success, Malcom shouted "Shutterbug!"

Simon activated his rear camera and saw the threat. A few feet off the ground floated a small, one inch round device with a micro-lens recording circuit. The small robot was hovering using magnetic repulsion waves just outside one of the tent windows. A small blue light on its top was illuminated indicating its recording activity. As it peered into the windows of the protective tent – they could hear a small beep emanating from it. It was watching everything they were doing.

"Damn! I thought I had found all of the launchers!" Simon muttered as he tried to determine where the spy device was filming. He watched on his hidden camera and shuddered when he saw the device had floated into the tent and was trying to peer around their backs, trying to see their work. The device desperately tried to peer over their shoulders to see the contents of the safe. Fortunately for them – their large, protective suits were blocking the device's full view. It hovered around to the side of Malcolm, then to the opposite side of Simon.

"It can't be much longer, it has to die anytime now..." Simon whispered.

"Yes, but the Secret Service cannot be far behind if this Shutterbug is here. Someone nearby is controlling it" he replied.

Simon knew Malcolm was right. He was going to have to act quickly when given the chance. All he needed was to wait for the heat and radiation to kill the device. Simon knew that Shutterbugs were not meant for use outside the domes – but they must have placed all of the launchers just for their dig activity. He cursed himself for missing one of the small boxes. Simon wished now that it was hotter inside the tent, so it would die sooner.

After another minute, he got his wish as he saw the device start to waver – smoke drifted out of its venting, and finally he heard the clunk as the small device fell to the ground. He looked around and saw the robotic device, on the ground, smoldering. He peered through the tent opening and down the road to the rest of the construction site. In the distance he saw a Secret Service hopper approaching. He had to act quickly, he had to act now to protect the data disc – if he could.

Simon thought for a moment, wrapped the disc in a protective bag, and unlatched the seal on the left glove of his protective suit as he whispered "Man, this is going to hurt." Simon held his breath as he heard the hissing sound as the cool air escaped. A small alarm went off in his helmet.

Without thinking, he pulled the glove back and immediately felt the heat and radiation start to burn his skin. His hand started to sizzle and smoke as he pulled the glove farther off of his once protected hand. He moaned in pain as he felt the burning of a thousand hot radioactive needles searing the very skin off his hand. He grimaced but continued to pull the glove back just enough to allow him to slide the small data disc into the sleeve. As soon as the disc was securely tucked into the sleeve, he looked at the blackened skin on the top of his hand, moaned, pulled his glove back over his burning hand, and then reactivated the seal.

The pain in his hand was intense, and the cool air of the protective suit was not soothing the burn – the opposite was true, as the pain worsened with the cold. He would feel this pain for quite a while he feared. He closed his eyes for a moment, and concentrated on the disc and what historical information he knew he would find. He kept concentrating, and attempted to fight off the building pain. He thought about how the sacrifice to his hand was minor, compared to the valuable piece of Council history he was now guarding.

The pair heard the hopper land outside. They watched as two black-suited Secret Service agents stepped out, and walked toward their tent. The agent's protective suits were much lighter, tighter, and thinner than the bulky, heavy suits they were wearing. The masks and helmets were a matching black, which prevented Simon from making out the faces of the officers. They wore small packs on their backs which provided cool air to their

7

streamlined suits. He noted the suits had the stars and fist insignia of the Alliance of Northern Order embroidered on the left chest. Simon could tell their suits would allow them to pursue anyone with great speed – they would be able to catch the two of them with ease if they had to run. He had no intention of running from this pair however – since they each had quite large and formidable looking blaster side arms in their holsters.

They entered the tent and Simon noticed one of the agents wore rank insignia. The officer spoke to the pair. "So, I see you found something? What is it?"

Simon concealed his pain and with his good hand took some of the papers out of the safe and held it up to the agents. "It appears to be various orders and plans regarding the events of the night of the bombs" he told them. "This has great significance to further identify the events in our history."

"I will see those…" the officer ordered as he extended an outstretched hand. Simon gathered, then handed the officer all of the metallic papers that filled the safe. The pain in his hand was excruciating – he hoped his face was not giving away his suffering. He stood up and noted the pair of agents were actually much shorter than him. He looked down at the darkened helmets trying to see the faces behind the masks.

The officer perused through the stack of papers once, then a second time. He went through them a third time and began taking pages from the stack and handing them to the other agent. Finally, he handed Simon three pages out of the stack of over a hundred pages of the documents. "You may use these in your research. The rest are propaganda papers created by our Supreme Commander as deliberate falsehoods…these are not to be read or ever mentioned."

Simon looked at the three pages given to him with disgust. "Well, gee…thanks…" he muttered.

"Be glad we allow you to have those pages. It is not like we need someone thinking they can rewrite history, hmm?" the officer told him. He then snapped "Now, you are finished here – I do not see anything else that needs investigation, and we need to clear this area so the crews can continue with the construction. We have a new space port to build. Pack up, and be gone within the hour."

Without allowing time for any rebuttal, they turned, and walked back to their hopper. They opened the doors, got in, fired up the magnets and jets, and flew away.

Simon stood up and saluted them with the middle finger of his good hand. A shutterbug rose from below the window and started to beep as it began to image the pair. Simon's other fingers quickly rose up to join with his middle finger, and then he turned his palm outward, and then moved it back and forth in a waving motion. "Have a safe trip back!" he shouted. "Jeez… alright let's get out of here. Nothing else we can do here…" He looked at his burnt hand. "And I really need a med kit."

"Shit!" Malcolm decried "They took all that documentation…bastards. How could they do that to us after all of our work?"

"It's okay…I blame it on short-man syndrome. Let them think they stymied us…we have what we need."

2

"This reminder from your Department of Motherland Security...your computer use is a privilege, don't abuse it! When using your computer, remember it is constantly connected to our Alliance World-Net. This connection brings you every item of information available in the world...all at the command of your fingertips. However, there are unsavory types that will try to use YOUR privilege to help our enemy, the South...Don't let them! Report any observed abuse of your World-Net to any on-duty Secret Service soldier and protect our home. Remember, unity is power and enforcing the rules brings unity!"

Simon locked the apartment door and made sure it was securely locked. He checked the security VID system – no, there was no one in the hallway. He walked into the kitchen -- all quiet here. *"Hmm, a sandwich would be good."* He thought about it for a moment -- then decided against it, as he had more important things to do.

He walked into the large living room, and looked out from the floor to ceiling windows. His view stretched across the city all the way to the dome projectors. The projectors gave a soft pulsing glow as their beams protected the inhabitants beneath them. He paused a brief moment to enjoy the view – the people below looked like small insects as they scurried about in the open areas below his window. Hopper vehicles flew by in organized chaos along their designated flight paths. The flashing lights of Council approved advertising signs lit the skyline – all promoting the Alliance, the Council, and a host of their crony corporations. Moving his head back up to the level of his floor, he took one more look, and then quickly closed the privacy shutters. He peered up and down at the shutters until he was convinced no one could see through the tan-colored screens.

He moved into his office and once again stopped. He glanced around the room as he evaluated the area. He walked over to the large bookshelf and looked over every book on the shelf. He examined every book – looking behind each of them, and then moving the books into different positions and locations. If there was a spy device behind any of the books, he would have found it in this exercise. He walked over to the adjacent wall, and looked at his collection of 20th century weapons. On the wall was a .38 revolver, a military .45 caliber pistol, an Uzi and Mac 10 all displayed as historic artifacts. He checked around every artifact, inspecting each nook and cranny of the defunct weapons.

He then walked over to the desk, and examined his computer console. He looked at the computer and lightly bit his lip. He took one more look around the room, then reached down and activated the device. As it booted up his eyes once again darted around the room. His eyes met with that room's set of large windows – the shutters were still open. He jumped out of his chair, rushed over to the window, and quickly closed the shutters.

He heard the chime as his computer finished its boot up sequence. He walked around to the center of the room and looked at the large faux leather sofa just a few feet from the wall. He inspected the large seat – he shoved his hands between the cushions, and ran his fingers along every surface.

Finally, he went to the last wall he had not inspected, and looked at the ornate mirror hanging in the center. He peered at himself for a moment, then stared to turn away – but he then stopped, and turned once again back to the mirror. He put two of his fingers behind the mirror, moved it away from the wall, and then peered behind it. Having not found anything, he gently put the mirror back, turned, and walked to the bookshelf.

He stared at the books while he thought about how he began this quest -- it was all because of the books his parents gave to him prior to their deaths. Those books had sat on the bookshelf for years. Then one day, he finally built up the courage to open them. They were all on subjects dear to the three of them -- anthropology and history. His mother was the historian, and she kept such an enormous collection of history books. He never had a doubt where his love of history came from. His parents loved their books, and they loved him. Then one day they were taken from him. He never forgot the day the Secret Service dragged them off and left him to fend for himself. His parents taught him well however, as he not only survived, but became a success – they would have been proud of him if they were still alive to see how he had turned out and what he finally discovered.

After they took them from him, all he had to remind him of them were the books. He could never bring himself to read them until two years ago. For some reason, he finally became compelled to get the book of United States history off the shelf and thumbed through the pages. He chose that particular book because it was his mother's favorite. The day he picked up that book was the day his life changed. He reached up into the shelf and pulled down a book with the title "The History of a Great Country – Our United States" He opened the book, and once again found little scribbled notes throughout. Single words, such as "Lies" and "NO, not true" filled the various Alliance censored pages. He got to near the end and found an old tattered note – the note that started it all.

The note was written by a group called the "People Against War", and it told of a secret that needed to be told – but first it had to be found. The secret was well hidden and could only be found by someone with the knowledge, cunning, and resources to not only find, but to use this discovery. The note foretold that whoever found the secret would be forever changed. He was determined that he was to be that person.

The note then gave the first of many clues – the first one was from the Star Spangled Banner. "The rocket's red glare, the bombs bursting in air..." was the first small clue. Simon decided to immediately go in search of the meaning of the clue. He soon discovered that he was not the only one searching for this mystery. Some were searching to discover the truth – but there were others that were attempting to protect and hide the secret forever.

He travelled to the location of Fort McHenry where the song was written and found nothing except the competition – all willing to do anything to find the secret. Simon realized that this was not the correct place but just a dead end in the maze and moved on. Using numbers written in a scattered manner on the page where the note was located, he was able to determine the true meaning of the clue. Using the numbers as coordinates, he found an abandoned missile silo – this is where he found a key.

He turned the page and read some cryptic notes and markings made by his mother. Those notes gave Simon what he needed to continue, and to decipher the second part of the clue: "the bombs bursting in air". More numbers written in a pattern that only he would able to determine, were also included with the clue.

This clue led him to the center of the country where the South had exploded the first bomb over the center of the nation – in the hopes to destroy communications via electromagnetic pulse. Simon had determined the exact spot for maximum disruption of all electronic circuitry, and traveled there. As he predicted, he found a locked box that was opened by the key found in the silo. In this box the next clue was found – and the chase continued for the next year and a half – that is until the other day at the construction site. Now he was about to get the answer that had been the focal point of his life, and also had consumed the lives of many of his fellow historians.

He lightly shook his head, and then placed the book back onto the shelf. He then turned to the middle of the bookshelf. In the middle of the wall furnishing was a picture from the 20th century -- Munch's "The Scream". He pried it away from the wall and it swung open. Behind the painting was a security safe. He entered his private code into the locking mechanism, and it quietly clicked. He opened the door and removed the data disk he found at the dig site, along with a reader for the disk.

Leaving the safe door open, he turned and once again looked around the room. He turned back to the door and closed it – yes, he was sure he was alone and not being watched. The room was silent except for the slight hum of the computer console, and the clicking second hand of a 20th century mechanical clock that sat on his desk. He walked to the front of his desk, and faced to the back of the computer. He reached down and disconnected the network interface. In an electronic female voice, the console delivered a loud message:

"A World-Net connection defect has been detected. A technician will be contacted in five minutes if the cause has not been resolved. While your console is not connected to the World-Net, you are in violation of Council order 55-8-94-4 forbidding unmonitored computer activity. To prevent an unwarranted trial and prison sentence, you should now shut down your console until help arrives. Live wisely and by the rules. Long live the Supreme Commander and the Council of Order."

"Shit, I'm sick of those Council announcements!" he screamed out. He began to think that this work might someday help to change things for the better. Realizing his time constraint, he quickly ran around to the other side of the console, and sat down. He inserted the disk into the reader, and the reader into a computer input bus. He then activated a decoding program. His palms were sweating with anticipation, and he fidgeted as he waited for the disc reader to slowly interpret the data. He realized he was acting like when he was a little boy and he had just found his father's adult data disc for the first time. He felt he was once again that child who was about to sneak a peek at something forbidden – something that he knew he should not be looking at, but was going to anyway, and did not want to get caught. The program searched the disk and located a number of different types of files. It began decoding documents, and displaying the file names and type on the screen.

One was of particular interest to Simon – it was a list of names. He opened the file and looked over the names – he recognized all of the names on the list. At the top, there was former President O'Shay, Vice President Melroy and a vast number of others – all were in top positions in the government – that is up until their deaths. Next to the names, were actions taken. For O'Shay it said "brake failure", next to Melroy's name – "tainted medications". The list of names and incidents went on for page after page.

"My god, it all makes perfect sense..." Simon muttered.

The decoder program finished with another file that caught Simon's inspecting eye -- It was a video clip dated July 4th, 2029. "I have got to see this one" he whispered as he activated the video viewer.

On the video was the now Supreme Commander, Gregory Shrubway. He was at a table with four Generals – each General sitting two on each side with the President at the head. A Sergeant stood in the background standing guard. Simon noticed the Sergeant had a large blaster pistol in a side holster.

"Now is the time to strike and smite our enemies! Now is the time to take control of the world as is destined by our Lord and God..." The President told the Generals.

One of the Generals stood up. "Mister President, we believe you are no longer of full mental capabilities. I for one, will not assist you in this folly of destruction. I and the other Generals agree that you should go...you should be removed, and that we should take control of the government. Now, stand down."

The President smiled at the four Generals, he then spoke softly to them "Well, if you want to go against the will of God..." He nodded at the Sergeant who quickly took out his blaster and fired a quick shot to each General before they had a chance to react in self-defense. Four flashes lit up the video screen. When the flashes cleared, every one of the Generals were dead.

The President commanded to the Sergeant "Now, take the keys from him and remove the control box...I have the codes, we really didn't need them for that." The Sergeant took the keys out of the corpse's pocket, unlocked the chain connected between his now-lifeless hand and a briefcase, took the briefcase, and then handed it to the President. He opened the case, took out a red envelope, and entered the codes. The President gave a countdown and used his thumbprint to activate the launch sequence. Monitors on the wall showed smart bombs being launched from various locations.

"My god!" Simon shouted as he realized he had just witnessed the day the world completely changed. He had just watched the start of the war with the southern hemisphere.

"*A World-Net connection defect has been detected. A technician will be contacted in one minute if the cause has not been resolved. While your console is not connected to the World-Net, you are in violation of Council order 55-8-94-4 forbidding unmonitored computer activity. To prevent an unwarranted trial and prison sentence, you should now shut down your console until help arrives. Live wisely and by the rules. Long live the Supreme Commander and the Council of Order.*"

"Damn!" He immediately inserted a data crystal into the console, and copied the video and selected documents to the device. He then deactivated the decoding program, removed the data disc reader, and then the data crystal. He ran around to the back of the console, and with shaky hands plugged the clear fiber cable back into the computer.

"*World-net connection restored. Follow the rules and support our leaders. Long live the Supreme Commander and the Council of Order.*"

He grabbed his communication device and entered the code for Jenkins Nethim, President of the Pre-Council Historical Educator's Association. A bearded fat-faced man answered.

"Simon, what has you calling me at this time of night?"

"Hello Jenkins, I'm wondering when the next meeting is scheduled."

"Next Thursday, why?" he asked.

"I have something to present, something really important" he said with a slightly breathless voice.

"You finally found it, didn't you?" Jenkins replied, now he too showed excitement in his voice. Simon nodded in return. "We can definitely fit you in. I will arrange for confidentiality, also."

"Thank you my friend. This is what I have been trying to find all these years."

Jenkins fat cheeks turned red, and a large smile crossed his face. He couldn't hide his excitement. "I and the Association look forward to your lecture. Good night, my friend."

"Good night, and thanks" he said as he disconnected.

He looked to the ceiling, and smiled as he realized he had finally found it. Now all he had to do was survive until Thursday. A noise in the other room startled him back to reality. "Crap, what's out there?" The realization of the disc in his hand created a slight pang of panic in his mind. *They can't find this!*" His eyes darted around – he spotted the safe. He ran to the metal box, quickly opened the door, threw the disc, the reader, the crystal, and slung the door shut right as the office door opened.

"Simon?" A fluffy-haired blonde woman stuck her head around the door and into the room. She noticed Simon quickly closing the safe and moving the painting back into place. "What was that?"

He turned to find his girlfriend, Betsy Hallton as she stood at the door, smiling at him. She wore a tight, white vinyl skirt – which was extremely short, and showed off her long shapely alabaster legs. She also wore a matching top that showed off her large, artificially enhanced chest. Simon instantly remembered she had been working all day slinging artificial meat-food sandwiches at a local eatery. Her eyes were adorned in two shades of blue eye makeup applied in the latest style -- horizontal stripes. Her lips were full and bright red from the lipstick she wore.

He mentally beat himself up for forgetting she would be coming over after work. She gave his silence a bewildered look. He forced a smile then answered "Oh nothing dear, I was just...adjusting the painting." He hoped she did not see what he was actually doing.

"Oh...okay..." she said slightly confused. "Hey, want to go out to dinner? I'm starving!"

He sighed inside as he thought that perhaps she did not see, or did not care what he was doing. "Sure, what do you want?" he replied.

"Well...I really want to go somewhere where we might be able to get a glass of real wine! Can we please?" she pleaded.

He thought for a second then smiled at her. "Well, real wine is really expensive. But you know, that's a great idea! We need to celebrate anyway."

"Celebrate?" she asked with confusion. "Celebrate what?"

"I'll be speaking to the Association next week. I'm going be telling them something really big, and really important. It should propel me to the top of all historical professors. I might even become famous...if I'm lucky that is."

"Oh, how impressive! I always knew you were smart. I'm very lucky to have a boyfriend like you!" she shrieked with giddy. "Wait, I need to change..." she began to remove her clothes.

Simon's eyes opened wide as she stripped totally naked in front of him – there was no modesty whatsoever. She then turned, and ran into the bedroom. He started having second thoughts about that dinner he just promised, and he started to follow her into the bedroom. His mind was now set on an evening with her and the Pleasure-Matic. He had not even gotten to the office door however, when she returned from the bedroom dressed in a skin tight white plastic jumpsuit. "Okay, ready!" He was shocked how quickly she had changed. After a moment of slight mental disappointment, he walked up to her, smiled, and kissed her on the cheek. "Okay, let's go."

"This is so exciting...Will you tell me what your presentation is about, my sweet professor?" she pleaded.

"No...well...maybe...maybe just a hint after dinner...for sure next Thursday before I present. One thing I can say now...it will change the way you think of this world, forever."

3

Remember, terrorists are everywhere! Your wonderful Supreme Commander and the Council are waging a war against an enemy – your enemy – and they need your help in winning this war. If you see anyone suspicious, or performing acts of sedition against your Alliance, report them immediately to any Secret Service soldier. The South has spies and terrorists everywhere – it could be your neighbor, your teacher, or even your best friend! You never know when or where you will run into our enemy – so report them! It is the only way we can prevent the South from getting the upper hand on all of us. Remember, only you can make our Alliance safe. Unity is power!

"Don't worry sweetie, you'll knock 'em dead" Betsy whispered to Simon as he looked over his notes in preparation for his speech. The pair sat in the back of the banquet room waiting for Simon's big moment – the culmination of the years of research, diving into danger, and digging into the true history of the Supreme Commander and the Council.

Simon was visibly showing how nervous he was – sweat was dripping down his brow, and his hands were slightly shaking. Betsy took a napkin and wiped up the flowing drops. She looked at his wavy brown hair, and noticed a few strands out of place. She licked two of her fingers and wetted the troublesome hairs to lock them into place.

She then stroked his thin face with the back of her hand "There, all better. You look so handsome!" she told him.

Simon forced a smile to his face. "Thanks sweetie, this is such a big moment for me. Everything I have worked for...researched... has gone into what I am about to present."

She stroked his face again and smiled. "I'll be right here, so just look this way when you need a boost!"

"And with that, I have nothing to worry about! This will be a fantastic presentation..." he boasted.

She looked at the program "Pre-Council Historical Educator's Association." She looked up and around at all the historians sitting in the room. She wondered if they all would believe in what Simon was about to tell them. She wondered if all of these people could indeed accept the fact that Simon had discovered the truth about how the current government had been formed. She also felt a slight pang of guilt over what might become of his discovery.

The master of ceremony now approached the podium. It was the Jenkins Nethim. "I would like to continue the festivities this evening with a very special presentation by our esteemed colleague, Professor Simon Piccolo. He has come across some fascinating new information that will be of interest to everyone. I think you will be surprised… and shocked… by what he has found and it will definitely make you reconsider everything you have been teaching. I will also ask that the doors now be secured… from this point, no one may enter or leave. This will allow us to discuss the topic freely…without any secrets being leaked… our conversations will stay within this room. I will also ask that the staff once again do a sweep for listening devices." He waited for the nod from the staff security officer, and then said. "Yes, it's that serious. Now may I present our distinguished colleague, Professor Simon Piccolo!"

The applause was deafening to Betsy as Simon stood, and walked up to the podium. It appeared to her that he was now in a daze. He was greeted by Jenkins who after shaking his hand leaned back to the microphone. "I see our distinguished colleague is once again wearing one of his all too famous outfits. Tonight, just for us… I see he has concocted… a leafy collage, is it?"

Simon laughed nervously as he approached the podium, slightly embarrassed that Jenkins decided to note his latest outfit creation – a tight fitting, shiny white top, with holographic green leaves embossed on the front. The embossed leaves moved when viewed at different angles giving the appearance of looking through a tree filled forest on a breezy day. Betsy thought it was a good choice, considering his topic.

The room went silent as Simon cleared his throat. He adjusted the microphone upward to match his height, and then cleared his throat again. Betsy felt as nervous as her boyfriend. She knew that now was the time, his big moment – when he would reveal all of his research. She also knew this would probably be the most important moment of his life – it was also going to be the moment of his biggest downfall. With a pang of sadness, she looked around the room to see if she was being watched.

"Ok, as we say in our classrooms...let's review what we know so far. In 2024 the United States absorbed Iraq's elected government after defeating the Islamic State in the region. After Iraq was absorbed, our country's name was changed to the United States Alliance. We were told that this new...ALLIANCE...would create a deterrent to terrorist countries and organizations. This alliance would prevent any organization from using any U.S. Alliance territory as a terrorist base of operations."

"Then in 2025 President O'Shay, Vice President Melroy, and other top-level cabinet members began to die...all died by mysterious causes. It was rumored that terrorists were involved with the deaths...but of course, it was never proven. And thus, with a vote of Congress, the then Speaker of the House and former President, Gregory Shrubway was reappointed back into the position of President."

"Let's move up a few years... June 2027... the Treaty of Venice was signed. This treaty was an agreement by all countries stating that all Californium 252 bombs, the WMD of choice, would be eliminated. Russia and China joined with the Alliance to sign this treaty. Little did these two allied countries discover...that the current Alliance was STILL secretly building the bombs... as a matter of fact, the bombs were improved with smart technology. Now, they could seek out their targets after being launched from anywhere. When they discovered our deception, the two countries threatened to break the treaty if production did not stop."

"Hmm, yeah... that did a lot of good... as on July 4th, 2028, the first smart C-bombs were launched against the two former friends and superpowers. With the power of these new bombs, every major city in Russia and China were totally obliterated. At the same time, smart C-bombs were launched at Iran, France, Pakistan and India. Billions of people died at the turn of two keys, and within only a timespan of five minutes."

"Moving on to 2029...when the "Ultimatums of Liberty" were sent to all of the now-decimated countries. And what happened? The threat worked...as all of the countries in the northern hemisphere agreed to join the United States Alliance and follow the lead of our President. Then upon the complete agreement with Congress, the United States Alliance was reformed into the Alliance of Northern Order. The office of the President was disbanded and Shrubway became the Supreme Commander. He also formed the Council of Order at the same time."

"Finally, we have always taught that the countries of the southern hemisphere were evil, and did not agree with the ultimatums...thus, they were deserving, and because of that, were subjected to the eventual attack from the Alliance. When they did attack, the one thing the Supreme Commander or the Council did not anticipate... the South had the ability to thwart our attacks. To the Supreme Commander's dismay, the shield technology that our scientists had developed here in the north had been identically developed almost simultaneously in the south. Shrubway came close to executing every one of our brilliant minds in an effort to stop the leak of technology to the south. There has always been some debate as to those possible leaks of technology...but whatever happened, even the thought of a leak did nothing but raise the level of paranoia."

"In any case, the bombs were launched at Rio de Janerio and other major southern cities in a sneak attack. Fortunately for the South, they had that technology, as it rendered our bombs ineffective. After Shrubway's attempt at a sneak attack, the countries in the south formed the Southern Hemispheric Union... and we have been at war with them ever since. No... nobody lived happily ever after..."

Betsy watched as Simon measured the crowd, he took a long pause before he continued. "Three years ago, I was studying a cache of old historical books. In one of these books was a letter. This letter was signed the "People Against War" and told of a hidden agenda that was planned, and carried out by the Supreme Commander and his minions. The letter also stated that if I dug around old military sites I would find the proof of this plot. I'm happy to say that just a couple of weeks ago, I discovered the hidden proof of our true history."

The people in the crowd gave a loud gasp over his announcement. Betsy saw him give a slight smirk of confidence – she returned a smile to him which then turned to a slight frown as soon as he looked away. She softly said to him "You have their attention now, my Simon... unfortunately." She looked at the centerpiece on the table in front of her. It was a representation of the fall flowers that used to exist before the war. The flowers were arranged in a collage of gold, tan, and russet colors. In the center was a wire card holder with a plastic card. On the plastic card was the number five. She removed the card from the holder and looked at it. Once again, she looked around the room. She checked to make sure no one was watching. She opened her purse and dug through the bag until she found an identical card with the number five written on it. She took the card, and put it into place on the wire holder. She looked at the direction of the card then pressed an imbedded button built into the card. A small blue light flashed toward her indicating the circuitry in the card was active.

She took out a communication device, entered a code, and an image appeared. In the image was the podium with her dearest Simon giving his speech. She entered some codes into the device and then spoke. "You should be getting the image now." The device beeped two times. She bit her lip as a slight pang of guilt came to her heart. She felt an acid feeling as it started to swell in her gut.

Simon was still speaking. "Now, the first thing I found was a plan describing a detailed plot. This plot was devised to take advantage of a weakness in the U.S. Constitution. Up until this time, there had never been any previous consideration that, there would *ever* be a possibility of a former term limited President wanting, much less devising a plan to regain his former power."

Simon pressed a button on the podium, and activated a computer display behind him. On this display was an image of him holding a number of scorched but readable sheets of metallic paper and a data disc. "However, newly discovered historical documentation shows that such a plan was indeed devised...and acted upon by the now Supreme Commander Gregory Shrubway."

"Shrubway's first goal was to plant a number of his subordinates into positions throughout the three branches of government -- Justices, Senators, Representatives and even Cabinet members of the O'Shay administration were planted members of Shrubway's complex scheme. With this network of cronies in place, he ran for a House of Representatives seat in his southern home state...he won by a landslide. Now that he was in office, Shrubway used his now established network to gain the position of Speaker of the House. All was ready now... the plan was set to be implemented."

Betsy adjusted the place card as Simon switched the display to an image of a list of names in an electronic document. "In 2025 he initiated the well-developed plan...it began with the assassination of President O'Shay, then Vice President Melroy was also killed. This activity was followed up with the deaths of most of the major cabinet posts. The operation was carried out swiftly, and with stealth. Some were shot...some lost their lives in explosions. The President died in a car crash...others died in some very mysterious, and forever unexplained ways. No one knew who was ultimately responsible for these deaths until now. The list in the image behind me was discovered with a number of documents in a locked safe in the area formerly known as the city of Denver Colorado. I was barely able to smuggle these documents out...the Secret Service was always watching."

"In these documents, was an overview of the plan, and this list. This list shows the people who were assassinated, what order they were to die, and how they would die. This evidence proves without a doubt, that this was a well devised and orchestrated plan by Shrubway and his cabal."

Betsy heard the crowd start to grumble and voice complaints. They were starting to realize that they had been lied to, and fooled all these years. Simon was feeding them the food for thought that they needed to rethink their pre-programmed view of history. Simon now had a cocky smile on his face as he looked at her. He then took a drink, and cleared his throat. He waited until everyone had calmed down before he started to speak once again.

"Shrubway suggested that a terrorist cell had infiltrated the upper levels of government and suggested that the time was here for a leader who would deal with the killers. By using his established network, it was suggested that the Congress vote to appoint Shrubway back into the position of President. Shrubway gladly accepted his promotion back to the Presidency in a speech to both houses of Congress. His speech was all about returning with experience and the knowledge to get revenge on the terrorist organizations responsible for the assassinations. He also brought his former Vice President back to fill this now vacant position. Now in power, with his large network of loyal contacts in Congress, and the judicial branch... Shrubway was able to persuade the two bodies to modify Article 22 of the Constitution to give him unlimited terms... all under the guise of defeating the terrorists, and protecting the country. He also spoke to the populous to convince them that he was the only one who could do this task. By using his charisma, Shrubway convinced the major bulk of the population to follow his suggested plan. "

Once again, the crowd grumbled with disbelief. Simon took another sip of water before continuing. "With his power base now firmly established, Shrubway slowly began to manipulate Congress to erode the rights of every American. Spying on citizens became common place... surveillance a norm, and arrests of suspected terrorists became the fear of all citizens. The Secret Service became its own branch of the military service, performing any dirty task needed or requested by the President. The size of this branch dwarfed the other four branches of the military. This part of history we all knew; however, it should be remembered that his manipulation of the country was not going unnoticed. His then-allies, Russia and China noted the changes in the population being led by the returning president. They saw the rampant frenzy being whipped up via nationalism. Through their well-established spy network, they discovered that while in Congress, Shrubway had appropriated money to develop a secret anti-missile defense system despite the treaties of 2019 forbidding them. In addition, instead of decreasing the number of fission bombs, he had actually put billions of credits into the discovery of an efficient method to create vast sources of Californium 252. With a stockpile of this volatile element, he instructed the national scientific and industrial complex to create the first of many Californium bombs, which became known as C-Bombs. These new super weapons became the mainstay of the U.S. arsenal. "

He changed the display behind him to show an image of an early C-Bomb. "This was the super weapon that Shrubway had his technological community create. These were the weapons Shrubway used to conquer the northern hemisphere. I know this for a fact, because I have seen the historical image with my own eyes... and now you will too." The display changed at Simon's command to the grainy video he found on the data disc. Sounds of shock are voiced from throughout the room as realization of what they were viewing sunk into their minds. A tear came to Betsy's eye when she saw the start of the war that caused the historic destruction to her home planet.

After the video ended, Simon gave a moment for the images to sink deeply into the minds of the audience. "After the first round of bombs were launched, "Ultimatums of Liberty" were sent to all countries of the world to join with the United States Alliance or die. Caught unaware, almost every country in the northern hemisphere knew they would be destroyed – there was no defense against these new super weapons. They all agreed to join, and would follow the orders of the American President. To ensure his complete power base, the President along with his new Secret Service attacked and killed all but his most loyal members of Congress. In December of 2029 with the loyal members and supporters of his cabal, he formed a new order of government and named it the Council of Order. Shrubway took total control as the Supreme Leader."

He once again changed the display to show a map of the globe with vast dark red areas that stretched across enormous portions of all of the continents.

His voice cracked slightly due to the sadness and sorrow in his heart. "What was not considered, was the damage all of those bombs would do to the planet. When the bombs were used, radiation spread throughout the globe. People in remote locations were spared from the bombs, but killed by the radioactive cloud. Many plant and animal species were driven to extinction from the deadly floating cloud. Some species did survive, but were severely mutated. Oddly, some fauna and flora species somehow escaped totally unscathed. To this day, scientists are still trying to find out how they managed this survival. Luckily, the half-life of Californium is quite short – the 252 isotope used in C-bombs has an estimated half-life to be 2.6 years and the cloud dissipated quickly after an explosion."

"Outside of the areas of the cities protected by the particle shields, the landscape is barren and burnt. The shields are the only protection that the remaining cities have to protect against attack by both human warfare and the burning death zones created by the bombs. Man cannot live outside in the death zones

-- the lack of Ozone causes fatal sun burning and the radiation sears flesh within minutes unless environmental shells are worn. Some can survive for short periods of time when advance sunscreens are applied and by avoiding the super-heated hot zones."

"Even with this knowledge, some still try to go out on their own without protection to find a safe haven. These "extremists" are many times found somewhere inside a death zone, burned to a crisp. In many cases, their bodies are never found."

"If this wasn't enough, our bombing of the planet pissed off nature. Now, massive ion storms caused by the explosions circle the globe. Getting caught in one of these storms unprotected is fatal.

On a positive note... yes, I am not just Mr. Doom and Gloom... they have discovered that some death zones are starting to cool and recover, albeit slightly. In those places, we are starting to see some remnants of the recovery of nature. Scientists predict however that if the earth recovers it will likely take longer than man's time on this world. Thus, the shirt I wear tonight is in remembrance of the beauty of nature, and a somber note of what we have lost due to this missing part of history."

Betsy noticed that a tear had dripped from Simon's right eye. She knew he was visualizing what the Earth was like before the bombs, and the war. Behind him now appeared an image of a map of the current transportation system. "Travel between cities and other protected locations are now achieved by hopper vehicle or tube travelers. These are the only safe methods to leave a protected area and travel through a death zone. However, not even a hopper or tube traveler will provide adequate protection in the event of an ion storm. For this reason, all travel is monitored and timed to avoid these storms."

The display changed again and now showed two icons. Betsy recognized the first and largest to be the stars and fist symbol of the Alliance of Northern Order. The other was in the shape of Brazil on a background of a large star. She assumed it was the symbol of the Southern Hemispheric Union.

"Since the bombs failed due to the shielding, these weapons have been abandoned and instead the two hemispheres have returned to the former barbaric methods of warfare death... exploding bombs, ray and beamed weapons, and good old-fashioned hand to hand fighting. The battlegrounds have become the unfortunate countries in middle of the globe, the countries along the equator. These countries essentially are no more... they are waste lands... lands of burnt cinders."

"The Alliance of Northern Order and the Southern Hemispheric Union... the SHU... have been working on ways to create better weaponry and improving the armor to protect the soldier. Despite all of the two superpower's technical capabilities, there have been no further advances in any weapons that would give either side an advantage. It has been rumored however, that there is still research that may instead improve the actual soldier instead of his tools. This ground war has been continuous from its start in 2031 up until now -- 2058. There appears to be no end in sight for the end of this war."

Now on the screen was an image of a man that Betsy did not recognize. Simon pointed at the image while he continued. "Okay, so now you've heard my opening lecture for my first night of class... now something else that maybe you didn't know. I found this photo... on the disc. As you can see, this is the same face as the person we saw in the discovered video. Thus, this is the only time anyone outside the Council has seen the face of the Supreme Leader without his veil of shadows."

She watched Simon as he smiled at being able to shock them once again. At that moment, her communication device beeped. She answered the device and a shadowy figure appeared on the screen.

"We have all the information we need from the camera now. We wish to continue to monitor the situation in the room. Now is the time to perform your final task as ordered." She sternly looked into the camera of the device "You WILL do what you promised won't you? You will get my son from the Councilman like you told me you would, right?"

The face of the man on the screen became slightly clearer, enough for her to see a smile on his face. "Of course... you will get everything you deserve. I suggest you perform your final task and leave there now. The planned exit will be clear and open. I will contact you shortly regarding your reward." The man's smile turned to a snarling look of anger as he told her "Now do what I tell you!" The transmission ended suddenly with a slight indicator beep.

Betsy took out a mirror and checked her fluffy blonde hair and makeup. She then stood up, walked around the back of the room, then along the side wall to the stage. She then ducked behind the stage as Simon looked at her. He flashed her a smile, and a wink. She smiled back with as good of a convincing smile as she could muster. She felt horrible to be doing this to him, but she had no choice. He was still speaking and she slowed her parting steps as she approached the back stage exit.

Simon continued. "In this hemisphere, the Supreme Leader has purged the lands of anyone that might be a southern sympathizer. This includes anyone from Africa, Australia, South America, Central America, southern Asia or anyone of Hispanic or African descent. Even good, law abiding citizens have been thrown into death camps simply because they have a southern sir name or their skin color is too dark. Originally the Council set up internment camps as in the same manner that occurred in the war in with the Japanese in early 20th century. But later the camps were discarded and the prisoners sent to death camps to save money."

"With the latest scientific advances and medical breakthroughs, a human body can be repaired, or have parts replaced... thus allowing a person to live indefinitely. Unfortunately for the planet, these breakthroughs have allowed the Supreme Commander to continue to not only live, but to thrive physically. Thus, the Supreme Commander can provide the stimulation to keep this personal war going as long as he chooses. My personal opinion is that the human race will become extinct before our leaders decide that this war is pointless and futile. They will never make the right decision to end the conflict."

"I am angered that we have been lied to. I am angered that I have taught all of these lies for so many years. I hope you feel the same and can help me to eventually right the wrongs, and correct history. I thank you for your time...and will now take your questions, one at a time."

A standing ovation rose throughout the conference hall. After the applause calmed and the audience returned to their seats, a hand in the audience rose in a quick and stiff manner.

Simon noticed, and acknowledged the man in the dark room "Yes, you have a question?"

The man shouted "How do you suggest we correct the errors in history without being killed ourselves?"

Simon looked around as he thought about – then answered "This is our quandary. How do we change history? How do we do it so we do not become victims of our own untruths of history? How do we change what people currently think? How do we not appear to be southern sympathizers? These are questions I now hope you can help me answer."

Betsy had slowed down to finish listening to Simon's speech, but now she had arrived at the exit door. *"Couldn't you have just been a normal professor? Why did you have to question everything?"* With a tear in her eye she turned to her boyfriend and mouthed the words "I am so sorry my sweet Simon…" She began to push the exit door open, but then stopped, and turned back to look at Simon again. She then reached into her purse, and withdrew a small, black box. She opened the box, and released five small Shutterbug devices that immediately took to the air. With tears of guilt dripping down her made-up cheeks – Betsy turned away, and closed the exit door behind her.

4

"Need to get from one side of the motherland to the other? Then AllianceTram's Tube Traveler is for you. Our state of the art Traveler will get you where you need to go with comfort and ease. We have your comfort and safety in mind, with beam protected tracks for every mile you need to go. The smooth magnetic ride of the Traveler will also get you there rested, and at peace. And for a trip across the ocean, we have a protected water tube ready to get you from the poisoned coast to the red cliffs of Dover. Try an AllianceTram Tube Traveler today! Always remember to travel with your security pass and clearance ID at all times. Some citizen class restrictions apply. For citizens who can afford transport dues only please... discounts offered to our military and Blessed travelers. AllianceTram is not responsible for health hazards of excessive magnetic force exposure."

The Tube Traveler streaked across the death zone on its way to sector 15. Although it was called a tube, upon closer inspection, the Traveler did not move through a tube at all. The "tubes" were metal rings supported by ground based stands. Connecting the rings were steel bars that went from one ring to another in a spiral manner. On the Traveler were cables mounted on a rotating frame. These wires were spun in the opposite direction from the spiral wires on the tube. Solar generated electrical currents were sent through the wires – which when combined with the metal shell of the Traveler, formed a powerful electromagnet. When the magnetic force from the Traveler's wires hit the opposite magnetic force from the tube's wires, the Traveler would become suspended in the center of the tube. Then electricity was pulsed through the wires using computer control. The repelling magnetic forces pushed the Traveler, which allowed it to be propelled down the tube at great speeds. Because the Traveler was suspended on a rotating frame, the passengers inside were provided a smooth and speedy voyage. To protect the tubes against the forces of radiation, heat, and the ion storms that constantly roamed the planet – small protective beam projectors were attached to the tube supports. In the event of a storm, the projectors would increase their protective force field in an attempt to protect the tube as best possible. Although, sometimes the storm won out, requiring a quick repair job by transport crews. In the event of a major storm event, the transport would be rerouted to an underground "safe haven" bunker.

Simon stared out the window of the Tube Traveler as it shot across the barren and burned landscape. He noticed the pulsing glow from the numerous hot rocks still dotting the landscape. He was still amazed that after all these years there were still cinders burning out there. He had convinced himself that the Earth was refusing to heal itself. He always found himself in awe when he saw the destructive force of the bombs that still cause the planet to burn. Even after all these years, he could never believe his eyes when he looked over the devastation that was once a living and thriving valley. His thoughts were interrupted by the attention bell and stopping announcement.

"*Arriving at sector 15 city...the Traveler will be stopping momentarily. Live well, live proper, live by the rules of our great Council.*" with the announcement bell ringing again in conclusion. Simon slightly cringed at the announcement, then looked around hoping no one noticed.

He gathered his compression bag, stood up, and stretched his arms above his head. A long loud yawn escaped from his open mouth. It had been a long and successful day, and he was exhausted.

He looked at his reflection in the window – he admired today's shirt selection. "*It got rave reviews at the conference. Yes, a nice choice, but not as good as the old standby*" he admitted to himself. "Old standby" being his favorite shirt, and a trademark of his style -- a dark blue stretch top with holographic stars in the patterns of his favorite constellations as seen in the 1900's. Simon always liked to wear these outrageous tops as they got him noticed -- maybe not always in the best of ways, but his students always enjoyed what he wore. His classes would have betting pools as to what wild thing he would come up with every semester. He needed to come up with something for the upcoming semester as the next wager pool would be formed soon.

The Traveler came to a full stop, and the doors opened. Simon exited and got onto one of the personal people movers, and rode it until he arrived at his apartment building. He entered the building, rode the elevator to the 24th floor, and walked to his apartment door. He used his identi-key and opened the door.

"Betsy dear, are you here?" he called out. He glanced around but did not see her. He assumed that she had left the conference to go to work.

"Odd..." he thought "she is almost always home from work by now, and she is always predictable." Betsy was not the brightest star in the sky – if her intelligence was rated as the light intensity of the heavenly bodies, he assumed she would probably be a dark star. But she was young, pretty, and was fun to be with at times – so Simon kept seeing her. He looked down at the white flooring and noticed red spots. "Did she find the celebratory wine I bought, and drank it without me?"

He looked around his living room, then the bedroom. She was nowhere to be found. He called out for her again. He was getting both concerned and angry at this point. He wondered where she had gone off – he was hungry and wanted to go out to celebrate. He walked into his office. "Betsy?" he called out.

A voice answered him but it was definitely not Betsy's voice, unless she had had a sex transformation recently. "Hello Mister Piccolo" the voice calmly said.

Startled by the manly voice, he ran to the nearest wall and reached for the Uzi hanging there. Even though none of these weapons worked, he hoped this invader would not know that minor detail. There was a large man standing at the far wall, looking out the window. He was at least 6 feet 5 inches tall, and had a slight build. He wore a black uniform with a long black cape. The cape had a hood that partially covered his face.

"Please Mister Piccolo... do you really expect me to believe that weapon works?" The man chuckled as he questioned Simon's choice of protection. "Mister Piccolo, put the weapon down and have a seat. My name is Jared Mosley, and I am with the Secret Service."

Simon's heart sunk into his stomach, he now realized that somehow, they had found out about his research. The large man walked from the window and sat down in Simon's comfortable desk chair. He pulled the hood off of his head. His skin was pale and ghostly – Simon wondered if he was perhaps albino. There was a bead on a wire around his neck – pearl with the number 88 on it – he was Blessed. Jared rocked back and forth while he studied his prey – bright white eyes looked him up and down.

"Did Betsy contact you?" he finally asked the large man.

"Actually, yes in a way. We paid Betsy to keep an eye on you, and to let us know if you performed any acts of sedition -- which judging by your speech, you have now done. You do realize that your educational exemption from statements of counter culture does not cover speeches of sedition and anarchy against the Council don't you?"

Simon nodded in agreement -- he never thought the Council would move to cover up and silence him as an educator. "How can it be sedition if what I spoke of is the truth? I have proof after all..."

As he spoke, he looked across the room where his safe was located. However, where his safe once hung in the wall, was now only a molten puddle of steel steaming and sizzling on the floor. The painting covering the safe was burned to a crisp. All of his evidence was gone. His heart sunk into his stomach as he realized what a fool he had been. He did not think far enough to realize the treachery the Council would perform to silence dissenters.

Jared looked over at the site of the safe "I do not see anything in the way of proof." The man stood up and removed a pair of energy bracers from his belt then sighed in disgust. "Simon Piccolo, I am placing you under arrest for the crime of speaking sedition and of promoting terrorism. Please do not resist, or I will kill you."

Shocked, Simon shouted "Terrorism? How can giving a speech be terrorism?"

"You spoke lies about the Supreme Commander and the Council" he replied "You spoke of false reasoning regarding our struggle against our ultimate enemy, the southern hemisphere. Thus, you are inciting acts of terrorism. Now, please do not resist any further. I have a hopper waiting for us on the roof."

Simon sighed and held out his arms so the bracers could be placed around his wrists. They instantly crackled and glowed while they pulled his arms together. Jared took out his blaster and pointed it at Simon, then motioned him to walk ahead of him.

A cold chill of a thought came to Simon – he stopped, turned to his captor and asked "You know what I did and where. I hope you are only punishing me for this and not anyone else in the association."

Jared coolly smiled and said "Mister Piccolo, by giving that speech you involved every single person in that conference room, every educator is now involved. You have also involved anyone working in that hotel. We have already arrested every one of them, and they will be summarily punished...be it by prison time, torture... or death. Either way, you have more important things to be concerned with... your own life."

He motioned Simon to continue walking to the door of the apartment. As they approached the door he turned around and looked at his apartment – a tear came to his eye. He knew he would never see this place again. Somehow, despite this dark moment, Simon knew that somehow, he would find a way out of this mess. He always had in the past -- he was good at surviving and making things better when he had screwed up.

He looked at Jared. "So, what did Betsy get paid to turn me in? It had better have been a lot of credits."

Jared gave a pained look. "Ms. Hallton was going to be paid some credits, and be granted a special request for her service to the Order. My orders were then changed based on something in her past that could not be overlooked. However, I don't think that should be of concern to you now."

Confused by his answer, Simon shrugged his shoulders, and disregarded him further. They took the elevator to the roof and walked to the hopper waiting in the middle of the rooftop parking pad.

The hopper was one of the few methods of travel across a death zone. It was a luxury item for the rich, or those in government since they were quite expensive to purchase. The average hopper was very sleek and streamlined. They ranged in size from 2 to 8 doors. and would hold the same number of people as there were doors. There were hoppers that had a larger capacity, but those were only used for transport of large amounts of people, and had a history of being very unreliable due to weight versus lift problems.

The hopper used magnetic technology to create a repulsive force to lift the hopper off the ground. Once it was hovering, the hopper used fission jets to move the vehicle in the desired direction. From there the hopper would be navigated like a boat or spaceship – force moved the hopper forward, and an opposite force slowed or stopped the hopper when needed. Fission jets provided steering for the hopper by pointing the jet's force away from the desired direction, thus moving the hopper in the direction required. The hopper's controls were all computer controlled – thus, a simple movement of a stick or wheel would allow for driving of the hopper without significant training. This particular hopper was a New-Ford, and was reflective silver in color. It was a typical Government Issue type of vehicle.

The door was opened for Simon, and he entered and sat down inside the hopper. This hopper was a 6-door model, and he was seated in the middle section behind the driver. He started to look around, and was shocked when his eyes caught a glimpse of something covered under a blanket in the section behind him. He detected a few strands of blonde hair, and saw an arm exposed. The arm was covered in a white jumpsuit – the same jumpsuit used by meat food slingers. His hands trembled as he fearfully peered further into the back seat. He found what he had feared – the exposed hand was bloody and he realized it was Betsy's hand. Betsy had been executed.

"My god, you killed her..." he said out loud as the hopper stated to lift off.

"Yes..." Jared blandly said, then continued "unfortunately I was instructed not to be kind or gentle when I terminated her. She had made a Councilman very upset when she demanded to see her son...who is a Blessed one." Simon knew of the attempts of the Supreme Commander and the Council in their acts of selective breeding that created what they called the Blessed. This was their big attempt at creating a super race. "Even the mother of a Blessed does not have the power to push the father around... that is when he is a high-ranking government official... and thus the mistake that caused her ultimate fate. But don't worry, I am sure you will be joining her soon" Jared said with a cold tone in his voice. He then gave a weak chuckle, and asked Simon "We do need to make a stop at the corpse recycling plant. You don't mind do you, Mister Piccolo?"

Simon ignored his bad attempt at humor. Jared chuckled again, then moved the controls. The hopper with the helpless Simon trapped inside rose up, and flew away.

After flying for a few hours from town, Jared took the hopper in for a landing. Simon had been mindlessly staring out the window, but was now noticing the ground getting closer.

"Where are we?" Simon asked "I don't recognize any of the landmarks as being near a city dome"

"We have an ion storm coming... so, we need to stop and wait it out. I'll buy you dinner... how would that be Mister Piccolo?"

Jared actually had a small smile on his face. Simon assumed he was going to get a very large bonus, and perhaps a promotion for his arrest. As a matter of fact, he assumed he had no reason *not* to be happy and celebrate. He wanted nothing to do with this man's free meal – however he did find he was hungry despite his situation. He decided he might as well get something from this man who was surely going to have him executed or imprisoned. "Well, I might as well spend your money" he replied to his request.

Jared smiled "Yes, that's the spirit!" Simon was surprised to see this big man had any form of a personality.

The hopper landed at a small protection town in the middle of a death zone. These towns were built underground, and were constructed for the sole purpose of waypoints for hoppers and Tube Travelers during ion storms. These towns consisted of a refueling station, meal service automats, and rental sleep tubes. After landing, the hopper doors opened – instantly the bracers crackled and glowed as they locked his arms back into place. He could move them, but only a few inches in each direction.

"I set the bracers lower so you may eat" the agent said. "However, should you try anything I may turn the power up enough to crush your wrists. If that doesn't stop you, I will kill you flat out. Do you understand?"

Simon nodded to acknowledge the instruction, and the threat – he had no intention of putting up a fight.

The automat was a large room, very sterile looking, and everything was colored bright white. A typical style of any building owned and operated by the Council. There were tables and chairs set up throughout the entire room – all composed of stainless steel and white plastic composites. On the far wall from where they entered were the food preparation consoles.

"How about a nice steak?" Jared asked his prisoner.

"Sure...fine..." he replied absentmindedly.

Jared went to the console and punched in instructions, then waved his ideni-key as payment. Two plates appeared in slots below the device controls. He returned to the table with the plates and set a plate down in front of Simon. They had picked a table in the back of the automat -- Simon preferred to not be seen in this manner.

The "steaks" were actually synthesized protein with mottling and coloration to give the appearance of a T-bone steak. There were also synthesized flavoring, and even smells. But when one ate the steak, the true nature of the supplement became apparent – it was in no way anything that came from a cow. Cows disappeared after the war along with most farm animals. What animals were found after the initial attacks were sent into bunkers to supply fresh meat to the Council and to the war effort. Many of the remaining animals had been shipped out into space on the Starlight Space Ark. Thus, the rest of the populous was left with supplements for nourishment. It was adequate, but not enjoyable.

While he choked down his food, he looked at the large man sitting in front of him. "Jared, a name reserved for a Blessed?" The man looked up slightly and gave a small nod in acknowledgement. Simon noticed his hand was scarred -- he wondered where that damage came from. His gaze caught the attention of the agent who gave him an angry glare.

"It was a gift from the South, those people who your speech was protecting" the large man whispered.

"Wait, are you telling me you fought in the war? I thought that no Frogspawn ever fought on the front lines?"

Jared gave him a hateful look. "I will ignore that insult, since I am taking you in. However, since you asked, I did fight in the war for a brief time. I am one of the oldest of the Blessed. As a nobleman, I volunteered to help lead the fight in the war effort. My parents felt it would be good for one of our kind to lead the charge. I was injured in the battle for a village in Chihuahua. After that, they decided that the Blessed were meant to lead the troops as commanders...not soil themselves as foot soldiers."

"In other words, they decided that your kind did not make good fighters, and pulled them back. Use the Normals as cannon fodder, as you enjoy the back side of the battle in comfort."

"In other words, we were bred to be leaders. You Norms are meant to do our bidding. But I paid the price for you." He now had a cold, threatening tone to his voice. "Because of what they did to me, people like you cannot speak the kind of garbage as was in your speech. Because of them, your freedoms are gone. In an hour, we will be proceeding to the judicial complex...after that you will be tried, and convicted of terrorism...this, I am certain." He gave an evil toothy smile to Simon. "Enjoy your steak Mister Piccolo...for it will be your last."

Simon stopped eating and pushed his plate away. "You sure know how to wreck even a bad meal."

After Jared finished his meal, they returned to the hopper and sat in silence for the rest of the hour. Not a word was spoken by either of the two men – it was an uncomfortable silence. Simon just stared out the window to the blank rock walls of the cavern. The storm finally passed, Jared started the hopper, left the town, and continued north to the judicial complex.

This complex was also underground. It had been secured to prevent any attacks, and to thwart attempts at freeing its prisoners. The hopper entered through a concealed tunnel, and flew a mile underground to the landing site. As soon as the hopper landed, Simon was met by six guards. Each guard wore a white uniform that indicated they were part of the corps that protected the judicial branch of the government. Jared did not say a single word to him – he simply walked off as soon as he presented his prisoner to the guards.

Simon was led to a cell, which was empty except for a single chair in the middle of the small white room. He assumed this was an interrogation room, but no one ever came – no one spoke to him at all. After many hours, the six guards returned again. They did not speak a word, only motioned for him to follow. He was taken to a trial room. The room was dark except for the platform that he stood on, and the judge's podium high above him.

A bell sounded, the judge walked in, and sat at a seat behind the large podium. The judge was a large man who wore a black hood like an executioner. Simon had a bad feeling this was really not a trial at all.

The judge spoke in a digitally modified, growling voice while looking down at Simon. "Simon Louis Piccolo, you have been charged with sedition, and crimes of terrorism against the Order. I have seen the evidence of the speech given by you. How do you plead?"

Simon cleared his dry throat, and announced "Not-guilty, Your Honor."

A long moment passed for Simon until the judge replied "Very well, you have been found guilty of your crimes as charged."

Simon burst out "What? Don't I get to present my defense? Don't I get ANY form of trial?"

A shooting pain ignited throughout his body as the platform he stood on crackled with pulses of plasma energy. He could no longer speak as his nervous system had been completely disrupted. The judge looked down at him as he slowly spoke "I sentence you to imprisonment at the Kansas City Work Camp until such time you are declared dead. May our Supreme Commander, the Council of Order, and our lord and god bless you a quick and merciful death, Simon Piccolo."

The judge stood and stared down at Simon, his hands clutching the edge of the podium while he leaned against it to loom over his victim. Simon glanced up at the judge and noticed his hands were scarred. "*My god, this was a total set up! Jared was my accuser, judge, jury, and executioner!*"

The plasma was turned up again, and after a few seconds he passed out. While the plasma was still affecting his system, he was dragged, and thrown into a prison transport hopper. He would be at the rock mines even before his nervous system would begin working again. Simon Piccolo would never taste freedom as he currently knew it ever again.

5

"Have you felt that your body is just not as vital as it used to be? Well, maybe Body Replacement Company is for you! Come in and get a free, no pressure evaluation. If you wear it out, we can replace it. You name it...heart, lungs, knees, and nearly every joint in a Human body can be replaced with efficient lightweight titanium steel or advanced polymers. Not available for every class of citizen – as class restrictions apply, financial constraints apply. Patients need to know all facts before agreeing to replacement procedures. In some few cases, there is the possibility of rejection, improper installation, visible mutilation, possible future reliance on external machinery, and on rare occasion -- death. Talk to your physician before taking on any replacement regimen. Body Replacement Company is not responsible for any problems that may occur from accepting this type of treatment. Be sure to read all two hundred and forty-seven pages of the risks, dangers, and waiver of liability statement prior to signing your replacement agreement. So, stop by, or comm us, and find out what we can do for you – Body Replacement Company, the bionic experts!"

It had been months without a major breakthrough. Doctors Derrick Swanson and Stephanie Wilcox hovered over the genetic bonding device trying to figure out what caused the latest failure in their design. Derrick reached for a shop towel and wiped the sweat off his brow.

"It should work, the molecular intermix matrix is working perfectly, the molecules are inserted into our little virus critters and they are distributing the new DNA -- but we are still not getting the proper bonding." With frustration in his voice, he asked "What are we missing Stephanie?"

"We are so close" she replied "I'm sure it will just take another adjustment or two to find the proper sequencing. I think we have the matrix tuned properly at this point, so it must be in the process sequence. I will do some more work on our little carriers to make sure they are not the cause of the failures."

She spoke with confidence – Derrick detected this, and looked up from his work to see her smiling at him before she returned to her microscopic display. He thought she had a wonderful smile and it gave him hope that indeed he would figure this problem out.

With his large fingers, he disconnected, moved, and reconnected a few analog wires inside the device. He closed the lid on the device then returned to the computer panel. "Ok, I have readjusted the pattern forming buffers, and now will set the sequencing to match the buffers. I hope we have it this time." He manipulated the command sequence using the computer console, and rechecked his calculations on the display. After a few minutes he felt confident that he had everything correct. "Let's put a mouse into the test cage, and keep our fingers crossed!"

"Our subject…" she read the label on the cage, and then announced "is test subject 237. And he is a cute little thing." She blew a number of little kisses to the small animal in the cage before she took the mouse from the cage, and placed it into a plastic box on her workbench. She then took the box and placed it on the surgical table below the bonding device.

The bonding device was a large, conical-shaped machine. It consisted of a 3-foot large disk in the back, and then angled to a pointed tip on the front. The device's shell was a clear plastic material, and all of the internal electronics could be seen through the shell from the outside. There were many flashing lights on the inside to show the processing of information within the device. The tip was constructed of a glass-plastic hybrid material, which concentrated a beam that would be projected from the device to the test subject. The plastic in the tip was of a material that would stretch or contract as electricity and heat was applied or reduced -- thus changing the tip's shape to adjust the beam as needed during use. The entire cone-shaped device was mounted onto a wheeled floor stand that allowed it to be moved when needed for best beam coverage. Many large cables connected the bonding device to the various power supplies and computer controls throughout the room. The cables were attached to booms that kept the cabling out of the way while allowing the device to be moved easily if needed.

The room itself was a fairly standard lab for the institute. It was well lit, had a work bench on one side used for electronic parts assembly and other fabrication functions – this was Derrick's work area. The other side of the room housed a workbench with microscopic displays, life monitoring equipment, medicines, and other biological work supplies and was Stephanie's work area. In the middle of the room was the genetic bonding device on one side, and at the other side of the room, the control console for the device. Behind the control console was the interface to the massive super computer.

The computer – the Super Organic Array Parallel-processor, also known as SOAP and nicknamed "The Clean Machine" used bio-circuitry in a parallel configuration to form a synapse-style computer brain. The computer would actually learn from its mistakes, and was capable of some form of independent thought. This made it highly useful in the determination, breakdown, sequencing, and combining of DNA materials for the institute's various experiments. The computer itself took up many gigantic buildings throughout the crater that housed the institute.

The Institute for Medical and Defense Research was built within the walls of the former site of Crater Lake in Oregon. During the bombing, the lake that filled the crater was dried out by the intense heat of the explosions. With this giant crater now empty, it provided a perfect spot where research could be conducted in secret. A particle barrier, and satellite image scattering device had been installed to cover the crater. The institute was then built within the deep well of the crater, surrounded by the high walls. The institute consisted of a multitude of buildings that filled the crater. The supercomputer took up most of the crater with its massive organic parallel processor buildings, DNA storage matrix, and power generation plants.

One section of the institute housed the experimental subjects before they undergo testing. Another large section housed the subjects after experimentation. Both of these complexes ran deep into the ground with layer after layer of sleeping quarters in circular rings. The top layers contained the keeper staff housing, and security computer systems for the living quarter complex. The computer security system was housed in multiple layers for additional protection of the institute staff. In the center of these rings was a large open area that was used for recreation and exercise. In the center of these exercise areas were opaque roofs and flooring that allowed light to shine down into every exercise area of every layer of the living quarters.

On the opposite side of the crater from the experimental subject living quarters were the living quarters of the scientific staff. Next to this building were the scientific labs. The living quarters overlooked the complex and provided a quiet place to contemplate, and provide a productive after-work environment. All of the buildings were connected by underground tunnels, but most of the staff preferred to use the sidewalks outside.

Derrick Swanson was a molecular physics engineer. He had been at the institute for over a year, and was considered one of the foremost experts in molecular disintegration and reintegration. He had been the primary architect for the food processing integration machines used throughout the northern hemisphere. Now, the Alliance hoped his knowledge of the process of removing and returning the molecular bonds within substances would make this project a success – but so far all of his work had only met with frustration.

His father always told him he was built for manual labor – like a ditch digger. He proved him wrong by getting his degrees and instead worked with fine microcircuits. His green eyes currently were quite bloodshot as he had looked at way too many miniature circuits this day. His brown hair was a mess from him constantly running his hands through it in frustration. He had started to neglect his body as he had not seen the exercise parlor in quite a while – he had no time for those trivial time wasters. He was tired and needed rest badly, and it showed. *"Just one more test should do it..."*

Stephanie Wilcox was a bioengineer and genetic sequencing expert. She had worked for many years in the process of teaching the giant SOAP super computer the intricacies of human and animal DNA and gene sequences. She was also the authority in determining the medical requirements to manipulate a DNA molecule. In addition, she was the creator of a super strain of retro viruses that they had used to insert manipulated DNA into host subjects. She was not quite as tired, and not quite as nervous as her partner. She knew that they were close and they would figure out the error of their ways soon enough.

She was calm and collected in her thinking. She always acted in a professional manner and it showed in her appearance. She had developed some blemishes on her cheeks recently – perhaps from too many nights staring at a genetic code display while leaning on her hands. Today was no different as she stared at her monitor biting her plump pink lips in deep thought. Her work was currently her life, and nothing else really mattered. She felt that stress was the bane of progress, and should be avoided at all times. Derrick appreciated her attitude, and she always made him feel good about himself. She made a final check of the vital statistics of the test mouse in the box.

"Our subject is doing fine, doctor" she proudly announced "We can proceed when you are ready."

Derrick flipped a few virtual switches and entered a few computations into the computer console. "Okay" he said. "Let's take a few molecules from our test subject."

He activated the device above the mouse. The device lit up and began to emit a mild humming noise.

"Activating molecular sampling now" he shouted out.

He once again flipped more switches and a mild light emitted from the tip of the device onto the head of the mouse. The mouse noticed no change as a few DNA samples were removed from his brain. The device tracked the mouse and followed its every move – its precise beam pinpointed, and was locked into place for the entire experiment.

"Sample obtained and locked in the computer matrix" Stephanie announced over the hum of the machines.

"Okay, let's pick a donor and introduce the molecules for bonding."

Stephanie searched through a computer database and selected a suitable set of DNA strands. "Okay, test subject sample 556 will be our donor." Stephanie announced over the machine's hum "This mouse has improved brain functions over our current mouse. Now placing the sample into the bonding matrix."

The hum increased as the supercomputer began to draw power, and start its work analyzing the two DNA sequences. The computer worked for over an hour at making every theoretically-possible combination, then determined the final matching and combination of each segment of genetic material. When it had completed its final computations, the display indicated to Derrick that matching was completed.

"Okay, start the bonding sequence in the matrix please, Stephanie"

She typed commands into her console to instruct the supercomputer which DNA samples to take, and bond to the test subject's DNA. She pressed the command to initiate the bonding. The complex was filled with the loud wailing sound of SOAP, as it performed the billions of calculations, along with the sounds made as all of its fusion reactors were brought on-line to power all the massive circuits required to process the bonding. After a few minutes, the hum lowered to a mild level and the computer consoles indicated the bonding process was complete.

"Okay, we are ready to integrate and initiate mutation." Derrick announced "Keep your fingers crossed."

"I have my fingers AND toes crossed Derrick. Now inserting the DNA into the super bugs for transferal and mutation." She had a big smile glowing across her plain face. After a few more minutes of work by the massive machine, she yelled out over the loud whine of the computer "Okay, retro viruses are ready for insertion!"

Derrick returned the smile to his working partner, and he began entering the sequence of commands on his computer console. He continued to press virtual switches at the console until once again, the bonding device glowed and hummed. The beam emitted from the tip and hit the mouse once again in the head. After a few moments, the device shut down, and the lights turned to a dim glow as the computer shut down. The noise in the room went to an almost deafening quiet.

The mouse sat quietly for a few seconds. "Did we do it?" Stephanie asked with anticipation in her voice. Suddenly, the mouse began to violently convulse, and within seconds a noise is heard like that of a popcorn kernel exploding. The mouse's remains now covered the inside of the box. Nothing was left of the mouse, except for the mess.

"Damnit! What went wrong? That sequence should have worked!" Tears began to flow from his bloodshot eyes. He put his head down on the desktop of the control console. He began to mutter meaningless words about failure.

Stephanie jumped up, and ran to him. She placed her hands on him and rubbed his back and shoulders to comfort him. "He almost survived" she whispered in his ear. "I am sure it is something minor that we can adjust to make it work. You and I will do it Derrick, have faith please!"

Her soft voice, and massaging fingers on his back did calm him. He raised his head off the desktop, and looked at her. He felt he could melt into her arms if she would let him, but he knew this was just the heat of the moment – nothing else. She now massaged his shoulders – she could feel how tight he was wound, she knew he needed rest. She was worried if he didn't rest soon he would break down.

"Derrick, maybe we should call it a night?" she suggested.

He rubbed his forehead, and looked at the computer screen once again. "Maybe you're right... I AM tired."

Something on his monitor caught his eye. He started to watch the bonding sequence replay – he watched it repeat over and over. After he watched it repeat six times, he stopped it at a particular point in the replay. "Steph, look at this. Notice the mutation process occurring?" His voice was filled with excitement. He started the replay loop again.

She watched the replay a few times. "Yes, the mutation process has started... nothing unusual about that... I am not sure what..."

"Except..." he interrupted her "Notice WHEN this mutation is happening."

She looked at the time log for that frame "My god!" she gasped. "The mutation started before the bonding was completed! The viruses were still multiplying at the same moment that the tissue began to mutate. That could cause the reaction we witnessed. Is that what you were thinking also?"

He nodded his head in agreement "Yes, the mutation is happening before bonding is complete, thus throwing the entire process into a jumble, which is causing extraordinary mutation at an accelerated rate and boom! No more mouse."

She pondered the thought for a moment, then as if a light went on in her head, her eyes lit up before she shouted "A stasis field! That would place the subject in a suspended state, thus preventing the mutation process from occurring until we WANT it to occur. That should prevent the blow up and allow for normal mutation using the new DNA sequencing." She continued to ponder on her idea for a moment, then said "Yes, I'm sure that will work."

"How long can we keep a living creature in stasis though?"

She took a stylus pen out of her lab coat sketched a few notes onto a computer pad, then took the pen, and scratched her strawberry blonde hair while she thought about the question. "Mmmm, a mouse can take maybe 15 seconds of stasis... a human being much longer... maybe a minute."

He smiled. "That should be long enough. How long before we can test...?"

She patted him on the head "Only after you get some rest. Now scoot!" She pointed to the door. He gave a brief pouty-face, then obediently obeyed like a trained dog. He stood up, ran his fingers through his hair, looked at her – she was still pointing to the door, demanding his departure. He waved at her without saying a word, turned, and walked out of the lab to his quarters. Once there, and with the help of a medicinal aid, he got some needed sleep.

The next morning Derrick awoke early, and gulped down the quickest food he could find so he could arrive at the lab as soon as possible. But when he arrived, he discovered that Stephanie was not yet there. "Damn" he grumbled to himself "She is going to sleep in on purpose I bet...Well, there's plenty to do in the meantime...Much to prepare." He brought up the virtual computer console and began to enter his calculations and commands for the next experiment.

Stephanie arrived a half hour after Derrick. She laughed at his excitement over the possibility of success. "Well, I see a little sleep has given you a whole new outlook on life!" she proclaimed.

"Not just sleep, but the possibility of success" he replied.

She smiled at him. "Well, let's get to work then!" She sat down at her console, and activated the virtual desktop. She then ran through various files, and selected a test subject and a donor subject. She announced "Okay, I have both subjects selected."

She got out of her chair and walked to the racks of test subject mice. She went to a cage and grabbed one of the mice.

"Test subject..." she read the cage number "287." She then walked over and placed it into a plastic test module box. "Now, you live through this and I will get you a huge yummy piece of cheese" she said in a voice reserved for little children. She walked across the room and placed the box on the table below the device emitter. "Okay Derrick..." she said with a smile "We're ready to begin." She then began to enter computations into the computer console.

"Right..." Derrick announced. "Sequencing DNA sampling from our test subject mouse." He typed on the console and flipped virtual switches to sequence the process. The device lit up and began to hum. "Obtaining sample now" he said as he flipped switches to activate the device. The bonding device lit up brighter and hummed louder, and then emitted the beam out of the tip, and onto the head of the mouse. After a few seconds, the device stopped the beam, the hum faded, and lights lessened.

Derrick read the console "Okay Stephanie, the DNA is in the bonding matrix... we are ready to proceed."

Stephanie started to enter commands on her console. "Okay..." she said as she selected a donor subject "Let's try subject 556 again. I have a feeling our test mouse will appreciate that level of intelligence." More commands were entered on her console, and then the supercomputer activated the fusion reactors. The room, as well as the entire complex was filled with the loud hum of the computer working, and the power plants fulfilling the machines power needs, as it once again worked at completing its computations.

Like before, the reactors shut down, and the crater became quiet once again after the bonding computations were calculated. Then after a short while, the two DNA samples were bonded together, and were once again inserted into the retro viruses.

"Okay, we are ready to get it right this time Derrick" she said with confidence. "Activating the stasis field on your command." She prepared to press the command buttons on his request.

Derrick flipped more virtual switches and commands, then shouted out "Okay, in ten seconds activate stasis field. 10...9...8...7...6...5...4...3...2...1...now!" They both simultaneously flipped virtual switches. The mouse suddenly stopped all movement, as if it was frozen in time. The beam activated and emitted from the bonding device, transferring the manipulated retro viruses with the modified DNA to the mouse's brain.

"Only 10 seconds of safe stasis left, Derrick." Stephanie shouted.

Derrick began to sweat "Let's hope that is enough time." He pleaded with his computer console "Come on, bond faster... go viruses, go!"

"5 seconds, 4, 3, 2, 1..." she counted down. As she reached the count of one, the console indicated bonding is complete, and the device powered down.

"Kill the stasis field quickly!" he ordered.

When she flipped the switch to disable the field, the mild high-pitched noise of the stasis field went quiet, and the mouse began to move. Stephanie checked the vital statistics of the mouse. "Vitals are normal... so far, so good."

The mouse curiously moved around inside his plastic box. Derrick monitored the virtual display of the mouse's brain for activity. Thirty seconds seemed like an eternity to him, when suddenly he began to notice mutation activity. He watched as the mutation process began. "Come on baby, live through this..." he pleaded with the mouse in the box. "You have made it this far..." Another thirty seconds go by, and the mutation is occurring, but very slowly. "Should it be this slow, Stephanie?"

"It's very possible that performing the bonding in this manner may also slow the mutation process..." she answered, then continued "which has to be a good thing."

They waited for hours while they watched the progress. The mouse continued to live and the mutation continued in its brain. The hours turned into days – they kept watching and monitoring. They took turns between sleeping, eating, and watching – they formed a 24-hour vigil, constantly monitoring their test subject. Finally, after a week the mutation process stopped, without reason or warning.

Stephanie checked the virtual imaging of the mouse's brain. "Our little friend's brain has mutated fifty one percent, and the mutation percentage has not moved any further in hours. I think we should take a sample for testing."

Using the bonding device, they removed a single cell of the mouse's brain, and placed it into the molecular analyzer. As she looked at the image of the brain cell, Stephanie's blue eyes lit up, and a big smile graced her large pink lips. "I think we've done it Derrick!" She jumped up and down and began doing a happy dance.

"Is there a way we can prove the bonding really occurred? Not that I don't trust what we are seeing."

"Ohhh, always the skeptic" she scolded him. "Yes, I think there is a way to test the mouse for bonding success. Test subject 556 is very special. He was taught the pathway through a few special mazes. No other test mouse has been able to learn this. If our little friend did get a proper bonding and mutation, then he should be able to learn and navigate the maze."

He smiled. "Thanks, this will indeed prove the bonding worked."

She went to a nearby closet and brought out one of the special mazes. It was much more complex than most of the mazes used for standard mouse training. It had an entrance on one end, and an exit with food at the other end – but the twisting pattern of the corridors always made it very difficult for the mice to navigate. Stephanie put the mouse in the entrance corridor, a movable door blocked the mouse from entering until its human masters granted access.

"Okay, if this mouse indeed has gotten some of the brain functions of 556, then it should take no more than 60 seconds to navigate the maze, and find the food." She set a timer, and activated the release countdown for the entrance door.

When the timer reached zero, the entrance hatch flipped open, and then the timer reversed and began to count up from zero. The mouse looked at the door for a second without moving. This caused a brief panic amongst the two scientists – until the mouse smelled the cheese at the other end. To their surprise, the mouse zipped off into the maze. It ran quickly, as it made numerous twists and turns through the confusing set of corridors. The mouse made a few wrong moves, and hit dead ends a few times. However, after a short time, the mouse found the exit, and the food. The mouse began his well-deserved feast as the timer stopped at 185 seconds.

"Well, not as fast or as efficient as 556..." Stephanie proclaimed "but he did find his way through. Prior to the bonding, he was not even able to make it halfway. He got lost and stuck every time."

"Can we call this a success then?" he sheepishly asked. "We will need to report our progress to Zardonagon."

She became giddy with excitement, then said "Of course we can silly...we did it! Our friend's original brain never found the exit!"

She ran to him, grabbed him, gave him a big kiss, and a long hug. He wrapped his arms around her, and returned the hug. The corners of his closed mouth begin to move up, finally forming the largest toothy grin on his now happy face. He had quite a few things to be happy about today.

"C'mon doctor, let me buy you a celebration dinner..." he ordered as he jerked his head toward the door.

"Lead on doctor, I am one hungry girl... be ready for the check when I'm finally done eating!"

He offered his arm, and she took it. They walked to the door at such a pace, they were almost skipping. He stopped to turn out the lights, and looked around before he locked the door. His gaze happened upon the computer monitor, he turned, but then returned his gaze in a double take. *"I could have sworn it just said 67 percent"* he focused a third time at the monitor *"no, it is definitely still 51 percent..."*

Stephanie gave him a concerned look "What's wrong?"

"It was nothing... just my tired mind playing tricks. Let's go!"

They closed, and then locked the door behind them. They spent the next few hours having a wonderful time at dinner. After dinner, they said their goodnights, and went to their quarters for a good night's sleep.

Stephanie woke up early the next morning. She was excited to check on her test subject. She was ready to write up her observations in her report. She got dressed and ate a quick breakfast. She arrived at the lab and laughed when she realized the door was locked. She had beaten Derrick to work this morning – for once.

She unlocked the door and went into the lab. She went to the maze where they had left their test subject. She gasped as she looked at the maze – it was broken. The door had been jimmied, and the mouse was gone.

"Oh, my god!" she cried out. *"Did someone really steal our test mouse?"*

She began looking around the floor for the mouse. Her gaze then wandered to the cages holding the other test mice. Her eyes were bulging almost out of her head from the sight before her.

She contacted Derrick on the communication device. He answered with a sleepy look on his face. "Good morning sunshine..." he said, but then saw the look on her face. "What's wrong?"

Tears flowed from her eyes. "Derrick it's terrible..." she sobbed "every one of our mice is gone"

"Gone...someone stole our mice?" he asked.

"Yes, every cage door has been unlocked, and opened. The mice that were in the cages are gone!"

"Shit!" he shouted. "Okay, call security and then we will have to report this to Zardonagan"

Her tears stopped slightly, and she forced a crumbled smile onto her face. "So somehow Derrick, you have just made a bad situation even worse…" she said with a joking annoyance in her voice.

"Sorry…" he mumbled "but he has to be told…We're gonna need more mice…I'll be right there."

The communication device shut down. Stephanie took another look around, and let out a huge sigh of despair. She sat at the console, contacted security, leaned back in the chair, and looked at the ceiling searching for an answer to her predicament. She could not find a clue or answer up on the plain white surface. *"Well, I guess it will be back to square one in the experiments and theory proofs. And, it will be all day messing with security…great."*

She sat and looked around the room for some clue – but then the strangest feeling hit her. She felt a draft in the controlled environment. She stood up, and wandered around to look for the source. In the far corner near the cages, she found a small hole in the wall.

"What could this be?" She said as she examined the hole. "This is the oddest thing. Perhaps this is how our thieves were able to disable the security." she deduced in her mind. "Well, it is a matter for security to deal with."

6

"Every day your Alliance is finding new ways to defeat our enemy, the Southern Hemispheric Union. Our scientists are hard at work trying to develop a human that will be even stronger than any known Normal person and possibly, but doubtfully...even stronger than any of our Blessed humans. Also, our spiritual leaders are looking for ways for our lord and god to provide the power, to help our forces to strike down the enemy. Even our Supreme Commander himself said that our salvation and the key to us winning the war would be with the religious side of our society, not the scientific side. He realizes however, that scientists must try to find the secret to victory – even if they will more than likely fail without divine intervention. For those citizens unfortunate enough to turn their backs on our society and promote evil, the only way they will find salvation is in one of our glorious experimental programs – one where the foul and vile of our society can redeem themselves and provide a service to our Alliance, the Council and to our Supreme Commander. This leads me to remind you that The Council of Order wants you to obey the rules. After all, unity is power and not following the rules and degrading our unity will not only hurt you, but could put you in line for one of our leader's glorious experimental programs. For the Alliance News Network, Maxwell Simpson reporting."

Doctor Catherine Harmony stared dully at the images that flashed before her eyes on the computer monitor. Faces, names, and life stories flickered at a methodical rate into her now-numb brain. "Certainly, ONE of these people will meet the criteria for the experiment... I only need one..."

She turned to her assistant Michael Fair and sighed in frustration. "I think we will never find our person..." she told him while letting out another sigh. "I guess that wraps up this prison... let's do the query search on the next prison... perhaps our man will be there."

"Very well, doctor" Michael replied as he entered the parameters of the next query search "I have entered the parameters for the next search at...Kansas City Memorial Penal Work Camp. It will be a few minutes, how about a quick snack break?"

She pondered on his suggestion for a moment, then stood up. "Yes, you're right, I think a few minutes away from the terminal will not slow the process down, and I could use the break."

Her young assistant walked over to the food dispensary machine, and entered the codes for a pair of simulated Turkey sandwiches. The machine dispensed the food, and he met Catherine at the table near the office window that overlooked the institute grounds. She just sat at the table, and stared out the window past the darkness of the sleeping institute. Her eyes fixated in fascination at not only the fluctuating glow coming from the shield generators, but also the constant glow of the death zone that could be seen over the top of the dark crater walls surrounding them. He sat the plates on the table, which regained her attention. She turned back to the table, and then picked up the sandwich.

She took a bite of the mostly white-colored sandwich "Yum, this was a great idea Michael, thank you for reminding me to eat!"

"My pleasure doctor! It's part of my job after all...making sure you're in tip top shape to do your work!"

"How is it I could not get an assistant like you until 3 days ago?" she asked the young man. "I could have used a good person like you for years."

He laughed. "Just consider yourself lucky now..." he joked confidently. "I guess I finally decided I needed a good steady job!"

The two sat quietly for a few minutes while they enjoyed the food. They both drank stimulant drinks to maintain mental sharpness.

Michael examined his new employer, and as he had done over the past three days – his gaze turned to her hair. Her hair was such a deep tone of dark brown that it almost appeared black, except for a natural set of bright white stripes. These stripes started just above her temples and normally would naturally hang down around the front of her face. The white locks of hair would have hang down, if she had not always had pulled them from front to back. When pulled back in the current manner

– the two long white locks of hair formed something that resembled the stripes of a skunk.

She took another bite of food and caught him staring. "Michael…" she scolded "you're staring at my hair again. Perhaps you should just talk to me about it. Is it offensive or something?"

"Oh, heavens no!" he replied, feeling embarrassed. "It's just… well, I have never seen anyone with the coloration of hair such as yours. It's very attractive, but I must admit that I have never seen anyone else wear their hair in this way. I hope you don't mind me asking, but since I have started working for you I have always wondered… why you have those stripes at such a young age… and why you don't cover them."

"OH, now you flatter me! Well, to really understand, you have to know about my travels while I was working on my doctorate degree. As part of my research, I travelled to the far eastern sectors of the northern hemisphere… in search of the old techniques of mental training. I spent time in China and Tibet seeking out the Buddhist and Taoist monks. They were rumored to have survived the bombings, and were living somewhere in this mountainous territory. With only a survival suit, an anti-grav pack of food stuffs, some various supplies, and a Sherpa to carry my stuff, I went in search of these mysterious and secluded monks."

"I spent years searching for the monks. I was about to give up when out of nowhere they just appeared to me. It was almost as if they were watching me the whole time and knew what I was seeking. The monks told me that I had a purpose that would someday require their training. Then… they simply offered to train me. I originally thought that the training was given so I could cure others, but since then I have wondered about the true reasons behind their motives. I now surmise that I was trained for this particular project. The monks always said the silent ones would need my help during the most critical of times."

She took a bite of sandwich, and chewed slowly while she thought about it for a moment, then continued after she swallowed. "I've always wondered who the silent ones were. Could they be the sub-human results of these experiments?"

"It's very possible doctor… but how would they have known?"

She pondered on that for a moment before answering "That is one mystery we may never know the answer to. I have a feeling those monks had some extraordinary ability that foretold of the future." She took a short sip of her drink. "Anyway, I trained and studied for many long days and nights... training that lasted years. Sometimes, I would train without even eating or sleeping. I found that there were times I just really didn't need the food or rest. One day, I fell asleep after a difficult training session, and woke up with these skunk stripes. I had no indications of my hair turning before it happened...it just changed overnight. The monks told me the stripes were due to my newly found abilities. They told me that this is where my ability would focus, the stripes would act like an antenna for directing mental energies toward the healing of others."

She took another bite of sandwich, and then rinsed it down with a sip of the beverage. "I swore to the monks I would never cover these stripes... and now I consider them a sign of authority and knowledge. Besides... in my opinion, they're kind of cute!"

He chuckled and gave her a big smile. "What else have you learned to help in your profession?"

"Well, the monks suggested I learn hypnosis, but it was something they could not teach me. So, after leaving the monastery I traveled to the European continent. I found the last master of the art of hypnosis -- Marko "Mentallo" Pascall. After my training from the monks, I found hypnosis quite easy to grasp and master... and thus, within a year, I was an expert in the art. I can now actually send a person into a deep state of sleep, obtain their memories and experiences and manipulate their mind to act or behave in a prescribed way. I find it is actually quite powerful when combined with concentration and meditation techniques."

"So, this was all prior to you graduating?" Michael asked.

"Yes... I returned to the ANO homeland, and finished my degrees in Psychiatry and Psychology. After that, I settled into setting up my practice in zone 1. I felt the former city of Washington DC and the seat of the Alliance government would have plenty of people who needed my help... and boy, was I correct! There were plenty of people who needed my healing practice. I never really thought much about it... I would accept patients, cure them and send them back to society. Life was good and normal... and I made a good amount of credits. I lived in a nice apartment, in a good part of the city, and even dated sometimes. I really could not ask for more."

"So, you then just left your practice, and came here?"

"No, but I did leave my practice for a while. For a few years, I was hired by the Alliance Space Force. I sometimes wondered if perhaps that work caused me to be noticed by the Council... anyway, I was put onto a rocket and was shot up to Starbase Prime as the chief psychological analyst for the crew of the Starlight Exploration Program... the Space Ark. I analyzed an endless list of people who had been selected that would eventually go up into space, who would be exploring and eventually colonizing new planets. I worked with the crew members as needed, ensuring that they would mentally survive the trip and be able to flourish when they arrived at a habitable planet. Those thousands of humans, most of them Blessed, took off with Starlight... to this day, they have not been seen or heard from again. After the Space Force lost contact with Starlight, the project was done as far as I was concerned, so I took a chemical rocket back to Earth and returned to my zone 1 practice."

"So, what brought you here then? Why would anyone... besides me... want to work in this god forsaken place?"

"Well, life was normal for me for a while... until the day this tall, large man... dressed in black, showed up at my doorstep. That was the day my life changed. The man was a Blessed Secret Service officer, and he had a message that was only for my eyes. The message demanded that I immediately go with him to Council chambers. Well, what could I do? I had to of course follow their instructions to the letter! So, I went with the man, and was escorted to the hearing chambers of the Grand Council of Order. The Council granted me 30 seconds of their time... pretty generous actually. I was told that my talents were needed for a project of great importance to the Order. They told me that this project was full of failures and setbacks, and that they felt that part of the failures was due to mental instability. I was told I would be tasked with working with one special patient, and this patient would receive my full undivided attention and training. They felt that if I trained the patient to use mental art abilities, it would help to keep their mind intact while the transformation process occurred. Also, they thought that through my training this one patient would be able to hold onto their human side, and thus would be able to communicate to their human masters."

"Ahhh... so thus the reason we are spending all this time finding one single prisoner. I was wondering about that!"

"Yes, If I succeed in helping one person hang on to their human side, this will allow for the creation of human-animal hybrids that will have the mental capabilities to not only understand and communicate with their human masters, but will allow them to carry out complex and dangerous military assignments. Even though I was *requested* to help... well you know... you do not refuse a request from the Council... that is, if you wanted to continue to live!" she lightly chuckled.

"Wow! That's a fascinating story doctor." He thought a moment, then asked "So you use those hair stripes in your practice... how if I may ask?"

"It's easier if I show you... give me a moment."

She closed her eyes and began to concentrate. After a few seconds, her face emanated a look of total relaxation. Michael thought he could feel the energy that flowed from all parts of the room into her body. After a few more seconds, the two white stripes of hair began to softly glow. The glow started as a mild yellow, but then grew brighter, and finally glowed a bright white. The glow continued for a minute, and then she opened her eyes and looked at him. There was energy flickering from her hair stripes – there was also a mild glow and total look of calm in her eyes.

"See..." she spoke with a resonance in her voice that filled the room "now I'm in a state of total relaxation and concentration. I can make the mental energy flow to any point in my body, or to another person if needed. I can maintain this state as long as needed to help a patient heal."

Michael had a look of total amazement in his eyes. He could not believe a human could focus and control internal energies, external energies, and auras with their mind – but there she was, doing exactly that in front of his eyes.

"And..." she looked him straight in the eye, and then said, "I can shut it off with the blink of an eye." The energy suddenly stopped, and the glow immediately went away. "Ohh!" her voice spoke in a state of sheer happiness "I feel great now!"

"Words cannot describe it doctor..." he spoke with sincerity, and awe in his voice "that was one of the most amazing things I have ever seen. Could you teach me that?"

She gave a light laugh. "Maybe someday... after we find our subject and I work with them to success. But this person must be the perfect choice. Everything depends on this one person."

He could tell she was serious about this. She had to be completely certain of her choice, since a wrong decision could mean not only the end of her career, but possibly the end of her life. It was well known that the Council did not accept failure easily. Many a scientist or researcher ended up "missing" after failing at a pet project assigned to them by the Council. She was a Normal, she knew what could happen... and she had no intention of becoming one of those missing person statistics.

She always assumed that her talents would never be noticed by the Council, after all, who would need the services of a Psychoanalyst with knowledge of ancient mental arts? Certainly no one would ever need training in the Zen art of deep meditation, Taoist concentration, visualization techniques, or the technique of hypnosis – all long thought to be lost, and also well forgotten. No, she always felt safe in selecting these mental techniques as a primary function of her counseling practice – but nothing else.

She pondered for a moment, and then said "I sometimes wonder if perhaps I used my curative process on a member of the Council. You know I would never know since no one has actually ever seen the faces of the Council except for inside members of their secret circle. Or perhaps, maybe when I worked with their offspring... the Blessed... maybe that was enough for them to give me this assignment? Oh well... nonetheless, I'm now stuck in this project... and I must succeed to get out of it."

Then the realization that she still did not have a test subject came to her. "*God, what did I do to deserve this? I still have not even come close to finding someone!*" She worked herself into a mental panic for a brief moment. She did a light moment of meditation to calm herself, as panic was not what she needed right now. "Okay, we must find this person..." she muttered out loud as she meditated "and we must find him soon."

Michael heard the concern in her voice. "Are you sure we should continue this evening? We could always use some sleep, and start fresh again in the morning."

She thought about that for a moment before answering "No, I don't know how much longer Zardonagon will wait for us, we have to keep going until we run out of current records."

Saying that name sent a chill down her spine. "*Edward Zardonagon... that creep...*" she thought to herself as she pictured that old, haggard, mean, and evil looking person in her head. She found herself recoiled from him the moment she met him, she could never totally pinpoint what she felt about him that first day – she was not sure if it was because he was Blessed, or was there something else about him. In any case, from the time she met him, she had realized her exact feelings about him. She felt his experiments were horrid – turning human beings into forms of animal hybrids. Not only did he create these hybrids, but in the process, he caused them to lose whatever was human inside. They never would speak, or act like a human in any way, shape or manner after he had finished with them. They were most likely pure animal – they were definitely not human. He had since labeled them "Sub-humans" and she hated him for creating those poor, pitiful creatures.

He only saw those poor creatures as failures. Many times, she had witnessed him going into a rage after a failure, and in the process destroying the poor mutated creature. She always thought that perhaps it was for the better, since now they would not suffer. But it was more how, and WHY he destroyed those poor creatures that repulsed her. One method he enjoyed, utilized a beam he developed to cause their DNA to break apart – the creature would painfully turn into a puddle of jelly. She was not sure if they were still alive or not at that point – she hoped they had already died by then. Then again, it was not like they had a reason to live after that experiment anyway.

Sometimes she witnessed him using his finger injector to poison the creature into death. She could tell that it was quite painful. Regardless of the method, she always felt sadness for the deaths at the hands of this madman. Yes, she felt he was a madman – he was the classic "mad scientist" of old 19th century motion pictures. She felt he was even beyond her help, not like he would ever admit he needed help, or would ever ask for her assistance. She was glad that the prospect of counseling him would never occur. She shuddered at even the thought of hearing and feeling his deepest thoughts and desires when under hypnosis.

So here she was, working with that disgusting creature of a human being known as Edward Zardonagon. He despised her because she was given carte blanche from the Council for anything she needed to make this project a success. This included finding just the proper person, no matter how long it took. She had a small staff that was available for anything she needed. She had the records of every prisoner, in every prison camp in the entire northern hemisphere. She had been searching for just the correct combination of mental capabilities and personality for the experiment.

She needed a person with a high intelligence quotient – as only through intelligence, and her training did she feel that one could force their human side out after a transformation. She also needed the proper personality, one that could get along with her for training, and one that would allow for the flexibility to adapt to their new hybrid form. It was that combination that was preventing her from moving onto the next phase, which was actually beginning the training process.

She stood up from the table and walked over to the mirror and gazed at herself. "Oh god, I look like shit!" she decried. She ran to her desk and grabbed a jar of skin rejuvenator from her compression bag. She applied the clear cream to her face, which immediately started to tighten her tired skin, and faded the dark circles under her large brown eyes. She was tired and it showed, but she had to keep going. Her skin was a light alabaster, she had no need or desire to use colorant, to create the "zone-walking look" that so many women were sporting now. She felt the dark skin look was much too dangerous, and brought out way too much attention. No, her light skin was just fine. The rejuvenator was doing its work, as she watched her skin return to its normal smooth and flawless look.

Her fixation on her appearance was broken by the computer's signal chime. The query of the next prison facility was complete. The list of names was now shown on the multiple computer displays. "Okay, let's sort the names by IQ please" she told Michael as she returned to the monitor. He entered a few commands, and the names were rearranged based on a predetermined algorithm of IQ, age, and crime – it was important after all, to avoid working with a murderous lunatic.

The first face appeared on the monitor, and she examined the information for a few minutes. "Yes!" she shouted "This one will do just fine. High IQ... and appears to have a good behavior record. Alberto Rullotoni... check his status for me, Michael."

He queried the prison database for the prisoner's current status. His face changed from happy, into a pained look. "Sorry doctor, he died yesterday."

"Dammit!" she cried out in despair, before she regained her composure. "Okay, moving on to the next person then..." she said as she entered a command and displayed the next face.

She looked at his biography for a moment, while mumbling "High IQ, good..." then sighed and said "but way too violent. No, this one won't do at all. Michael, think we will ever find "mister right" for this project? HA! Mister Right... that will never happen for me in any way, shape or form!" Her attempt at humor caused her to expel this unusual giggle from her open mouth.

The first-time Michael heard this giggle, he was shocked. He had never expected to hear this manner of noise from a professional doctor. However, since then, this giggle no longer affected him. He nonchalantly answered "Oh you will find Mister Right... in BOTH ways...professional AND romantic I'm sure doctor..." he advanced to the next potential test subject.

She smiled at his positive outlook "Oh, I suppose that I will eventually..." her voice faded to nothingness when she saw the face of the next subject appear on the screen. "My god is that really you?" she asked the face on the computer screen, obviously not expecting an answer. She read the biography: Simon Louis Piccolo, age 46 former educator of modern history in south region 4, now sentenced to death for anarchy and terrorism.

Michael looked at the doctor staring at the screen "You know him?"

"Yes" she answered "I took Modern History from him when I was in my undergraduate studies. He was a wonderful instructor, and a great person... My god Simon, what did you do to deserve this?" She continued to read his biography, and reached the section of containing his IQ score. "198! Wow, I knew you were smart... but you have now amazed even me, professor." She smiled while speaking to the computer screen. "Michael, check his status... and PLEASE don't tell me he is dead!" She was close to praying for him to give her the answer she needed to hear – alive. She feared he might already be, or will soon be dead, and had a deep concern for his life. The Kansas City facility was for the sole purpose of removing unwanted criminals from this existence.

He typed up some commands, and then smiled. "Shows he is still alive and well, and surviving in the KC work prison. Shall I make the arrangements for pick up?"

She snapped an answer without a second thought. "Definitely! I will check out a hopper and go there tomorrow! He has the personality and intelligence to make this work. He CAN survive... I'm sure!" Her mind was now awake and alert. The thought of working with her former professor, and such an intelligent man, gave her the hope that this project could be a success.

She muttered softly to herself "I'm sure he would not remember a quiet student such as me after all these years..."

"What was that doctor?"

"Oh nothing, I was just reminding myself that he will not remember me, and that I need to stay totally professional when we meet." She giggled, and a large smile grew on her face as she stared at the face on the monitor. She then spoke to the face "We are going to save your life, and change you at the same time. You are now mine, Simon Piccolo!"

7

"Today our brave forces suffered a defeat at the hands of our southern enemies. The forces of the south launched a counter offensive against our forces defending the Isthmus of Panama. According to Central America Commander Oxford Omandy, one of our heroic Blessed... the southern forces somehow managed to sneak past our patrols and surround the encampment at Colon forward base. With the troops surrounded, they pushed the force to the edge of the radioactive waters of the Atlantic Ocean. Having nowhere to retreat, they had a choice of surrendering, suffering a painful death in the ocean, or fighting until dead. The brave forces of your Alliance chose a fighting death over the dishonor of surrender. With this defeat however, our enemy now has control of a key strategic position preventing our military forces from advancing any further into the enemy's homeland. In addition, we lost over 2000 of our brave troops. Fortunately, all Blessed commanders and field leaders were able to escape, so they could continue to lead, and take the fight back to the south in the future. With this defeat, our Supreme Commander wants to remind all of you that our troops now need you more than ever. Work harder and faster to produce the components needed to supply our troops. Reproduce selectively and produce only quality children, as we need them in our armies. Last but not least, always live within the rules and live in unity with the Alliance – after all, unity is power. For Alliance News Network, I am Connie Dahlia."

The creature thrashed around the table, both in fear and suffering. This once-human being was no longer anything like his former self. He now had a round tube shaped body. Segmented joints were imbedded into the creature's skin from the tip of the tube which was formerly his head, all the way to where his stubby, worthless legs now dangled. Two large, bulbous, hazel-colored eyes stared up into his face. A large maw of a mouth opened and closed as it attempted to breathe while fighting the configuration of his new body. He struggled to adjust to the restraining straps that had reshaped themselves to conform to the new body shape – they reshaped and then shrunk down to a size smaller to prevent movement.

Doctor Edward Zardonagon stood over this creature, and looked at it with a cold calm face. He examined the thing that his transformation experiment had produced. The calm on his face suddenly turned into a storm. His gray eyes blazed with fiery anger and rage. "WHAT THE HELL IS THIS MESS?" he screamed out. All of the lab assistants in the room stopped their chatter and the room went into total silence. Every one of them turned, and looked at their boss – their faces had looks of both fear and worry.

The creature's eyes opened wide, and a giant, tooth-filled mouth opened and let out a hissing scream. It was in horrid pain, and this caused Edward's rage to build even further. A frustrated Edward grunted and held up his hand. On one finger was a thimble-like device, with a long golden needle. He flexed his finger slightly and a small drop of liquid dripped out of the tip and onto the creature. He lowered his hand, and with a grunt he sunk the needle of the device deep into the head of the creature. He rotated the needle around inside its head to inject the poisonous fluid into his brain. After a few seconds, he stopped pushing the needle. He waited another moment before he pulled the 4-inch-long, wide-tubular needle out of the flesh of the wormlike creature.

The pain in the creature's eyes told of its suffering. It wiggled, and the hissing scream continued as the poison in its body was slowly and painfully killing it. Edward smiled as the creature writhed in pain and agony. Edward justified to himself that this was a fitting fate for such a failure of an experiment. Finally spitting its last breath in the direction of Edward, the creature's mouth closed and its movements stopped. Its suffering was now over – it was dead.

Edward looked at his staff – the rage still in his eyes. "What a waste of protoplasm and conversion energy" he muttered. He looked at the dead creature again, then with a boom in his voice yelled "I NEVER want to see that combination in this room again. Do I make myself clear?"

Every assistant in the room shook their heads in agreement and replied with a hearty "Yes sir!"

Edward turned to walk out the door, then stopped and turned just enough to look his staff in the eyes. He focused his stone-gray eyes on each one of them. In each person, as his eyes affixed, he stirred both fear, and loathing. Finally, he softly said "If this animal type ever shows up again, it will be one of you on the table next time. Am I clear?" Once again, each assistant muttered a "Yes, sir" as he turned and walked out of the lab.

He stormed down the hallway until he reached the door to his office. He entered his office and after the door closed, he started to throw anything he could find. He threw everything, across the room – books, pens, papers, and glasses.

"Damn, damn, damn! Why must I be surrounded with incompetents?" He walked to the bar and poured himself a large glass of recently refined scotch whiskey, and quickly gulped the drink down.

He activated his computer, and queried "Data query... categorize the animal types that historically have resulted in failure..."

A moment later, a list was displayed. The list was categorized by species type. There was a mixture of vertebrae and invertebrate failures, every bird and reptile had failed – none of these failures surprised him. It was however, the list of mammal failures that surprised him. Animals such as Deer, Antelope, and Moose were all failures. He would have to analyze why that occurred.

He then returned back to today's failure. He thought about the animal type chosen and wondered how that happened – he could have sworn he had removed selections like todays from the database. He knew someone had to be plotting against him. "Why do they do this to me?" he muttered. "They are sabotaging my work to make me look bad... I know it... I will get them for this!" He threw the now empty glass against the far wall. It hit a computer display – a small explosion followed as the display was destroyed. Sparks flew from the unit as the liquid remains from the glass dripped into the electronic components, and shorted them out. He stopped his tantrum at that point, and looked at his now damaged wall display. He walked to his desk and pushed the call button.

"Yes doctor?" the voice on the other side of the communication device asked.

"Umm, my computer wall display has developed a malfunction...I will need a replacement...immediately!"

"Very well...I will have a replacement sent up right away."

Edward disconnected without saying another word. He walked over to the bar and poured another scotch into a new glass. He sipped the drink calmly this time while he walked to the windows and stared out across the campus of the institute. The liquor was doing its work, as it calmed his nerves. He continued to stare out the window for another moment, then walked to his desk, and sat down with a hard thud into the soft, simulated leather of the chair. He reactivated his desk computer, and quickly glanced over the bulk of his communications. There was a message in his email box that caught his eye:

"Doctor Zardonagon, I have finally selected a subject for my experiment. I will be picking him up immediately, with training starting upon arrival and completion of intake processing. Dr. Catherine Harmony"

"Great... now I'll have to put up with that bitch bothering me with her mental training nonsense... that is, until I can somehow get her to fail." He tapped his fingers on his desk while he peered over the communication again. "Yes, there must be something that I can do to help expedite her departure." He took another sip of his drink, then a small smile flashed across his old, gray-skinned face. He now relished in just thinking about the possibility of her failure.

He then sighed, put an image of Catherine on his screen. "Although, I will miss you when you are finally gone, Catherine. You have a fine body... and are pretty good looking. Maybe I can get you into bed one time before I send you packing." He let out a small chuckle as he realized how his piggish thoughts pleased him so.

He closed the communication, and then fidgeted his fingers, while at the same time rapping them on the desk top. He realized his nerves were shot. He took another drink, then opened and dug into his desk drawer until he found a bottle of pills. His hands were shaking as he managed to open the bottle, and removed two of the pills. He swallowed them quickly down, and then washed them down with the remainder of the scotch. He returned the bottle to the drawer. Sitting in the drawer was his blaster. He swore he heard the weapon calling to him. He picked up the blaster, looked at it for a moment, and then popped the barrel into his mouth. Sweat now poured down his forehead as he wrapped his lips around the beam emitter, while he contemplated pulling the trigger.

His finger started to slightly squeeze the trigger. Before the weapon discharged however, his moment of self-pity and destruction was interrupted by the door buzzer. "CRAP!" He yelled around the barrel of the gun. He pulled it out of his mouth, and threw it back into the desk drawer. He then reached across his desk, and activated the view screen. It was Derrick Swanson. He activated the door intercom, and barked "What the hell do you want Swanson?"

"Umm" Derrick stuttered "I... we need to speak with you for just a moment, doctor. Sorry to be disturbing you."

Edward looked closer into the monitor, and noticed that Stephanie Wilcox was standing behind the large man. "*Ah, he brought the tart with him!*" He let him sweat for a moment, then said "Very well, come in." He pushed the button to automatically open the door. He checked to make sure the blaster was securely back where it belonged before closing the drawer. "*I guess the world is blessed with this Blessed for yet another day.*"

Derrick and Stephanie walked in and were surprised to see the condition of the room – broken computers, and glassware were strewn around the room. To them, it appeared like an ion storm had hit recently. "Are... are you alright Edward?" Derrick asked.

"Of course, I'm fine... just had to think about some important things for a while." His gaze turned from Derrick to Stephanie. He said to her "Stephanie, it's good to see you."

He smiled and looked her up and down. He noted how much of her legs were exposed by her mid-length, brown skirt. He examined her legs – short but still slim, and showing enough of her knees and lower legs to give him a start. He took in the slightly round shape of her calves, his eyes finally moved up to her face. He took a long stare at her young face and thought "*plain, but cute.*" His eyes then moved back down slightly, just enough to take in the sight of her breasts – they were covered with a white blouse, a ruffle ran down the front. A small, brown bow completed the collar of her blouse. She was wearing a lab coat, which slightly covered her chest to him. He noted however, that it was open enough for him to put his mind into full-imagination mode. He sat and stared at the young doctor while he imagined her naked. He began to fantasize about pulling on her short blond hair, and forcing her head in various positions.

Stephanie noticed his gaze and realized he was undressing, or perhaps raping her in his mind. She recoiled inwardly, and subconsciously wrapped her lab coat around her in a motion of self-protection. She discovered that she had subconsciously taken a small step back from the lecherous man.

"Doctor, sorry to disturb you." Stephanie said with a slight frosty tone in her voice.

"Well... sit" Edward barked as he pointed to the two chairs in front of his desk "What is it that made you decide to disturb me?"

Derrick was outwardly nervous as he told him "Well Edward, we have good news and bad news..."

"DON'T PLAY GAMES WITH ME DERRICK   !"

"Sorry..." Derrick mumbled, then continued "the bad news is that someone apparently has stolen all of our test mice. Not a single one is left."

"What makes you think someone stole them?" Edward queried "Why would someone steal your mice anyway?"

"Well... I'm thinking because of the good news. We were able to perform a successful DNA bonding on one of our mice... it mutated perfectly." Derrick was now beaming with pride.

Edward eyed Derrick with suspicion before saying "I might propose that perhaps you disposed of the mice to cover up some true reason... perhaps failure?"

"NO" Stephanie shouted "Derrick... I mean... we... actually did a successful bond. We watched the mutation... 50 percent!"

"Did you really do anything Stephanie... or is it that you let Derrick do all the work, and you are just riding his coattails?" He laughed inside knowing he was pulling their strings like a puppet. He was enjoying them as they squirmed and danced.

"Now look here..." Derrick interrupted as he stood and moved closer to Edward "she was as crucial to the success..."

"SHUT UP AND SIT!" Edward demanded and pointed to the chair. Derrick immediately stopped speaking and sat down. *"Oh, this is too funny... I really have this big man by the balls!"* He let a small laugh slip from his tight lips.

"What's so funny?" Stephanie asked the doctor. She noticed he had the smile of the snake that just ate the rat. She could tell he was very pleased with himself.

"Oh nothing..." he told her nonchalantly. *"Now for the grand slam... perhaps the answer to my problems."* He then gave Stephanie a serious look and said "However, the loss of your mice might just be a good thing. If you indeed have had the success you say you have, then I think you should continue your experiments... but this time on humans."

"WHAT?" Stephanie yelled, as she jumped out of her seat. She stepped quickly to Edward's desk. He stood up to meet her at the side of the desk. "You cannot make us start human experimentation, it's..."

"I can... and I will, Stephanie." He cut her off as he put his wrinkled, gray-skinned face into hers. He stared deep into her eyes and noted that she was filled with fury and anger. He found her anger exciting – it caused his adrenaline and testosterone to freely flow throughout his body. He could smell the hormones of her anger flowing through her, and it excited him. Her anger brought the feeling of his youth returning into his fading body.

"I cannot believe you would do that. I cannot believe you would make us harm another human. Don't make us do this!"

Edward continued his stare and spoke softly. "Stephanie, we are at this institute for one reason and only one reason... to build a better soldier. Raw human beings no longer will do, thus we perform our experiments. That is the way it is... so get used to it."

Stephanie was in a total rage at this point, Derrick just sat in shock – he had never seen her so angry for all the time he had known her. "You make me sick... you're disgusting..." she spat without thinking.

"I see you are starting to appreciate me, Stephanie." He said, then chuckled. His mind and his mood shifted to this young girl in front of him. His thoughts were now totally removed from the current conversation. *"Perhaps it is time to move on to more pleasant things..."*

Still staring into her blue eyes, he softly told the young woman "You know I have an ability... I can feel, smell, and sometimes even taste hormones that are given off by another human being." He smiled at her, then flared his nostrils, and took a deep breath through his nose as if smelling a warm apple pie, fresh out of the oven. He savored the smell of the scientist in front of him. "You my dear, are giving off one strong scent. Your norepinephrine... your flight or fight hormones are strong. You must be very angry with me. However, I am finding your hormones exciting. I wish to explore them further."

Stephanie gasped in shock. She realized that he was standing so close to her that she could feel his energy aura invading her space. But she also was close enough to notice an even worse invading presence – he had developed an erection. It was bulging through his slacks, and slightly poking into her. She jumped back – her face showed both shock and sickness. "You're a lecherous bastard. How could you harass me in such a manner?"

He laughed. "Remember, Supreme Leader Shrubway eliminated all harassment laws years ago. I can't be accused of that. And even if I could... well, I am Blessed after all..." He once again stripped her with his eyes. He licked his lips slightly, then suggested "I think perhaps we should discuss this. Perhaps you should stay tonight and we can discuss this..."

"Absolutely not doctor... there are staff prostitutes for that purpose. I suggest you call one right away."

"Now, now my dear... I could force you to stay..." he suggested with an evil smile is on his face.

Derrick stood up at this point "Edward..." he shouted.

Stephanie raised her hand to stop Derrick. She was determined now. Her blue eyes gave Edward a freezing, stone-cold gaze. With a slow, icy tone in her voice she simply said "Then I quit. Find yourself a new Genetic Engineer..." She turned and started to walk to the door.

Edward loudly laughed, and then said "Alright, you sure have spirit. No need to up and quit on me. Your right, I over stepped my bounds... however, you two WILL start your experiments on humans immediately. Now go." He pressed a button on his desk and the door slid open. He waved his hand in dismissal.

The pair of scientists left the room – he pressed the button again, and the door closed. Edward walked over to the bar and poured another drink. "Bitch... no stupid little girl shoots me down, and gets away with it." He sipped his drink, and then laughed out loud. "You will solve my problems for me. Then I will take your ideas, and the credit... then, we will see how you will feel about sleeping with me you little bitch. Yeah, see how you like that... little miss plain girl... bitch." He smiled, sipped again on his drink, and turned to once again gaze out the window.

He laughed again while he thought out loud "Perhaps she is right about one thing..." then turned to his desk, sat down, and activated the communication device. He ordered "Send a prostitute to my office immediately!"

He then looked over to a small refrigerator at the bar. His fingers twitched slightly on the desk as he continued his stare. Finally, he stood up, walked over, and opened the refrigerator. He reached inside and pulled out a jar of pink berries. His fingers tapped on the lid of the jar as he considered his options. After his consideration, he opened the jar, and pulled out one piece of the large pink fruit, and popped it into his mouth. He chewed and relished in the feeling that immediately started to creep into his brain. He popped a couple more berries into his mouth before placing the container back into the refrigerator. He then walked over to a cabinet near the bar, opened it, and then pulled out the Pleasure-Matic machine. He checked the connectors and wires on the device before saying "Ahhh, now I am ready for a whore. Where the hell is she?"

*   *   *

Derrick and Stephanie walked down the corridor away from Zardonagon's office in total silence. Finally, Derrick broke the silence. "Stephanie, are you alright? I've never seen you so angry."

She turned, and saw the look of pure concern in Derrick's eyes and on his face. She took a deep breath then smiled at him. "Yes, I'm fine. I was a little surprised actually. I've heard that he can turn on any woman like that... but I had never experienced it before. He really frightens me sometimes. If he didn't have the complete backing of the Council..."

"I understand, try to forget about it now. Hey, how about we go relax at the Automat? I will buy us dinner and drinks... hmm? Sounds like a plan, yes?" He gave her a big smile and jerked his head in the direction of the food automat.

"Oh, how can I refuse an offer like that from someone as nice as you? Okay, lead on Doctor!" She had given up on her anger. A small smile returned to her face.

"I'll tell you what, we'll have a nice meal, and maybe some drinks. Then call it a night, and first thing tomorrow morning start our selection process. Since we have no choice in the matter, we might as well go jump into it with gusto!"

She sighed, and smiled "Yes, absolutely. Let's go!" She took his hand and lead him down the corridor. She knew he would help her to forget what just happened. He would bring her back to the reality of work. That is what she liked about working with him. She felt she was quite fortunate to have him as a partner, and he was the sole reason she was still working there – especially after what had just happened. If he were not there, she knew she would have just upped and quit, or worse she might have killed Edward. Once again, she felt yet another connection with Derrick – one she hoped she could explore further someday when they had completed their project work. As they quickly walked down the hall, a thought occurred to her. This thought stopped her dead in her tracks. "What do you think happened to our mice Derrick... did he take them?"

They began walking again as he pondered her question. He then shrugged his shoulders, and said "Don't know... we may have to write this theft off as a mystery. He sure didn't give us any answers."

"Yes, I wonder..." she muttered.

8

"Today, a number of terrorists were tried and convicted of crimes against the state. This gang of thugs... disguised themselves as instructors... educators of our children. They used their positions of respect and knowledge to poison our children through the use of deceitful teachings and lies. Fortunately, they were discovered, captured, and arrested. Now that they have been sentenced... they will either be executed publicly... in just a few minutes, or sent to prison. This guarantees that our Alliance is safe from these would-be destroyers of our youth. Our Council gives great thanks to the brave souls who discovered and turned in these vicious criminals. These brave citizens are proof that through unity is power. Live within the rules and don't end up like these criminals. Maintain vigilance against these factions of fiends, and turn in anyone who does not conform. And now, the executions – parents, you may want to remove your children from the room."

It was 6AM, and Simon once again awoke to the morning dose of government brainwashing.

"It's a beautiful day at Memorial"

"It's a wonderful day to work"

"Be thankful you made it yet another day"

"Be blessed by the Council, and live today!"

"Work, work as hard as you can"

"Work and live...that's the Council's plan!"

The song did its damage – no matter how hard he tried, he could not get that song or the words out of his head. The song played and was heard everywhere – there was no escaping the mind-numbing melody. He tried covering his ears, but his attempts were to no avail, as the melody simply slipped around his fingers, and into his ear canals. The sonic properties of the song were created in such a way that no resident of the prison could block, or remove themselves from the music, or the lyrics. It was another day, just like every day at the Kansas City Memorial Work Prison, also known as "The Rock Pit".

He gave up on trying to continue his rough sleep, so he sat up and stretched – his hands hitting the concrete of the six-foot wide tunnel. His back ached, and despite his sleep, he still felt tired – as sleeping never really brought his mind to a proper rest. With sleepy eyes, he stood up, bumped his head against the top of the pipe, crouched lower to avoid another encounter with the hard surface above him, and slowly walked down to the main complex of tunnels.

He approached an intersection of the two six-foot tall tunnels, and heard a noise. He stopped dead in his tracks, shut off his pocket light, and listened. He realized what he heard was whimpering, just around the corner of the intersection. He went back to his sleeping area and grabbed a rock that he used as both a pillow and a weapon, and proceeded back to the intersection. He raised the rock above his head and slowly peered around the corner, then reactivated, and shined the small pocket light into the shadows. Below his gaze was a portly older man – a man whose face he recognized.

"Arthur? Arthur Manes, is that you?"

The man looked up, recognized Simon, and gave a weak smile and a nod. "Is it my luck that I ended up in the one place that has an ally? Did I really stumble upon you Simon, my good friend?"

"You did, my friend... you did..." he reached down and offered the older man a hand. With some effort, he stood up. Simon looked at him – he was in his seventies, had a gray beard and matching long scraggly hair. His pot belly told Simon that he had only just arrived. No one maintained their weight at the prison. His clothes were torn however, so he assumed he must have barely gotten away from a clothes thief.

Seeing his friend made him realize that the general population of the prison had grown – grown to a point to where it had reached even this remote location. He would have to find another safe area to dwell he realized. *Well, so much for this spot...*" He sighed upon the realization that eventually, there would be no safe place to hide, and no place to escape the violence.

He brushed off the dust from Arthur and helped tie his shirt back into a partially cohesive covering. "When did you arrive?" he asked.

"Just two days ago. They simply dumped me out in one of the tunnels, and closed the hatch behind me. They only gave me these clothes and nothing else. I have not eaten since I arrived, and as you can see... almost lost the shirt off of my back last night. I barely was able to push my way out of the man's grasp, and then I just ran. I ran and did not stop or look back. I hoped I had evaded him... that's when I found this tunnel, and this dark corner. I crammed myself into the corner and barely let out a breath. This morning however, it struck me... I had lost everything, and was going to die here. Everything I had was now lost... my teaching, my wife, my home... all gone. It had been so long since you disappeared and were thought dead... then they took most of the others, but not me. It had been over a year, and so I thought I somehow managed to have been forgotten by the Order. But then they arrested me this weekend and decided to make me an example. I would say I was lucky they did not publicly execute me, but then again... this is as bad as death, isn't it?"

Simon shook his head. This place was like hell on earth, but somehow, he had survived so far – survived only through using common sense and his intellect. He had managed to avoid most of the vicious criminals and gangs that roamed the prison. He found the most remote areas, and hid there – only coming out to do work duty or to purchase survival supplies – food, clothing, pocket light, and sunscreen.

The thought of food brought a grumble from his empty stomach. "Do you know where to get food or supplies?" Arthur shook his head no. "Come on then... let me give you the nickel tour of your lovely new home." They walked through a number of twists in the concrete tunnels until light began filling the tunnel – it was an eerie red glow that filled the passageway with light. They came upon the exit of the tunnel, where Simon stopped and put his hand in front of Arthur to prevent him from further progress.

"This... is what used to be the city of Kansas City. As you can see, it is now a bomb crater. This city did not have its particle shield in place when the bombs fell... thus, no protection, and now no life. Except us that is..." He pointed out to the cliffs and rock spires that jutted out of the red sandy surface of the crater. "The explosions melted the silica that made up much of the soil of this area. When the silica melted, it trapped rare and valuable radioactive elements located below the city. Also, the fission material of the bombs themselves were trapped in the layers of the silica. To make credits here... and more importantly, to use those credits to survive, you mine the trapped elements. This whole prison was built to provide a place for us unfortunate ones to become slave miners."

Arthur looked up at the tall steep walls of the crater. "Can't we just climb out of here? I don't see any guards to prevent us from going up there."

"Possibly... it is a large crater... over twenty miles wide. However, those walls I estimate are over three hundred feet high. A slip would be as fatal as just staying here." He pointed to the tunnel behind them, and continued "We sleep in the sewer system of what was once the suburb of Blue Springs, Missouri. The pipes are the only spot that are fairly cool and mostly radiation free. They let us roam anywhere we want as they do not seem to be too concerned about us climbing out. I suspect they know that it is pretty much impossible to climb... and if we did, the radiation once outside the deflectors would finish us. After all, we are in the middle of a vast death zone... unless you've arranged a ride for us out there..." Arthur shook his head no. Simon pointed across the crater to a tall building built into the side of the crater. "Over there is the administration building. That's where the guards live. They also have food preparation facilities, and administrative offices. But don't go there, as they will both not let you in, or help you in any way. As a matter of fact, you have a pretty good chance of being shot if you hang out near that building for very long. Once, they shot the legs off of a prisoner that tried to get in. They left him there, where he became food for some of the rougher prisoners."

"Cannibalism?" he asked. Simon silently shook his head yes.

"The guards will not lift a finger to help you. Sure, they occasionally will stop a potential riot... it's bad for their profits after all... but otherwise, their only jobs are to make sure we are working and producing. Don't ever look to them for help." He looked at Arthur's pale skin before asking "Do you have sunscreen?" Arthur reached into his pocket and took out a small spray bottle of a greenish-fluid. "Good, always have that... sunscreen is life here. Almost more important than food...

speaking of which." He donned a pair of protective eye glasses, and noticed that Arthur had his standard issue. "Will need to get a better pair of those... for now, come on."

Simon and Arthur headed out into the crater, and walked to a food vending vehicle. Simon gave the guard working the vending station enough credits for two bowls of food. The guard slopped the yellowish-green muck into the bowls and handed them to Simon. He looked at the guard with a slight look of disgust – the guard ignored his repulsion to the substance. He handed the bowl to Arthur who gagged the moment the vile mush hit his palate.

"Yeah, it's pretty horrible... I don't think it's really food... but you get used to it, and it keeps you going... kinda." They forced their food down and returned the bowls for a small deposit credit. Then they headed back out further into the center of the crater. Simon stopped and pointed at a small cart that was roaming the crater area. "That is the water cart... always know where it is, and have the credits to buy drink. If you do not drink out here... you die." The cart moved across the crater like a perverted drink cart at a golf course – stopping on occasion to sell their precious wares to the fortunate working prisoners who had sufficient credits.

"Speaking of credits... I think it is time we earned some..." Simon lead Arthur to a rock spire a mile away from the main prison area. While they walked, Simon continued "Nothing is free here. If you need a necessity, you have to buy it. In order to buy it, you barter." Arthur looked at Simon with confusion. "The minerals trapped in the silica... gold and platinum. We can trade those for credits that we use at the prison store, drink carts, food wagons, and the cafeteria... by the way, avoid the cafeteria. Anyway, if you find an ingot of metal, bring it to a guard, and barter for credits. They will try to rip you off by the way... so be ready." He stopped and gave a serious look to Arthur "Also, our main purpose here is to find "Bomb Rocks". These are large geodes filled with radioactive elements. Those were the elements I told you about earlier... the ones that are reprocessed. They use them for energy production and of course, weapons. I warn you... there is a reason they call them "Bomb Rocks" ... if you manage to break the shell of one, you will die. They have an explosive force that will shower you with radiation... there will not be much left of you if you open one."

"Thanks, I'll be very careful... maybe I will not even look for them."

"You have to... you are required to find at least two Bomb Rocks a day. If you find extras, those can be bartered for credits. Any deficit will require a payment of your credits. That means, no food or water that day..." They stopped on the way at a supply cart, and rented two pickaxes for the day's work. As they walked to the spire Simon continued "I have determined a way of spotting the geodes while I dig. I have noticed, where ever there is a bomb rock, there is also a pattern in the soil right above the geode. Thus, when I dig, I feel the difference... then start to dig around the geodes... thus, avoiding my untimely demise. Also, this has helped me to earn a decent amount of credits... so, you can depend on me for help. But please, tell no one that I have stashed credits... it would mean the death to both of us..." Arthur shook his head in agreement. "Good... as despite my attempts to keep as remote as possible, I have still become noticed. Most recently by the Bronsky gang. They're a nasty group of thugs, headed by the Bronsky brothers... Mikey and Orville. You'll recognize them if you see them... they're big, strong, and mean. I once saw Mikey crush another prisoner's throat just for sitting next to him by mistake in the cafeteria. I mentioned not to go there, right? Anyway, they are the worst excuse for human society... which also makes them perfect residents of this prison. So, avoid them at all costs. I've tried, but unfortunately, I've also failed. Mikey saw me from a distance and has decided he doesn't like me, and now wants me dead. I wonder if it would just be easier to let him kill me..."

Arthur stopped and put his hand on Simon's arm, then told him "No, Simon... someday, you will get out of here... somehow... I know it. You have to live and survive for now."

The pair arrived at Simon's chosen spot to find Harvey Ramirez already working the spire. Harvey was an 83-year-old man who was sentenced to die here because he was deemed a threat to the state. The truth was that Harvey was simply of Brazilian decent. However, Harvey was also a full blooded American – born and raised in what was Texas before the war.

After the change of control of the U.S. government to the Council, it did not matter where Harvey was born. It only mattered that at one time his family lived in Brazil, and that he had darker skin. He was convicted as a terrorist, sentenced to work, and eventually die at the Rock Pit. So far, he had managed to survive his first year at the pit, just like Simon.

"Greetings Simon, a lovely hot day again isn't it?"

"Ah yes, the weather is the same as any day here. Hot with a possibility of an ion storm in the afternoon."

He looked at Arthur. "Who's this? New arrival?"

"Harvey Ramirez, this is Arthur Manes. Yes, he just arrived... he is also a former colleague of mine from the educational society."

"Pleasure to make your acquaintance Arthur... well, we had better get started. Those geodes will not unearth themselves!"

They all laughed, and found their spots in the large rock wall that loomed in front of them. They then began to look for their daily prizes. As they worked they chatted about life outside, and how someday they would figure out a way to escape and live. Their conversation energized the men, and helped them forget the heat and constant danger.

"Arthur, remember some of the songs of the old days of the republic? I've been teaching Harvey some of the classics. Hopefully, you remember some of those songs, as it's the best way to make the time go by quickly during the day. If that doesn't work... well, there are always the jokes..."

"No!" shouted Arthur, which caused the three of them to burst out laughing."

Their laughter was interrupted by a voice behind them. "Well, look who's having such a good ol' time... the smart one, the old one... and a new person?"

The familiar voice struck a note of panic is Simon – it was Mikey Bronsky. He did not turn, but continued to dig as the large bald man approached. Mikey had come to their work site alone. Simon assumed he was not worried about the three of them, and thus decided he didn't need his entourage of thugs.

He walked up to the elderly man and looked him up and down. "Let's see what we have..." He grabbed the old man by the neck, and with a single strong hand, lifted him off the ground. With the other hand, he searched his pockets to find a couple credits and his sprayer of sunscreen. "Two credits and sunscreen? Do you think that's enough to make me leave you alone, old man?" the large Bronsky asked Harvey.

"It's all I have... please... let me keep it!"

Bronsky let out a huge bellowing laugh, then peered at the old man being held in his huge grasp. "I'll tell you what, find me an ingot, and I might give you back your sunscreen...but your credits are mine. Call it your insurance policy to live one more day."

Panic showed in Harvey's eyes as he begged "I need my sunscreen, I can feel it wearing out... please!"

Arthur started to move toward the two men, but Simon stopped him with an open back hand. He softly shook his head in the negative, hoping to not attract Mikey's attention. He watched as the green gooey coating on Harvey had started to lighten in color – this indicated that the sunscreen had started to break down. It was evaporating ever so slightly every second – within minutes, he would start to burn.

Simon nodded his head to Arthur, then began picking at the soil once again while he tried to come up with a plan of escape. He knew any moment, Mikey would be gunning for the two of them. He feared the real possibility of dying if he could not come up with a plan. "*I need a plan, but what? What can I do to stop this guy? If I don't figure out something, Harvey will die... and more than likely, I will too... But what do I do?*"

His thoughts were stopped by a feeling underneath his pick – it was a feeling he had felt many times in the past. It was actually two feelings – the first was that of his pick finding an ingot in the soil. He bent over and brushed the soil from around the ingot. It was a platinum ingot, and a large one. Unfortunately, the second feeling under his pick worried him – this was the way the texture of the soil felt before he would hit a bomb rock.

As he peered at the ingot, he noticed the rocky surface of the bomb rock beneath. It appeared that the ingot was imbedded into the shell of the bomb rock. This would make it almost impossible to remove.

His thoughts were interrupted by Bronsky's rough voice "So, what do you have for me today, smart man? It had better be good... or you'll find yourself dead in one shake. You may find yourself dead in any case, since I really don't like you." By this time the large man had shaken Harvey unconscious, and had thrown him to the ground like an unwanted, overplayed sock puppet.

A shiver of fear raced through his mind, he knew he was doomed unless he thought of something – and then it came to him. "Mikey... I found something that will be of interest to you. You can have it... all you have to do is get it out of the ground. It's too heavy for me to lift" he told the enormous bald man now briskly walking toward him.

As Mikey approached, Simon realized that he is truly a disgusting example of the human condition. His nose was pierced, and sticking through the hole was the finger bone of a man – probably one of the many he tortured before finally killing like a bug. He had forbidden tattoos on his body. The predominant tattoo was on his bald head. It was a flaming skull with snakes coming out the eyes. This particular tattoo was considered a family tradition as it was the same tattoo worn on the head of his brother Orville.

Pushing Simon out of the way, he looked into the freshly dug hole carved into the hill. "Let's see... OH! That's a pretty one! I might actually let you live for this gift." His eyes were wide open, and were full of greed.

"Help yourself Mikey... here... use my pickaxe" He nodded ever so slightly to Arthur. He used his eyes to tell his friend *"Get out of the way!"* Arthur took his non-verbal cue and slowly moved to the side of the big man.

He handed the tool to the large man. He took the tool from his hand without removing his gaze from the large, shiny, lumpy hunk of platinum in front of him. Simon began to slowly step away. Mikey stood straight up, and began to flex his giant muscles in preparation of the work needed to obtain his prize. Simon's backward pace hastened, he was now almost around a rock when he heard Mikey shout "Come to papa, you beautiful baby!"

He swung the pickaxe and hit the ingot with everything his body could throw at it, but nothing happened. Simon could not believe his eyes, he thought for sure there was a geode below that ingot – he wondered if he could have been wrong? The large man bellowed out a huge laugh and reached in to pick up the large blob of precious metal. As he wiggled the ingot from the soil where it was stuck, a cracking noise was heard. Mikey stopped his movement, removed his grasp from the ingot and peered into the hole. A hiss began to escape below the shiny metal. Suddenly, the ingot burst forth, propelled by a gust of gasses from the ground. The ingot shot out at high velocity, hitting the large man, and embedding itself into his forehead. Mikey screamed as pain wracked his now bleeding forehead. He started to stagger when the geode opened up, and burst forth its deadly gale of gasses.

The gust of gas from the rock hit Mikey like a hurricane. The radioactivity quickly melted his flesh away as he screamed. Within seconds his muscles were melting, exposing his bones and internal organs. After a few more seconds the screaming stopped as the remainder of his body disintegrated – only his right hand, which somehow avoided the escaping gas remained intact. The now lifeless hand dropped to the ground with a splat as it landed into the large puddle of blood and liquid remains that was once Mikey Bronsky.

"Yes!" Simon shouted in celebration. He was happy for the removal of this awful person from the planet. "Enjoy hell, you..."

His celebration was cut short by the screams of Harvey Ramirez behind him. He turned to see smoke rising as the skin of his arms had begun to sizzle. His sunscreen had failed.

He rushed to the now smoldering Harvey "Where's your sunscreen?" he asked the old man in a panic.

"Simon, Mikey took it from me and I cannot afford to buy anymore! I think... I think I am going to die!" he shouted as the pain started to swell in his arms. He swatted at his arms, hoping to prevent the burning. Within moments his skin would actually catch fire, and from there his jumpsuit would follow in a fiery blaze.

"How do we help him?" asked Arthur in a panic. The smell of smoldering flesh was staring to make the pair of men nauseous.

"Always carry sunscreen…" Simon said as he took out a vial of sunscreen from his jumpsuit pocket and began to apply it to the old man's arms.

"No, don't waste it on this old man…" Harvey pleaded with Simon "If you use it on me, you'll not have enough and…"

Simon stopped him and pulled out another vial of the precious fluid. "Don't worry old man, I always have back up around here." He smiled and continued to apply the sunscreen.

Within moments of application, Harvey began feeling relief from the burning, and was recovered enough to resume work. They began digging, but only after a few minutes of work, the pair was once again interrupted – this time by an approaching guard in his hover cart. The guard pointed at Simon, and motioned him to come to the shade of the cart.

Simon sighed. "Man, I'm never going to get my quota at this rate!" he mumbled as he begrudgingly dragged himself to the guard.

"Piccolo, you have a visitor… some fancy doctor from a research facility wants to speak with you. Come with me now."

Simon was confused – who would want to speak with him, much less even know about his existence. In any case, who was he to argue with going into the air-conditioned administrative section.

He looked at Arthur. Knowing Simon's concern, he told him "We'll be alright… we'll see you when you return…"

The guard smelled him as he got into the cart, and sneered. "You will need to use the sonic shower before you speak with this doctor" he barked.

He smiled and replied "No complaints here… drive on." He put his feet on the dash of the cart, and put his hands behind his head, all while keeping a smug look on his face. The guard engaged the hover cart, and the pair scooted away.

The two men returned to their digging. They were only able to work for a few minutes before they sensed yet another awful presence behind him. They both turned slowly at the same time to see Orville Bronsky looming above him. He was accompanied by three large thugs.

"Have you seen my brother?" the large twin asked the scared old man.

Harvey could not reply since he did not want to be the bearer of bad news to this large man – he knew it would be the death of him. He just stood there shaking until one of Orville's thugs called to him.

"Boss, you had better see this."

"Arthur…" Harvey whispered "get out of here… they don't know you, go hide now…" Arthur took his advice, and ran.

The large Bronsky walked over and saw the hand of his brother lying on the ground. A tear came to his eye as he realized his brother was now gone.

He turned back to the old man with rage and hatred showing on his face. He asked "Who did this… who was working with you here today? Tell me now old man, or die!"

He muttered "It… it was Simon Piccolo. Please don't hurt me!" The old man began shaking uncontrollably – urine began to flow down his leg from fear of this large, evil man.

The giant man shook his fist to the sky, and yelled "Piccolo, I will make you suffer long and slow for this!" He turned to Harvey and whispered "However, you… old man, will die quickly!"

Orville took a pickaxe from the ground and quickly thrust the shoveled side into the top of Harvey's head, splitting it in two. Harvey gasped as the tool invaded his brain, severing critical nerves, splitting his skull and brain in half. Harvey immediately crumpled into a dead pile of flesh. Orville kept his promise to the old man – he did die quickly.

With a snort, he placed his foot on the now dead man's head for leverage, and pulled the pickaxe with a few jiggles of the handle. He wiped the blade clean with Harvey's shirt. After being satisfied with the now-clean blade, he turned to his thugs.

"First, go get that fat guy who just ran off. Then, find me Simon Piccolo, but don't kill him. Hurt him sure, but don't kill him… he's mine! He is going to die slowly and painfully!"

The gang members nodded and ran off looking for their prey.

*   *   *

Arriving at the administration center, Simon felt the blast of cold, clean air hit his face. "Ah, air conditioning... it feels soooo good!" he decried.

The guard laughed "Don't get used to it... as soon as this meeting is over, you will be right back out in the crater."

Simon hated the guard for ruining his moment of happiness. He frowned at the guard and turned his gaze straight ahead. After traveling for another minute, the cart stopped at a door.

Without looking at Piccolo the guard pointed at the door, and announced "Okay, get out and take a shower. Someone will escort you to meet the doctor after you are done. And don't take long... if you spend more than 4 minutes in the sonic shower it will become quite painful for you. It's programmed for prisoners that way." The guard had a happy smirk on his face as he told Simon that fact.

"Hey, what about my sunscreen?" he asked with indignation. "It'll get washed off, and I just applied it. Who's going to replace it?"

"Who cares? Not me, that's for sure. Perhaps the doctor will reimburse your expense for a new application."

"Right..." was the only word Simon had for this happy guard now relishing in the thought of his potential pain and expense.

He got out and entered the door. Once inside, there was a clean orange jumpsuit waiting for him on a stand, and the sonic shower all within a totally white room. There was a message on the monitor above the stand holding the clothing "Simon Piccolo owes 5 credits for new clothing, payable to any guard."

A heavy sigh escaped his lips. "Great, more expenses I can't afford. This is worse than the bills I had outside this hell hole!"

He removed his jump suit, and found he was also able to remove his protective underwear. They were called protective because they would only open when the electronic circuitry would detect the need to defecate or urinate. Otherwise they remained solid and could not be opened, removed or probed. This prevented unwanted advances by other members of the prison population. This underwear, along with chemicals added to the food, insured that there would be no sexual enjoyment by anyone in the facility. In the shower building however, the underwear was receiving a signal instructing disengagement. Simon felt the unbinding, and enjoyed the feeling of freedom he was experiencing without any clothing draping his body.

The shower felt wonderful. He made sure he did not give the guard the pleasure of going past the four minutes, and getting the pain of overuse. He exited the shower, and put on the fresh clothing.

"Well, not blue with stars... but it smells good!" he thought as he admired himself in the mirror on the wall.

Prison was hell, but he found that his body had developed nicely due to all the work he has been forced into during his stay. He thought as long as he could stay alive, he would be quite healthy and was turning into quite a ladies' man. That thought hit him like a brick wall, something he had not thought about in quite a while – women. If it weren't for a woman, he wouldn't be in his current predicament.

"Best to forget those troublemakers... not like I'll ever see one again anyway. Besides, these darn chemicals they've been feeding me would prevent any excitement anyway" he chuckled to himself at that thought.

He took one more look to make sure all clothing was in proper order, and left the shower building.

A guard sitting in the driver's seat of a cart was waiting for him. He looked upset as Simon hopped aboard the cart.

"I lost three credits on you Piccolo. Didn't you even want to take a long shower?"

Simon relished in the thought of this man losing money due to his diligence. He replied "Now what fun would that have been to me? Not like a long shower would have made me feel better."

Realizing that the previous guard had tipped him off to the pain timer on the shower, the guard showed his displeasure of being duped out of his money. "Forget it, let's just get you to the doctor so I can escort you back out into the crater where you belong."

He jerked the cart into forward motion, and raced to the administrative offices. Only a few moments of travel were needed before arriving at the offices. The angry guard prodded him through a door, and down a corridor to another door marked "Conference Room".

The guard opened the door and motioned for Piccolo to enter, which he did. Entering the room, he suddenly saw the one thing he thought and perhaps hoped he would never see again. In the room was a long table for meetings – on the opposite side of the table, facing him, was a woman.

She was professionally dressed in a dark purple skirt and matching jacket. She wore a white blouse with a matching purple feminine tie. The skin on her face looked flawless, and was a bright alabaster white. Her hair was a dark brown with two bright-white streaks starting from the high temples, and was pulled to the back of her head. He thought they looked like skunk stripes.

There was one thing he was totally sure of "*She is stunning!*" He knew he was true to his thoughts, despite being locked up for so long. If she was not appealing, the sexual calming drugs would do their work and he would not have any thoughts about her. He knew she was a looker – and the more he looked at her, the more it made him think about how she was mentally stimulating him.

A distant thought came to him about who she was. He pondered if his memory was as correct as he thought about the past. He then realized that she was only here because he is locked up in this pit. His thoughts brought shame to him due to his predicament, and he became embarrassed to be nothing but a lowly prisoner to this highly intelligent and beautiful doctor.

To the side of her at the table was a portable computer, he noticed his image on the screen with some information which he could not read. She looked him up and down, and gave a soft smile before standing and offering her small hand to him.

"I am Doctor Catherine Harmony from the Institute for Medical and Defense Research in sector 9".

He shook her hand lightly "Piccolo, Simon Piccolo... nice to meet you Doctor Harmony."

Her smile became even softer, and Simon thought that she had a look of recognition on her face as she released her light grip on his hand. She was looking deeply into his eyes, and he wondered what she was searching for.

"Please have a seat Mister Piccolo... may I call you Simon?" she said while gesturing him to a chair.

"Umm, yeah sure... Simon is fine"

He was flustered by this woman – he did not know what exactly to say. He was totally unprepared for this, and no longer knew how to react to not only someone with intelligence – but also to a woman with such an attractive look about her. He wondered if he had been locked up so long that he lost his ability to even deal with women anymore. His frustration showed to her as she once again looked him in the eyes.

She smiled warmly and spoke softly "Please relax and be comfortable." Eyeing the guard at the door she motioned for him to leave. "Please give us some time alone, will you?"

Begrudgingly he followed her orders. "I'll be right outside, use the panic key if you need me to take care of this guy..." the guard grumbled as he left the room while giving an evil glare to Simon.

Returning her gaze to Simon, she stared into his eyes, then looked away before turning to her computer screen. "Simon, it says here you are in this prison for life. Is that true?"

Her statement embarrassed and frustrated him. It also reminded him of the fate that awaited him back out in the crater. "Yes... and the way things are going... I'm afraid that might be a shorter stint than I was hoping."

She now looked concerned "Trouble?"

He nodded "Yes. If the work, or the heat, or the radiation doesn't kill me, Orville Bronsky will." He knew by now Orville would know of his treachery in the death of his twin brother, and would be out for painful vengeance.

She had genuine concern in her look now. Her voice had a slight tone of panic, and she now spoke with a sense of urgency. "Oh my, this is not good. Look, let me explain why I am here. I'm here on direct authority of the Council to select one subject for a scientific experiment. This experiment involves my training, and then direct manipulation of the subject's DNA. This manipulation will change the subject... forever. However, if you are the subject... you will be well treated, fed, and cared for... before, during and after the process."

Simon was confused "Let me get this straight. You want me to be a Guinea Pig for an experiment?"

She nodded in confirmation, and she slowed down the pace of her words "Yes, the first phase will involve my training in ancient mental meditation arts. With this meditation process, I hope to have you mentally prepared for the changes that will take place during DNA manipulation. I'll be honest with you, in the past, many test subjects have not fared well. So my proposition to you is a risky one. But in light of your circumstances... and the fact that you are indeed under a death warrant by the Order, I think that this would be a good alternative for you... especially since more than likely, you will live through the procedure. I see your IQ tests show you to be highly intelligent, and I feel this will help you in the long run. So, want to sign up Simon?"

He thought for a moment. "Exactly what are you a doctor of, anyway?"

She raised her head proudly and replied "Psychology"

He chuckled "A head shrink, eh? So, you think you can get me through this. Well, either way I am screwed... so what the hell!" He paused and thought a moment about Orville in the crater. "Ummm, can you get me out of here today?" A large smirk appeared on his face.

Between the look on his face, and his comment, a very unique giggle escaped from her mouth – it slightly shocked Simon for a moment. She then answered him. "Yes, I think we can get you out of here in a few minutes. I have a hopper ready to take us back. Do you need to go back for anything?"

He paused for a few seconds only for effect, then said "Ah, no... nothing back in the crater I can't live without. Let's go!"

She stood, and headed for the door. Simon stood, started following her, but then stopped himself in mid-stride. Catherine stopped, and looked at him with a confused face. "Is something wrong, Simon?"

"No... one second..." he thought for a moment then said "Ah! Row 10, seat 23, 14 years ago."

"What?"

"You must have been in your early 20's when you sat in Row 10, seat 23 in my class. I never forget the faces of my students. You did not have the stripes in your hair, and that threw me off, but your face is as pretty now as it was then! Yes, I remember you well."

Embarrassment over his compliment caused her to blush. She was also shocked he not only remembered her, but could recall exactly where she sat in the classroom those many years ago. "Wow, you have some memory... I think you'll be perfect to work with!" she admitted. "Let's get out of here Professor."

"After you Doctor" Simon gestured toward the door. The two met the guard, and with him in tow quickly walked to the waiting hopper.

"Work, work, work all day"

"All work and never play"

"The Council is the reason you live"

"Praise the Council for the hard work *you give..."*

Simon realized he would never have to listen to that horrid music again – at least he hoped they didn't play that stuff at the institute.

The waiting hopper was different from most he had ridden in the past. This one was a three-compartment model, and was much newer and nicer. As before, each compartment had clear protective walls to prevent moving between the sections. The guard opened the back section and motioned for Simon to get in. He followed directions and sat down in the back seat, then made himself comfortable.

Catherine sat in the front passenger seat, and turned to see how Simon was doing. She activated the speaker in the back

"All comfortable back there... need anything?"

He smiled. "No, just fine back here. But please keep the air conditioning running okay?"

She gave a nod "Will do, I'll keep you comfortable back there for the trip. Here we go!"

She motioned to the guard driving the hopper, the machine rose off the ground, and began its forward motion through the exit tunnel. It exited the tower, and Simon suddenly realized he was free of that hell. He wondered if Harvey was alright, and hoped he would not die too soon, or too horribly.

Although tempted, he did not turn to look out the rear window. He was never going to return there, and he never wanted to look at that place again. He felt bad leaving Arthur alone there, but he had no control over either of their fates. His life had suddenly changed – he was going to live, albeit perhaps in a different way. He looked at the doctor in the front seat – he realized he was actually looking forward to working with her. *"Yes,"* he thought *"life may end up being different, but it was once again on the upswing."* He settled back in the seat, and within minutes he fell quickly into a deep sound sleep – the first sound sleep he had experienced in over a year.

9

"At Alliance Health, we care for those who were not fortunate enough to be born with all facilities. We are concerned for your loved ones, and provide an atmosphere that is conducive to learning and growing. Alliance Health is one hundred percent backed by your Supreme Commander and the Council of Order, both for the treatment, and curing of the mentally disabled and mentally or emotionally impaired. With new discoveries in treatments being found every day, we promise to provide the best most modern care available. Discover what Alliance Health can do for your disabled loved one today. Class restrictions apply, financial restrictions apply, and not all citizens are approved for care at Alliance Health. Check with your insurance provider, if you have one, about Alliance Health today."

It was a dark night after lights out at Booshae Memorial Prison for the Criminally Insane. Galen Woods sat in his cell, and looked out the small window. He had nothing better to do, sleep was really unimportant – life was really unimportant, and he was bored, as always. Galen did not really know why he was there, but the nice man told him he needed to live there, so he did. Galen knew, soon he would finally tire of staring out the window and go to sleep. He would then wake up in the morning, eat, and help Mr. Simms in the factory putting the clothes into the large round thing. That is all Galen needed to know – it was all he knew to do.

*   *   *

That morning, Derrick and Stephanie arrived at the prison. They were to meet with Warden James Franco about a set of subjects for their project at the Institute. Derrick felt they were fortunate in their funding. The primary purpose of the Institute was for defense and the creation of weapons, and yet they were funded for medical research. The Council's recent decisions stated that it was important to provide medical cures for the incurable – the habitual criminal, the mentally deficient, and the insane.

He and Stephanie had finally made the big breakthrough, the one that proved that DNA could be bonded together, and then inserted into a subject. This bonding would then cause a mutation of the brain. Through this mutation, the subject would receive the benefit of the donor's brain functions, which they hoped would improve both the thought processes and intelligence of the subject.

Although to date, they only had success with lab rats. But it was enough to make Edward Zardonagon press the issue. He had ordered them to begin human experiments, thus ending their studies on lesser animals. Since his order, they had spent the past week finding subjects for their first batch of experiments. Through their search, they had located some good potential subjects. They both had high hopes that through their research, these subjects would benefit, and become productive members of society once again.

It was only a short hop from the Institute to the prison. The two scientists had been up all-night sifting through, and selecting their potential list of first subjects. Derrick had met with Stephanie after a short two-hour rest, and now were headed to meet their subjects.

"Warden Franco says the people we picked should make excellent subjects for our experiments. I really hope the profiles match the people...if they do, they will indeed make good candidates."

"That's wonderful! I'm so confident we have the correct computations required to insert the genetic materials correctly, Derrick... I can feel our success!"

"You do know how much I hope that your intuition is correct... don't you Steph?"

"Oh, we *will* succeed doctor. I can see you getting the next Council science award!"

She showed an aura of total confidence in her being. Her attitude was affecting him too, as he was starting to feel slightly confident – until his natural cynicism took over. "Well now..." he wiggled his finger at her in disagreement, and gave a small chuckle "let's not get too far ahead of ourselves. I think we first have to get a few human successes... then we can dream of awards!"

She had a large smile on her face, and her blue eyes were wide-open in excitement. He looked at her, and his gaze stared deep into her eyes. He came to the realization that she was beautiful – at least to him. He smiled back at her with confidence, but his thoughts were instead drifting to potential moments they could spend together – when work was not the forefront of their time together.

He felt the feelings growing inside him. He knew he would have to quell these feelings for now. They had formed a friendship through their work, and he never wanted to ruin that relationship. So, he kept telling himself that friends they would always be. But sometimes he wondered if she felt anything for him. *"Get it out of your mind!"* He pushed his desires out, and hoped he would never give his feelings away.

As they flew into the prison grounds the hopper entered a large tunnel that opened, and immediately closed behind them as they passed through. This is the only entrance into the prison. The hopper's auto pilot engaged, and drove the vehicle deeper and deeper into the center of the mountain. The lights of overhead lamps flashed into the hopper's cabin as they made their way into the center of the mountain complex. Derrick relaxed his grip on the steering controls, and then sat back as they watched the tunnel walls race by their hopper windows.

While they waited to arrive, Derrick started conversing. "I'm told that they picked this location so they could house the prison on the cliff side of this mountain. They put windows in the cells, and they even open. It seems kind of cruel however, as the fall from those windows is quite long. But I guess it prevents escapes..."

"Seems cruel..." she replied. "They can look out at freedom, but never achieve it until they die."

"I'm sure they count on some of them falling... keeps the population down. I guess if one was to go down to the bottom of the cliff, they would find piles of bones from hundreds of prisoners. We'll be going to the administrative offices in the middle of the mountain for our interviews. The closest we will be getting to the cliff might be the warden's office, which is also on the cliff face. "Ah, here we are" he announced as the hopper slowed and finally came alight in front of a large metal door.

Warden Jacques Franco was waiting at the door to greet them. Standing there was this stocky man with a dark bicycle mustache, and expansive smile on his face. He had light skin, dark eyes, and he had quite a happy look about him. They surmised he must really enjoy visitors – perhaps real visitors are few and far between for him. He was wearing a brown, plaid, two-piece suit, with a plain brown tie, a white shirt, and shiny faux leather brown shoes – perfectly polished and kept. His clothing matched his shoes, and was clean and well pressed, showing his attention to personal and professional detail. With a big smile, he took Derrick's hand, and shook it vigorously.

"Welcome Doctor Swanson!" He then looked at Stephanie, and his eyes lit up. "And you must be Doctor Wilcox..." He dropped Derrick's hand, and without removing his gaze from Stephanie, quickly grabbed her hand to shake it softly He then immediately took her by the arm, and walked her to the door. "It is not often we get such distinguished visitors. Come to my office."

He dragged Stephanie off to leave Derrick standing alone with all of their briefcases and equipment. With a huge sigh, he grabbed the cases, and ran off in pursuit.

They walked down the entrance corridor to yet another metal door that was the final door restricting entrance to the prison.

"Please press your fingers against the sensor for a DNA reading... this will allow you to unlock the doors, and disable the laser defense system. Each one of us must pass through the entrance one at a time. As the system must identify each person passing, it is imperative we only pass one at a time. You will see slots in the hallway walls, celling, and floor... these are the portals for the defense lasers. You *don't* want to activate that system... if anyone was stupid enough to try to get in or out without their identities being verified... well, there would only be bits left after the system finished with them." The pair of scientist gave a worried look. "Don't worry... you will pass safely. Now, let's go inside, shall we?"

One by one, they pressed the sensor, a light acknowledged their identities, the door opened, and they each passed safely through the door into the mantrap. The mantrap should have actually been called the deathtrap. It consisted of steel doors at each end and polymer walls, floor and ceiling. As Warden Franco had told them, they saw the polymer hallway had slots that allowed for the array of lasers to shine through. If anyone were to not validate their identities, then enter through either door, the doors would lock and a grid of lasers would slice the poor victim into small bits regardless of who they were. It was not built to capture, but to clear another cell for someone else in the event they were foolish enough to try to escape via this passage.

After the three had proceeded through the mantrap, they walked down the corridor to yet another door, with another DNA sensor lock. This was the door to the Warden's office. "Here we are..." he placed his finger on the sensor opening the door lock.

Derrick and Stephanie followed the Warden and each placed their fingers on the sensor lock, which allowed the door to unlatch, open, and for them to enter the office.

The Warden's office was lushly appointed with rare hardwood on the walls. There was a wall of monitors that displayed the various cameras throughout the prison. This allowed him to view or check the status of any part of the complex. The bookshelf on the far wall was filled with books – Derrick noted that most were classics that most thought were destroyed in the first bombing. Music was softly playing in the background. A large rare hardwood desk appointed the center of the room. Behind the desk sat a large comfortable chair that could swivel and look out the floor to ceiling windows over the cliff and into the valley below.

"I have a fine selection of lost wines and pre-war Scotch. Can I offer you a glass?" Jacques pointed at the large bar of various bottles. "Perhaps, you would prefer something more southern?" he smiled as he walked over to the bar and pointed to a bottle of contraband southern Brazilian rum.

"I think I will pass, I need to think clearly for this... but thank you" Derrick told his gracious host.

"I had better pass too" she also told the Warden.

He sighed. "Very well, then I suppose you want to take a look at possible subjects. All work and no play, eh?" he smiled with an evil grin, walked back to his desk, and then activated the monitor screens.

The screen focused on a large young man with brownish, blonde hair. He was a fairly attractive man, and was very tall and muscular. The one thing that stood out to Derrick was the slight bulge in his forehead. He surmised that this likely indicated some form of brain deformity.

Jacques pointed at the screen "This is Galen Woods, he is a life resident. He was convicted of murdering a clerk at a store. He is also mentally deficient."

"Really... is he violent?" Derrick asked.

"No, but he has the comprehension of a 6-year-old." he replied. "We really don't know what he can or cannot learn or remember. He works at the one job he knows... and works hard. That's all we care about. He's in the laundry facility currently... would you like to meet him?"

Stephanie showed her excitement in her voice "Yes, can we see him right away? He looks like he'll be perfect for our experiment!"

Derrick chuckled "Well, I guess we had better go see him... right now."

Jacques smiled, and motioned them to a secured door on the other side of the office. The door automatically opened when they approached, which allowed access to an elevator car.

"This will take us up into the complex... follow me." Jacques entered the elevator, then motioned for the two scientists to follow.

The elevator moved quickly upwards then suddenly stopped. Stephanie gasped at the sudden acceleration and immediate deceleration. The doors opened to reveal a rock corridor ahead of them.

Jacques pointed to the rocks comprising the corridor, and told the duo "Besides their small windows to the outside world, this is all a prisoner here will see"

Derrick knocked on the rock wall and felt how solid it was. "I would not want to live here full time."

Jacques gave a laugh as he proceeded along the corridor, guiding the two scientists in the direction of the laundry facility.

When the door to the laundry opened – standing directly in front of them was the large young man they saw in the video display.

"Galen, these two people are here to see you."

Galen looked at them confused, as no one had ever come to see him. "Hi..." he muttered after he looked at them for a moment.

"Hello Galen. I am Doctor Swanson and next to me is Doctor Wilcox. Mind if we speak for a few minutes."

Galen replies "Only... ummm... only if it is ok with Mr. Simms. Ummm, he is... umm... my boss. I got to ask him... ummm... if I can talk to you."

He looked at the man running the laundry who acknowledged his acceptance with a nod.

"Ummm... okay, I...ummm... can talk I guess" Galen smiled as he sat down at the table with the trio.

Derrick asked "Galen, do you know why you are here?"

Galen looked a bit confused for a minute, but then nodded his head in confirmation. "Ummm... yes... I was told I did a bad thing."

"Mind telling us about what you did, Galen?" Stephanie asked.

"Ummm... okay...ummm... sure, I can... I guess." Galen replied.

Over the course of the next hour and a half, he told them about how he ended up in this prison. He told them the story about the two neighbor boys he played with. These two boys liked to make him do things that they would not do themselves – they told Galen they were their "special games". One of the games they liked to play was good guys and bad guys. They always made Galen play the bad guy. They would tell him to take guns, and pretend to shoot people. Galen didn't know any better, so he did. As the boys got older, they began to tire of Galen always being around. One day, they decided if Galen was going to always be there, then they should make him useful. So, they instructed him to be the bad guy, and use the gun like they always told him to during play. Galen thought this was their normal game.

That evening, they went to an all-night store, told Galen to go in, point the gun, and demand the storekeeper give up his money. They told Galen it was all in play, but they were lying to him. Regardless, he did what they told him to do. He walked in, pointed the gun at the clerk, and demanded the money.

He told the clerk "Ummm... give the money or bang-bang!"

The store clerk thought it was a joke, and told the boy to go away before he called the authorities. Galen did not expect the pistol to actually fire a beam when he pulled the trigger, but he also did not think his friends would replace his toy with a real gun. Galen still had not realized what he had done – he thought this was still part of the play acting. So, he took the cash, some Scrunchy Snacks, and walked out to the car.

His friends never thought he would actually pull the trigger, and when they saw the gun fire killing the clerk, they left him at the store to take the rap. Galen, not knowing what to do, decided to go back into the store and find some more Scrunchy Snacks. The police found Galen in the store, a dead man behind the counter, a gun in his belt, and cream filling on his face. The trial was not really a trial, but more a determination about which prison to send him to. It was decided to put him in this facility, where they would never have to deal with him again.

Booshae Prison was where all of the mentally disabled and insane were sent. The Council did not want to deal with them, but also did not want to execute them as it would look bad to the populous. So, they decided to just put them somewhere, and let them rot – a typical way the Council dealt with their problems. Many here had not even committed a crime, but only had the misfortune of being born with a defective brain.

For the few prisoners who were not disabled, who were sane and were just unlucky enough to be sent here, this was as good as a death sentence. Most of these prisoners would only be allowed contact with the disabled and insane prisoners. After a while this would lead these normal minded convicts to a "flight" down the cliff wall.

There was a board on the wall in the laundry office that listed the "flight pool". There were names of the prisoners, estimates on who would be the next to leave, and when. When one would take the flight to the bottom of the cliff, the guards made either cheers or jeers as for one lucky guard, he or she would now have a nice little bonus for the month. *"For such an up to date prison, this is really a horrible place"* Derrick thought to himself as he peered at the board from across the room.

Now that he had heard Galen's story, Derrick thought he would be perfect for their treatments, and also this would be a perfect opportunity for him. Perhaps this would allow him to escape this place and maybe actually have a life in the future. Yes, he felt they could give him a better life – a life away from this horrid place. He would have a new life as an intelligent member of society. Derrick and Stephanie would cure him, and help him to live a productive and happy life from now on.

Derrick took out a small computer from his briefcase. "Galen, I run a scientific study that requires live people for experimentation. I think you would be perfect for this program. I must warn you however, it is dangerous, but I am confident you will be fine. I would like you to come and participate. It will get you out of here, and grant you a pardon. What do you think?"

"Umm... what does that mean?"

Stephanie laughed "Silly, you can get out of this place and work with us!" she said, then smiled.

When Galen saw the smile, he returned the smile and said "Umm... you and Doctor Derrick are nice. I guess... ummm... I will do what... what you said you were going to do."

Derrick placed the computer in front of Galen. It had a pledge of participation with a signature line. "I need to you sign this then."

Galen looked confused at the computer. Jacques realized Galen did not know how to read, write, or did not have any idea about what Derrick was trying to get him to do. "We have his response on video... that is good enough."

Jacques stood up and motioned to the door "Now, if you will follow me please... there are plenty more people to view. I have one in particular... and we are short on time."

Derrick looked at his chronograph, and noticed that it took Galen over an hour and a half to tell his story. "Goodness, I didn't realize we had been in here so long. Yes, please take us to the next subject. Thank you, Galen... see you soon."

"Bye-bye Doctor Stephanie... Doctor Derrick."

Galen immediately returned to his work. He wondered what they said to him, he really didn't understand, but they were nice, so it didn't matter. *"Why did they say he was leaving? Where would he go?"* He thought that he would miss Mr. Simms. Galen told him he was going to miss him. Simms laughed, and then gave him a look of slight repulsion. He turned away from Simms without another word, and returned to his work – putting the white cloths into the big round thing.

Meanwhile, Jacques took the pair of scientists to another part of the prison. This particular area was tightly locked down with high security doors. The pair realized that there was a noticeable lack of windows of any kind.

"This is our high security area for our criminally insane. The people here all committed a capital crime, and are all quite insane I promise you. I have one in particular that should be of interest, she is totally out of it. She murdered a few random people before she was caught and brought here. Care to meet her?"

"Absolutely!" Derrick shouted.

"Oh yes, a criminally insane person would be the ideal test for our process" Stephanie said. "If we could cure one person of their insanity... well could you imagine the possibilities?"

"Of course, I might be out of a job!" Jacques gave a hearty laugh as he was far from worried about his employment stability.

The trio approached a triple reinforced steel door. Jacques placed his finger onto the touch pad to open the door. The three doors clanged, as large locking devices disengaged. The doors then slid open – one at a time, revealing a split room. On the closest side was a viewing area with chairs. In the middle, a wall made of polished stainless-steel bars, which protected the people sitting in the viewing area. On the other side of the bars was a room with a single chair. Sitting in this chair was a woman. She had short, black hair, and ghostly white skin as she had not seen the light of day in years. Her dark eyes were bloodshot, with large dark bags underneath. She didn't appear to be strong, but the pair of scientists knew that this look was deceiving. Around her neck was a choker type of necklace. There were vials attached to the back of the necklace. Every few minutes a slight hiss would be heard from the necklace. She sat in the chair calmly.

"This is Lisa...she has no last name that we know of. Don't be fooled by her calm appearance. Let me show you. I will turn her calming necklace off."

He pulled a control unit out of his pocket. Entered some codes into the unit, and then selected the command sequence for her necklace. After he pressed the button, the hissing from the necklace ceased. Lisa sat calmly for a moment, and then her dark bloodshot eyes gazed up in the direction of the spectators in the opposite compartment. A snarl appeared on her face, without warning, she screamed wildly, and then lurched out of the chair. She lunged toward the three people while screaming and reaching through the bars to get at them.

Stephanie gasped in shock over the rage and anger boiling over in this young girl in front of her. Lisa reached over and over through the bars, as she tried to get to any one of the three on the other side of the protective wall. She backed off for a second, and then wrapped her small hands around the steel bars. Suddenly, her biceps flexed and turned rock hard – veins bulged out through the skin of her arms, veins in her neck also bulged like they were about to burst, and she began to try to move the bars to get to the trio. To Derrick's surprise, he noticed the bars beginning to give and bend under her great strength.

"Umm, Jacques... perhaps we should sedate her again?" He asked nervously.

"Of course, Derrick. I just wanted you to see the real Lisa when the necklace is not active. She is quite violent... and quite strong. You need to realize and remember that... if you decide to take her."

He pressed a button on his control device, and the hissing sound was instantly heard from the neck device. Within seconds she was once again calmed – she turned away from the bars, slowly walked over to the chair, and sat back down.

"Whew!" Derrick let out with a whistle.

Jacques laughed "Do you still want to take her? She'll be a handful unless your experiments work."

Stephanie announced "Yes, we must help her... and I know we can!"

"Very well... I'll send an orderly familiar with Lisa to go with you then. For your protection and assistance... how would that be?"

"That would be very helpful... thank you Jacques" Derrick replied.

"Very well. Now we have a few more people for you to review... if you will follow me..."

*   *   *

The two scientists left that evening in the hopper. Aboard with them was a prison orderly, Galen, Lisa, and two other subjects. Jacques told them, that two more would be sent on a weekly basis. If needed, he would send more if they requested.

They left the prison satisfied, but they still had a nervous ride back. The pair sat quietly, while the hopper traveled automatically. They barely spoke – as they were worried a conversation might awaken Lisa in the very back. She was completely sedated, but they wondered and worried about what would happen if for some reason the necklace device failed while they were traveling. They called ahead and ordered a special subject cell be modified for her—they were going to take no chances until she was cured.

10

Simon needed a few days to rest and relax after his ordeal at the Kansas City Prison. But now his mind was fresh, he was clean, he had shaved his beard off, his hair was neatly cut, his teeth were clean and repaired, and best of all – he had eaten good food until he felt full. Yes, he was ready for whatever fate was going to throw at him. He actually was quite pleased with fate so far – after all, he was now working with Doctor Catherine Harmony.

He found her to be enchanting. He knew it was not his long prison stay, not the long periods of loneliness – there were other women at the Institute, and he found no attraction toward them. He also found he quickly had already forgotten the promise he made to himself to avoid women. He was actually looking forward to working with her. He knew there is a genuine attraction – he found her to be irresistible, and found he was unable to refuse any request she made of him.

He wondered if she would ever feel the same toward him. He assumed that she did not share his feelings – she was a true professional, and he doubted she would get involved with a patient. Also, there was the end of their work together, when he would be transformed into who knows what. Yes, he should just remove those thoughts from his mind – but for now, perhaps a little flirting would not hurt.

When Simon arrived at her office today, he found her reviewing personnel history files that had been recently sent from Council headquarters. He knew that she felt it was important that she know everything possible about her patients, and requested a constant stream of whatever information had been made available. As she read the report, her face had become stiff. As she continued to read the report, Simon detected a distinct chill in her attitude toward him. He could tell she actually had already read the files, but for some reason she continued to read them over and over again. He quietly sat uncomfortably in the chair across from her desk while he waited for her to say something.

Finally, she looked up from the monitor and stared coldly at him. After a long silent pause, she said "So Simon, it says here you were imprisoned for terrorism. I could never imagine you could do something this bad. I thought you told me you committed acts of political activism. Why did you lie? I was under the impression you had just done some minor acts. But no, you went and actually attempted to overthrow the government... really? You attempted violence, and actually tried to kill members of the Council... even plotted to kill the Supreme Leader? Maybe I was wrong about you. I wished I had received this secret file before I asked you to join. I'm now wondering if I made a mistake in picking you. I wonder if perhaps I should send you back. What do you have to say for yourself?" She had worked her brain into a lather – she was angry and was acting as cold as she could.

Simon suddenly felt even more uncomfortable sitting in his chair, and involuntarily wiggled slightly. He then let out a huge sigh. "It's this world we live in, and the government that runs it... we live in a world ruled by fear and deception. A world ran by those who will stop at nothing, or stoop to any level to achieve their ultimate goals. They will take a man and crush the life out of him... until he either lies down and dies, or decides to do anything to survive. One mistake can be the end of a person or at least of the life they knew. "

He gave a long hard stare into her eyes before he continued. "Now, let me tell you the story of a man, a professor to be exact. A college professor who was really, really stupid, and thought he could change the world. At least change history as we knew it."

He proceeded to tell her the story about how he discovered the web of lies the Council and the Supreme Leader had woven. How they had started the war on false pretenses. How he had found evidence to prove his theories. How he was deceived by his girlfriend and turned over to the Secret Service. How he had been accused and judged as guilty without a real trial, and sent to the death camp to either die or rot.

She could not believe what she was hearing – the stone appearance of her face softened and deep concern appeared in her eyes as she stared at him. "My god Simon, you really did discover that?" She stopped for a moment and considered the potential consequences of such a discovery. "Yes, I could understand why they would want to silence you. It must have been a horrible experience." She shut down the computer "Once

I read this changed story, I actually assumed it was a trick. I have always been able to see through the Council's deceptions. Besides, your aura is telling me you are sincere. That is another gift I have… the ability to see through deceptions in people. You speak to me, and all I see is the truth flowing from your aura."

She smiled at him warmly now. "You and I are both lucky that you were strong, and used your cunning and guile to survive until I could find you and get you out of there. Simon, I'm so sorry that I had to doubt you long enough to discover the truth about your history and intentions." The cold tinge had lifted from her voice, and her face was now glowing with concern and compassion.

Simon looked at her, saw the change in her disposition and smiled "I was indeed lucky to have been found and saved by you!" He stood up and moved in front of her, kneeled, and finally took her hand. He placed the hand on his forehead. "You are indeed my Joan of Arc – my savior. I will be forever in your debt." He then took her hand and gave it a light kiss. He felt the smooth skin of her hand, and the light sweet taste of her skin on his lips. He wanted more but he knew he had gone far enough. He released her hand, and then looked up at her. She was blushing and smiling.

"My goodness Simon, you really are a charmer!"

"I do try… and it is very easy with someone like you." He wanted to say more but placed her hand back into her lap and went back to his chair.

She gave a small laugh. But then her look turned stoic again. "Well, Sir Galahad, we unfortunately also have work to do. I now have complete faith and trust in you… and thus, I need to start to train you in my techniques."

"Ah yes, all work and no play" he decried. "But I can think of no better teacher than you for what I have to learn. I am your willing student. The tables have been turned; the teacher is now the pupil. I am ready… you may begin." He bowed his head again while he peered at her.

She giggled "Now stop Simon! We'll start your training, but not today" she announced "let's start tomorrow shall we? Today, I would just like to talk and get to know you better. Then later, I have to attend a meeting. But... I would love to spend some time and have dinner this evening. Would that be okay?"

Simon gave a small smirk "Well, let me check my busy social schedule..." he paused and looked up in deep thought before saying "Okay, I have an opening and would love to squeeze you into my busy schedule for dinner! Say between pacing in my cell, and rolling around in my uncomfortable bed. Yes, I think I can squeeze in some time then."

She laughed again. "I can see working with you will be very enjoyable and entertaining. I think we'll actually have some fun! I'm truly amazed you still have such a vibrant sense of humor after everything you have been through."

"Actually, I am amazed of that myself. Not sure why however..."

"I think it's your spirit, and sense of decency. Seeing how you react to adversity reminds me of a time I had to help a woman – she had been severely, but legally tortured in the course of her service to the military. They actually performed surgery on her un-sedated! It must have been horrible for her, and she had such anger in her heart after that. Fortunately, I was able to get to her quickly. She too was a decent person inside, despite her military record and her success in the business of war. Because of her inner decency, I was able to use meditation and hypnosis to remove, or at least bury the hatred that burned in her. I always wonder how she's doing..."

"Why don't you find out?"

"Well, if I could. But she was a Captain on the Starlight. I doubt we'll ever hear anything about that ship again. But I do hope she made it, and is still fighting and surviving. And, it brings me back to you. Your captivity, the deliberate misjudgment, and the pain you have been through... and yet you still smile." She noticed his eyes sparkled when he looked at her – she tried desperately to ignore the looks he gave her.

"Once again, it's the company that I am with!" He once again flashed a toothy smile, and she in turn smiled and softly laughed.

They spent the next few hours talking and enjoying each other's company. Like every good thing however, it eventually

116

had to come to an end. Catherine summoned a guard to escort him back to the living quarters, and to his cell. She bid a fond farewell, and motioned the guard to take him back. She noticed he continued to turn his head around to look at her while he walked down the hallway.

The guard walked him from the labs to the living quarters for the human population of subjects. His living cell was one of the larger units within one of the upper levels in the patient living quarter complex. The first twenty levels were used for the guards and keepers. The keepers made sure the food delivery and waste disposal equipment were functioning properly. They also made sure that the cells were kept clean by its inhabitants. Below level 20 were the patient's cells. They call them "patients", but in reality, they were prisoners. They were all at least treated well and fed decently, so Simon didn't have a problem staying there. He thought it sure beat the death camp prison in Kansas City.

He arrived at his cell, and cleaned up lightly. Then he pressed the button on the back of his cell, and the wall opened to reveal a passageway. This passage led to the recreation area of that level. Each level in the living quarters was arranged in a circular manner. Each patient level had an outer ring that provided passage between the cells for the keepers and guards. On the inside of the hallway ring were the cells. The cells were alternating keystone shapes joined together so they formed a ring around the entire level. Passage tunnels then connected the back side of the cells to the recreation and exercise area. This area took up the remainder of each patient level. The area had an opaque ceiling that allowed light to flow down from the upper levels. The center of the floor of each area was also of the same opaque materials. This provided light for the levels below. The opaque material was shaped in a large lens, which magnified the light with each level so the intensity never varied from level to level regardless of depth. Artificial trees sat in large pots surrounding the opaque discs. In addition, rocks and patches of carpet turf were placed to give a park-like setting for relaxation. There was also exercise equipment and benches for sitting. It really was a fairly relaxing place to be. Simon assumed they wanted to keep them happy – as any one of them could become the first super soldier of the future.

In this area, the patients could walk, exercise, meet each other, talk, play games, and sometimes even fall in love. Simon had already made friends in the recreation area. He found most of the patients were very nice, and normally very intelligent. One such person was Danny Drake.

Danny was a native Jamaican. Danny of course suffered from one issue that caused his problems with the Order – his color. Because he was black, he was tried for treason – all because the nations of Africa were part of the southern hemisphere. It didn't matter that Danny was from an island only a short distance from North America. He was lucky, or unlucky enough to not be on the island when the bomb hit and removed everyone he knew and loved from existence. So as a single survivor, he attempted to live in America and not cause trouble. The Council and the Secret Service had other plans however. When they started their "Southern Ethnic Purge" campaign, Danny was caught up in the ensuing police action. He was tried in a Kangaroo Court, and sentenced to death. This project at the Institute was his only hope for survival – just like Simon.

"Greetings mi good frien' Simon, how be you mon?" Danny said while shaking Simon's hand. He had a huge toothy smile on his face, and his dreadlocks swung from side to side as he heartily shook his friend's hand.

"You look like the cat that ate the bird today Danny. Why the big smile?"

"Yeh, mi very Irie – mi in lub" he announced.

"Danny please...speak in regular English with me – PLEASE."

"Aye, sorry – I forget, and it is my native tongue" he replied as he forced non-slang words out of his mouth.

"Thank you! So, you and Cora Lee finally hit it off? I knew you would you ol' devil, you" he surmised.

"Aye, jah know."

"That's just great... I'm so happy for you" he exclaimed. He thought for a moment, and allowed a somber look to slip across his face, before saying "You do know however, that you both will be changed..."

A pained look came upon the dark Jamaican's face upon that revelation. "Aye..."

"Danny!" Simon heard in the distance. He turned and looked behind him. He spotted Cora Lee Williams walking toward the pair. "I've been looking everywhere for you!" she scolded, then looked over to Simon and smiled "Hello Simon..."

To Simon, Cora Lee was a plain-looking woman. She was slender, and stood about a half a foot below Simon's gaze. Her hair was blonde, and looked like the corn straw from an antique broom. She wore a dress she had made out of the white jumpsuits issued to the patients. The keepers didn't seem to mind her modifying her outfit -- they may have even liked the variety in her outfits. Simon did not think she she he was actually pretty – but Danny thought she was beautiful, and that was good enough for Simon. He was glad they were happy. She walked up to Danny and gave him a big kiss, which he gladly returned. Simon turned his head slightly, to not seem like a voyeur.

After breaking her embrace, she turned toward her lover's friend. "How are you Simon? How's that attractive doctor you keep meeting with?" she had an evil smile on her face. Cora Lee had seen right through his façade, and knew he was attracted to Catherine. He wondered if Catherine read him as easily.

Simon let slip a nervous laugh "Well, I've been meeting with her and we'll have dinner this evening. As much as I would like to admit more – that's all that is happening right now."

"Well, you will get her to lub you, Simon" Danny proclaimed "if this guy can get someone as beautiful as Cora Lee then for sure a handsome man like yo'self can get dat doctor."

"We will see..." Simon's smile turned down slightly "but I have to remember that eventually I will change... and she will not."

"Maybe you two will hit it off anyway. Danny and I know we'll change someday... we hope we'll be lucky, and be transformed into a similar species... or at least compatible. But in any case, we'll recognize each other, and protect each other. We'll still find a way to love each other no matter what! I know Danny will protect and take care of me regardless of what I become."

Simon realized they truly had a special relationship. "Well, let's hope your transformations don't come soon. You have to take every moment to enjoy each other. Listen, I'm going to go get cleaned up, and get ready for dinner. I'll catch up with you two later."

"Lickle more. Link up with you layta" He said as he waved farewell to his friend.

"See you soon, Simon!" Cora Lee changed her expression as soon as Simon was far enough away. "Danny, I'm so scared we'll change and I will turn into something horrible... something that will cause you to no longer love me..." she had deep concern in her voice, tears were also welling up in her eyes.

"Don' worry dear... no madder wat, ol' Danny will take care of you."

"Promise me Danny, if I'm turned into a monster you'll put me out of my misery... please!"

"I kno that will not happen, but if it do... Danny will take care of you and relieve you of da pain. I hope you will do da same for me."

"Of course, my love." She sealed her promise with a kiss.

*   *   *

Simon arrived back at his cell to find that it was almost time to go to dinner. He cleaned his face, and straightened out his hair and clothes. When it was time, the guard came by to escort him to the scientific staff living quarters. He was then taken to her apartment. He rang the bell to find Catherine waiting for him. She was wearing a formal evening gown – bright sequins adorned the long, purple outfit. A low-cut neckline exposed much more of her chest than Simon wanted to see while in his current confinement.

"Hello again, Simon. I thought perhaps we could just dine here tonight... it's much quieter. If, however you prefer, we could have dinner in the cafeteria..."

"Oh no! Dinner here would be perfect. I could think of no better place, and no better person to dine with tonight." He flashed a smile that could stop a charging bull.

She smiled back at him and laughed "Oh good! I really didn't want to have dinner with you in that cold cafeteria. I much prefer this intimate environment where we can really talk and continue to get to know each other." She waved off the guard, who gave her a raised eyebrow, then stiffly turned and walked down the corridor.

Upon entering her quarters, he looked over by the set of floor to ceiling windows. A table was set with various items of food. There were candles on the table. Simon looked and noticed a bottle on the table.

He softly smacked his lips hoping for the correct answer to his question "Is that... is that wine?" The sound of anticipation filled his voice.

"Well, it is artificial... I couldn't get the real stuff today."

"Who cares? I have not had even fake wine in over a year!"

She laughed "I bet there are quite a few things you have not had in a whi..." she realized the mistake in her statement and stopped herself.

Simon noted her embarrassment to her thoughtless comment. "Yes, but having dinner with you will be more than fulfilling enough for a long, long time..." he flashed a happy smile hoping to ease her discomfort. "This will be a special night, where we can continue to get know each other better... at least I hope. There is so much I want to tell you, and so much to learn about you."

"I too was really looking forward to this evening I must admit. I also look forward to working with you. I think... no... I KNOW we will work well together."

"I know we will too, Catherine. Now, how about we dig in to that food. You're right... I haven't had some of these delectable items in a very long time!"

It was a wonderful night, just as they had predicted. It may have ended with Simon being escorted back to his cell, but he was still happy with the outcome. He had a feeling she too was pleased with the evening. He decided that indeed the future was looking brighter, no matter what.

11

"Project Brain Heal Experimental Log, day 1, subject... Galen Woods. Doctor Derrick Swanson, voice logging. It has been a week since Galen arrived with us from the prison. He has done very well adjusting to his new life here at the institute. He seems to make friends easily, and has become quite attached to another new patient... Simon Piccolo... who is involved with Doctor Harmony and project Nature Warrior. Today, Stephanie Wilcox and I hope to start the process of healing on Galen. We are going to introduce brain matter modified with merged DNA from a host subject. Doctor Swanson has set the computer to pick a random sample from the DNA stores that will be used as DNA source material for the merge sequence. It is our hope that through our previous animal experiments and discoveries, we will be able to successfully merge the sample with Galen's brain matter and see a positive mutation that will improve his overall brain capacity. We don't expect a full reversal of his condition, but at least we may see some improvement."

Derrick had shut off the computer recorder by the time Stephanie had entered the lab with Galen. He turned to the pair and smiled, then said "Hello Galen... good morning, Stephanie."

"Umm... Hello, Doctor Derrick" Galen had a very large smile on his face this morning – he had not a care in the world. Derrick wondered if he had any clue as to what was about to happen to him today.

Stephanie also smiled "Good morning, Doctor Swanson" she had a professional tone in her voice. She was smiling, but also had a worried look in her eyes.

"*Doctor Swanson? She must really be nervous... I don't think I've ever seen her so worried!*" He continued to smile at his partner while he pondered her concerns.

Stephanie walked Galen to the table below the projector and instructed him to lie down on the cold steel table.

Galen smiled, and then whispered "I think... ummm... I think he likes you Doctor Stephanie."

She smiled and snuck a peek at Derrick, then whispered to Galen "You think that do you? Well, Doctor Derrick is a good friend of mine, and that is all right now." He gave her a smile and a chuckle to indicate that she was wrong. She returned a jokingly annoyed look. "Oh yeah? We'll see... maybe later after we are done with this project. But for now... you're my concern! I want you to be comfortable and relaxed, okay? I'm going to give you a shot... it won't hurt... I promise."

"Okay... umm... go ahead Stephanie" he had a tone of total trust when he spoke to her.

She gave Galen the shot, and he drifted into a deep sleep. *"Please make it through this... you have to make it Galen!"* The thought of the mouse exploding in the box returned. *"No! Get that out of your head Steph! You'll make sure he makes it!"*

"Stephanie?" Derrick called out "Are you... are you okay? Do you want to wait and do this later? If you don't feel good about..."

"No, no I'm fine. Let's do this" she told him, then smiled "Thanks for your concern though. I'm just worried."

"I have run over the computations so many times... I know this is going to work! We'll do this and Galen will be better for it... I know it!" Derrick pointed to the brain monitor showing Galen's brain and his brain activity. It read 9 percent. "Can't do much worse than it already is" he proclaimed "As long as we keep him alive... which we will." He tried to keep as confident of a tone in his voice as he could. He was hoping he had fooled her at least a little – but he was just as worried.

Derrick started working at the computer console flipping switches and making adjustments. The bonding device started to glow and hum. He made more adjustments on the console, and then looked at Stephanie who had also started to set her medical sequences into the computer.

"Okay Stephanie, I'm ready here. Just give the word, and I'll pull a sample." He was now sweating with anticipation, excitement, and concern.

"Go ahead Derrick... take the sample, I'm sequencing the computer for donor selection now." She continued to flip switches while she activated calculation programs on her console.

Derrick activated the bonding device. It glowed and hummed louder, until the beam projected from its tip and pierced inside Galen's brain – pulling away a small cellular sample of his gray matter. After a few seconds the lights dimmed on the device, and the level of the hum dropped.

"Sample obtained, ready for computer random selection Stephanie"

Stephanie flipped a switch and a flashing of various names and faces flickered on her screen as the computer began its random selection of a donor. Stephanie bit her lower lip in deep concentration. She looked at Derrick who was in deep concentration on his terminal. She thought for a second while the computer continued its selective search. She reached over and began entering process commands. The computer stopped its search, and displayed the information on the screen.

"Okay, sample has been selected..."

"Great!" Derrick replied with excitement in his voice. "Here we go then." He began to flip virtual switches, and entered sequencing commands as the supercomputer began its job of combining the two samples of DNA into one. It replaced damaged DNA structure with good from the donor. The institute's reactors fired up and ran at maximum capacity. They emitted the all-too-familiar loud hum as they worked producing the vast amounts of power needed by the super computer. The computer determined what other attributes should be combined with Galen's brain matter, and made the molecular adjustments. Finally, when the combinations had all been calculated and completed, the reactors powered down, and the computer announced the process was complete.

"Sample is ready for insertion into the retrovirus. It's all yours now, Steph."

"Right... preparing super bugs for the DNA insertion... now inserting mutated DNA structure into virus structure." A few moments passed while the computer performed the delicate work of inserting the DNA into the hollow structure of the retrovirus. "Okay, now stimulating reproduction of the virus." She activated a beam inside a chamber in the computer's central complex that was designed to be an incubator of the viruses needed for mutations. It only took a minute of stimulation to produce the proper number of retrovirus needed for mutation stimulation. "Our bugs are ready for insertion, prepare your sequencing."

After a moment of running algorithms on his console, the computer was ready for the next phase. "Okay, sequencing complete... we are ready for insertion. Are we ready for stasis?"

"Yes, stasis field in 10 seconds... 9, 8, 7, 6, 5, 4, 3, 2, 1, activating!" she announced as she flipped virtual switches which activated the stasis field.

The stasis field activated, and Galen became virtually frozen in time. Derrick simultaneously flipped switches, and the bonding device glowed brightly. Once again, the hum became a loud song of work, and the beam flew from the tip of the device into Galen's now-quiet brain.

"45 seconds to go Derrick" Stephanie announced over the noise. "Come on Galen, stay with us!"

The beam continued to work inside Galen's brain – placing the retroviruses at just the proper spots to stimulate mutation. Derrick was sweating profusely now – watching the time like a mad hatter. The beam stopped, as all viruses had been placed in the projection chamber, then lit up and gave a soft humming noise as a different beam projected the viruses into his head. "Beam is now stimulating bonding. So... we wait... hope your bugs are potent Steph."

"Me too! 30 seconds..."

"Come on, come on!" Derrick pleaded with the computer. As if on command, the computer indicated bonding was completed. The lights once again dimmed on the device, and the room went quiet, except for the high-pitched noise of the stasis field. "Okay, kill the stasis field Stephanie..."

She complied, and the room went quiet. They both sat, staring at Galen in anticipation and concern. Derrick watched the brain monitor. It continued to read 9 percent. Stephanie walked over to Derrick's console and sat down next to him. She grabbed his hand, and squeezed it tightly while she worried for her patient. The pair stared at the monitor without saying a word.

Hours went by, and yet the monitor gave no indication of any success.

"Still 9 percent... did we not get a good bond?" she asked.

"No, it definitely bonded" he reassured her. "I saw the viruses bond in his brain. I wonder if the mutation is slower depending on the size of the brain? Man versus rat..."

"I guess it's possible. Why don't we try waking him and see how he feels?"

He nodded at her. She went to her console, and changed settings on her computer. Indicators showed that the level of anesthesia was being lowered. Galen's eyes began to flicker around in their sockets as he came back to a state of sleeping consciousness, and entered REM sleep.

She lowered the drug level slowly until it was at zero. Galen began to stir on the table. Stephanie stood, and rushed to the table. She stood over him and watched as he began to slowly open his eyes. He looked at Stephanie, and smiled. She gave a huge sigh of relief, and smiled at him. Derrick saw him smiling – to which he also sighed, and sat back in his chair.

"How are you feeling Galen?" she asked.

"Ummm... fine I guess. But... umm... hungry."

She smiled "Okay... well first you have to rest before you eat, okay?" He smiled in return before he nodded back off to a light sleep – a light snore emitted from his mouth.

Derrick told her "Well, let's get him into the observation room, and relax." He activated a robotic arm to roll over to Galen, pick him up, and move him into a room right off to the side of the lab. This room was all white, with a small bunk on the wall opposite from the door. The door was of a plastic material, with holes drilled throughout for communication to the patient – however, a steel door could be slid in at any time for emergencies or protection. Next to the door was a desk with a computer console. This way, the doctors could work with the computer without leaving the patient. The walls were padded in case the patient became self-destructive. All furniture could be gathered into the walls for further protection to the patient. The robot arm entered the room with Galen on its forklift-like attachment and gently laid him onto the bunk. Galen continued to sleep, still snoring.

*   *   *

Stephanie and Derrick almost wrote off the experiment as a failure after a week. Then unexpectedly, Galen's brain activity jumped to 12 percent. When the increase happened, they were both asleep at the console. The monitor alarm went off on the console, which startled both doctors to an abrupt awakening.

"My god, it finally happened! His brain activity jumped 3 percent."

Stephanie looked at the observation room monitor, and saw Galen sitting at the edge of the bunk. He was watching the pre-programmed entertainment on the computer console in the room.

His activity raised another 3 points. It was now 15 percent. It continued to rise, but much slower now. The pair would continue to see the activity rise a point every hour, but then slowed to only a point every few hours.

After a few days, Galen's brain activity was at 43 percent. Stephanie went into Galen's observation room, and sat down at the desk while Galen continued to sit on the bunk. She activated the computer console and called up monitors so she could continue to watch as she spoke to Galen.

He broke from his entertainment watching and said "Good morning Stephanie" he smiled while he greeted her.

"Good morning Galen, you look well today. Feeling okay?"

Galen looked at Stephanie with a confused gaze. "Well, actually I *am* feeling pretty good today. You know, you look very pretty today." Stephanie blushed and smiled. He then asked "Will I be able to go out into the exercise plaza soon? I miss talking with Simon."

Galen's sudden request caught her by surprise. "Oh my... you already want to start wandering? I think you had better just relax for a while longer Mister Woods!" she scolded with a smile.

"Oh... alright" he whined "I guess the doctor knows best!"

She was amazed at how far he had progressed – way beyond what they determined would be his maximum improvement. She made some final adjustments to the monitoring equipment. Then looked back at him and said "Okay Galen, I have a few things to do... but will come back later to visit okay?"

"Stephanie..." he said as she was about to leave the room.

"Yes dear?"

"Could you leave the computer on? I'm getting bored!" he pleaded.

"I don't see why not. There are some entertainment viewing channels that you can watch. Just press the button labeled "view". There is also the Web-Net where you can look at northern events or other information – help yourself if you can figure out how to use it! If you have problems, I can help you later, okay? I'm so happy with your progress Galen... you're doing so well" she reached down and stroked his cheek. He returned her touch with a squeeze of his eyes and a smile.

"I have you and Doctor Swanson to thank. Thank you for everything you have done to help me, Stephanie. I will never forget this." He flashed a large toothy smile at her.

When Stephanie left the room, Galen walked over and sat at the computer console. He activated the virtual keyboard and started typing. He found it quite easy to use, and immediately began typing at a quick speed. After a few seconds of practice, he was using the computer and typing on the virtual keyboard as if he had been using the computer for years.

"Now, let's see what this world I have just been reborn into is all about..."

12

"Are you ready to begin?"

"Yes Catherine, what do I need to do?"

"Well first, we need to put your mind into a condition of openness. Where you will be able to relax, and meditate into a state above consciousness. You will need to be in a mindset where you can float outside your body and become a mass of pure mental energy."

Simon stared at her with a puzzled look. "Just how am I expected to do that? I'm lucky I can close my eyes to sleep half the time now. After my time in prison, sleep and rest have been pretty minimal... much less putting my mind into a state of relaxation. Are you sure you picked the right person?"

She spoke to him softly and confidently. "Of course I did. Despite your negativity, I know you will succeed at this. All I really need to do is to put a few suggestions into your head and we will be on our way to begin your training."

"Suggestions? How do you propose to do that?"

"Through hypnosis of course. It's the easiest way"

"I don't think so. I don't think there's any way to put me under. I have had others try in the past... and every attempt was a failure."

"You have not had *me* try, have you? Now relax just a little... will you?"

Simon did as she requested. He shook his shoulders and let them sink into the couch. At the same time, he allowed his head to become heavy, which forced it to also settle into the comfortable pillow on the couch. "This is about as comfortable as I can get. Give it a shot..."

She looked at him, and concentrated.

"Don't think this is going to work... I really don't..." He noticed that waves had formed around her head. He was not sure what he was seeing, but it fascinated him. The waves flowed and moved invisibly around the room. He found them to be so beautiful that all he could do was stare and watch the waves float and move. They went out and around, forward and back. "Very beautiful, very nice..." he muttered. Then the waves stopped. "Is that it? I told you I didn't think I could be hypnotized."

"Simon, I hate to break it to you. But you were hypnotized for over an hour..."

"What? There's no way." He turned to look at the clock on the wall across from him. It showed 15:15. He had indeed been there for over an hour. "Amazing! I didn't even know it happened."

"That's how easy it really is. All I have to do is find the wavelength of your brainwave patterns, and then match my hypnosis technique to your patterns. Now, you have your first suggestion... one that will allow you to relax your mind. You will be able to let go."

"You didn't take advantage of me, did you?"

"You wish..."

"Yes, I do."

She gave a small chuckle, and then smiled at him. "Simon, I cannot make you do anything you don't want... you still have free will while under hypnosis. You only do what you want. Why don't you take a break for a few minutes? Rest for a bit, then let's do this again."

"You said I only needed to be hypnotized once. You said I now had the suggestion."

"Yes, you have the initial suggestion. But before you can use it, you must be willing to accept the suggestion and train your mind to allow for the meditative state. To do this, you must strengthen your mind... and we will do this with mental sparring. I will try to send you into a hypnotic state, and you will attempt to stop me with your mind. And, until you can prevent my suggestions, we will continue with the sparring until you can stop me. When you can do that, we can proceed to the next phase of your training."

He opened his mouth to speak, but she held two fingers in front of his lips to stop him. "You might as well accept the fact you will be training in this manner... besides, you can't stop it you know..." She stood up and said "We will begin as soon as I return... and you won't be able to stop or prevent it..."

Simon realized how correct she was, and how powerless he was to stop her. How could someone have such control over their own, and other people's minds? How could she have such an influence over his mind? What secrets would she discover or reveal about him, and could he prevent her from finding those secrets? He knew he would have to be a quick study, and to learn these meditation techniques as fast as possible. He did not want her to discover his deep thoughts, especially those regarding how he secretly felt about her. He was finding himself more attracted to her every day – but he would not, could not let her know – not unless she somehow revealed that during hypnosis.

She returned after a few minutes, and sat down on the ottoman next to him. He looked up at her and the waves were flowing around her again. "No!" he protested, but it made no difference. He woke up another hour later. The smell of green tea toyed with the senses of his nose. "Damn, you did it again."

"And I will continue to do it until you can put up a fight with your mind. Now, drink this tea... it will stimulate your mind and make you alert.

He took the cup and sipped at the beverage. He found the caffeine invigorating as she had promised. It also tasted quite good – he realized it had been quite a while since he had enjoyed a good cup of tea. The pleasant taste of the tea was complemented with a number of different mint flavors – all of which danced across his palate. He sipped on the tea without thinking and soon discovered that he had only taken a few minutes to drink every drop. He had a saddened look when she took the empty cup from him. When he looked at her again he found the waves were back. "Oh no, I won't fall for this again."

He tried to look away, but no matter where he looked he saw the waves flowing in the air. He tried to close his eyes and he swore they were even dancing under his eyelids. He opened his eyes wide and fought it.

"Yes Simon, there you go. Now concentrate on the battle against sleep... think of a small spot in the middle of the waves. That one spot is your escape. Run to the spot and aim to jump through it."

He lasted an extra 30 seconds that time. Catherine giggled as he fell back into a deep state of hypnosis. "Sleep for a while Simon… rest and we will try again tomorrow."

*   *   *

The sparring continued day after day. Catherine never let up on Simon for even a moment. When he woke from his hypnosis induced slumber she would give him a minute to recover mentally, but then started right back up with her forced hypnotic routine. He found he was lasting a little longer during the rounds. After a week, he was lasting minutes instead of seconds. Today he was determined to make it over ten minutes before she put him to sleep again. He arrived that morning ready for battle – at least he hoped he was ready.

"Good morning Simon, how are you feeling today?" Simon noted how stunning she looked to him this morning. Every day he was finding her more and more pleasing and enjoyable to look at. He was starting to think he was really falling for her. He found even when sparring that her face and appearance was a thing of beauty, and he was gaining strength from his feelings for her. He had hoped he never revealed any of these secrets to her while in a daze.

"Hello Catherine… The Torturer, I'm feeling fine." He had started to joke with her about her constant bombardment of sparring attacks, he was always thinking of little digs that he could jokingly throw at her in a vain attempt at a little mercy. It failed every time, at least so far. He realized after answering her that he actually *did* feel fine. He realized that this was the most rested he had ever felt. "You know, when I say I am feeling fine… I actually mean it. I just realized that for the first time in years, I feel totally rested and relaxed. Must be all the sleep sessions you've been subjecting me to?"

"Yes, you are starting to get some of the extra benefits to our training. Not only are you starting to resist my mental jabs, but you are also becoming totally rested and relaxed in the process. When I was trained in this manner, I found the same outcomes. They would spar with me and I would go back to my room exhausted mentally, but totally at peace. I would sleep like a baby… I would wake up early every morning totally rested and relaxed. I would find that each day, I would be ready for the next round as I hope you are finding too..."

"Actually, although you are relentless, you're right. I'm feeling better every day. And I'm finding that it's getting easier as we go. Did the monks train you in the same manner?"

"Yes, they did. You should feel honored that I'm giving you training that no one else has ever received from me. This "torture" as you call it, was the same training given to me by the monks in the Himalayas.

"I AM honored. So, maybe there is something to this punishment you are rendering to me after all, eh?" He gave her one of his famous evil smirks.

She replied with only "En garde!" Then started another mental assault. He held out ten minutes that time.

Later, he was sparring with her as usual. His mind continuously attempted to expand that small point of calm in the middle of the sea of mental energy waves. For a brief second, he found he was able to actually expand the circle – much larger than ever before. He wondered if he could thrust himself through the expanse of calm. He pictured his body leaping toward the circle of tranquility. As he imagined the image, he found the hole became bigger – or he surmised that perhaps he got closer. Once more, he imagined jumping to that spot of peace and to his surprise he reached it and crawled in. Once inside the void, he came to the realization that he had actually entered Catherine's mental energy and thoughts. He could have sworn he felt her attempt to push him out, she attempted to push him back into the endless waves. He decided to try something, and thought one word – "Sleep".

Catherine started to waver, her eyelids began to flutter. He thought again "Put your head on my chest and sleep..." Her head bobbed, her body wobbled, and finally she started to slowly lean into Simon who was lying on the chaise lounge. He guided her head to his chest, and then she fell fast asleep.

She slept for over an hour – her head on his chest, one of her arms had reached up, and wrapped her hand around his shoulder. A small happy smile graced her face as she slept. When she finally awoke, she smiled and hugged him tightly while still in a waking slumber. She finally realized the situation, quickly raised herself up, and straightened out the bow on her blouse. He noticed a slight blush formed on her cheeks as she realized what had just happened.

After a moment, she recovered from her embarrassment, smiled at him, and said "You did it! I accidently let my guard down and you slipped right in. You've made so much progress! We'll soon be ready to move on to actually training you in meditation." She then stopped, and looked at him with concern. "Simon, when you put me to sleep... you didn't put any other suggestions in my head did you? You didn't take advantage of me."

"I wish..."

"SIMON!" He gave a chuckle. "In that case..." Suddenly, Simon felt himself fighting to stay awake once more.

*   *   *

That next day Simon awoke to find his mind had suddenly opened. His thoughts felt like they would flow out from his head like a wild flowing river. With this renewed energy, he thought that perhaps he actually had a real chance to not only take her on full force, but maybe even get an advantage from time to time. He discovered that this day his sharp mind was right on target.

Catherine, had started the sparring in her normal manner – a direct assault on his mind from the moment he sat down. This time however, Simon focused his mind, and through steady concentration found he was able to push back against that small passageway that lead out of her hypnotic forces.

A surprised Catherine had a look of astonishment on her face. "Simon, I can't believe it... you are really fighting back today. I'm almost thinking that you are strong enough to..."

"Sleep now my dear. Put your head on my chest and wrap your arms around me."

Following his suggestion, she instantly laid her head on his chest, put her arms around him and fell into a deep sleep. She slept soundly for a long hour. Simon relished in the feel of her touch – her arms wrapped around him felt so good and warm, he wished he could somehow control it, and never let it end. But it did finally have to come to an end as she woke up – a smile once again on her face. She yawned and opened her eyes. After a moment, she realized the position she was in, and the surprise made her jump up from him like a spring.

She gave him a non-threatening glare. "You made me do that, didn't you? You made me put my arms around you. Wasn't good enough to make me fall asleep, eh? No, you had to make me sleep on you while hugging you. Oh!"

Simon grinned. "Remember… one cannot be forced into doing something they don't want to do. So, if you are correct in telling me that… then… I must assume you not only wanted to do that… but enjoyed it… at least from the smile on your face."

She rolled her eyes. "Please! Well, in any case… you beat me that time. You had enough mental control and force to not only attack, but to overcome me. I'm very pleased with your progress. Now, you're ready for the next stage of training. It is time to learn to mediate. First thing tomorrow, we'll start… okay? How about something to eat before you return?"

His heart saddened at the thought of leaving again for yet another night in the patients living quarters. But her dinner offer made every regret about going back to the living quarters fade. "Dinner would be wonderful…"

"Great, let's go. Oh… and I will not let my guard down again."

"We'll see…"

13

Galen's mutation appeared to have peaked at 48 percent. But to the pair of scientists, 48 percent was a major success – so much so, that they felt they should attempt the process on yet another patient. They had also decided that Lisa, the violently mentally ill patient would be perfect to be the next subject. They had already obtained a sample of her brain cells for computer analysis. They ran the simulations through the computer multiple times – determining the peptides that required either replacement or repair, and also identified in many places complete replacement of strands that they felt might be causing her condition.

They ordered an observation room be constructed next to Galen's room. When it was complete, they had Lisa moved into this new living space. The young woman was still under the control of the sedation necklace – she was still way too dangerous and still required that she be totally sedated at all times. They were not even sure if they could repair her brain to the point they would be able to remove that necklace – but they kept high hopes that she would improve enough to live in a non-violent state.

Galen woke up when they moved Lisa into the room next door. She did not say anything to indicate her presence – but he somehow knew she was there. He rubbed the sleep from his eyes and sat up. After a moment, he got up and went to the computer console and began typing a myriad of commands. The computer screen flashed and flickered while Galen typed. He stopped and thought for a moment, he could swear he heard Lisa speak to him from the room next to him. Did he actually hear her speak? No, it had to be his imagination, he thought. He returned to his furious typing – after he entered a few more commands he stopped and smiled. A web-net screen appeared on the monitor.

* * *

Later that day Stephanie arrived at the lab. Derrick was already hard at work.

Stephanie walked over to Derrick and put her soft, small hand on his shoulder. "Well, I see you're non-stop working again. Are we going to be ready for this afternoon?"

"Yep, everything's ready."

"Wonderful! I'm going to take Galen out then. He's progressed so well... I think he deserves a break."

"That sounds like a great idea Steph. He'll really enjoy seeing his friends again. I am assuming they are still there... and maybe still in human form." He scowled as he said that. The thought of project Fury Warrior disgusted him. Breaking down Human DNA and recombining it with animals was a revolting thought, but at least it was a project that *he* was not involved with. He was glad instead that he was involved in his current work project – something that actually might be a benefit to humanity.

Stephanie walked over to Galen's room and peered inside. Galen was sitting at the computer console, still browsing the web-net. He stopped his typing and looked at her.

"Hi Steph!"

"Steph? Now where did that come from?"

"I don't really know... it just came to me."

She laughed "Well, Mister Friendly... want to go out? I think you deserve it."

Galen's eyes lit up "Oh yes! I do so want to go out! Yes, please Stephanie... thank you!"

Stephanie issued her hand to the door lock sensor, released the door latch, and allowed it to slide open. Galen stood up from the console and walked to Stephanie with a huge smile on his face.

"Will we get to go to the exercise plaza?" he asked.

"Sure, why not!" she replied.

On the way to the door they passed by the door to the observation room that housed Lisa. Galen stopped and stared at her. Her black eyes stared back at Galen without blinking. She made no other movement or sound.

"Wow Stephanie, she is very beautiful... but she has so much anger behind those pretty dark eyes."

"I hope we can help her like we did for you. We hope she can live a better life soon."

"I know you and Derrick will help her, I can feel it" he said with conviction in his voice.

"Galen, you amaze me! I'm so happy with how well you have done." She spoke to him with glee as she felt so much joy every time she saw how far he had progressed, and how much better his brain was now functioning.

"Come on... let's go. I want to tell Simon how much better I am doing!" he pulled on Stephanie's arm, almost dragging her along as she tried almost in vain to keep up with him.

They arrived at the exercise plaza and Stephanie placed her hand on the security console to open the door. It was midday, and the sun was shining fully through the opaque rooftop. There were quite a few people sitting around while they enjoyed the beautiful, artificial day. Galen spotted Simon and Danny over sitting near a tree. He ran off toward them, leaving Stephanie in the dust. She smiled and laughed at his enthusiasm.

"Simon, I made it! I survived my friend!" he yelled across the plaza as he approached the pair of men.

Simon turned from his conversation with Danny and saw Galen running toward him. A huge smile formed on his face as he recognized his friend as he ran in from the distance. He stood and ran to meet him halfway. He gave Galen a huge hug when he finally reached him.

"Man, I thought I would never see you again!" he told Galen.

"I knew I would be fine. Steph and Derrick did a wonderful job. Their project works wonders!"

Simon realized that Galen was now speaking with intelligence behind his voice. He was amazed by the change in his once mentally challenged friend. "I cannot believe it! You're speaking like a college professor now!" The two laughed and again hugged each other. Stephanie finally caught up with the pair.

"Hello, you must be Simon. I am Doctor Stephanie Wilcox."

"Simon... Simon Piccolo... a pleasure to meet you. I'm amazed and so overjoyed with your success. I can't tell you what a wonderful thing you have done for Galen."

"Seeing Galen doing so well provides me with all I need to push me in continuing my work."

She looked at Galen – raised her arms, and then put her hands on his shoulders. She had to stretch on tip-toes to reach his shoulders – and even then, they towered above her smaller height. "Galen, I need to go do some work... it will be a few hours, okay? Mind if I leave you here with Simon?"

"It's Lisa, isn't it?" he queried. "You are going to try to cure Lisa today...aren't you?"

Stephanie was shocked by his assumption. "*How did he know?*" "Yes, we're going to try to cure Lisa today. I can't promise anything though... she may be beyond our ability to heal her."

"You will succeed... I know it... I can feel it."

"Well, I'm glad you have confidence..." she laughed nervously "Simon, mind keeping Galen occupied for a while?"

"It'll be my pleasure!" he said as he looked at his smiling friend. "Danny and I will take good care of him until you return."

"Okay, be back later Galen... see you soon." she waved a farewell to him as she left the plaza.

Galen and Simon went back to the tree where Danny was still sitting. Danny stood up, and hugged Galen. They all sat down, and enjoyed the restful atmosphere of the plaza.

"Danny, do you worry at all about the future?" Galen asked the Jamaican.

"Aye, Galen... constantly. I fear more for Cora Lee than myself, though. I have this feeling..."

Galen interrupted him "I understand. I have a feeling too... that you will be very important in the future. No matter what happens, remember that okay?"

"Aye, jah." Danny replied.

Galen turned to Simon "And Simon, you... will be important in the future. You must keep your wits about you. You will be fine in the end... don't ask how I can say this... I can just feel it." He looked at Simon with a dead serious look on his face.

Simon, slightly confused, looked at Galen, then to Danny, and then back to Galen again. "Sure Galen... but... umm, how do you know this?"

"I am not sure really... it is just a feeling, or perhaps just a hunch. But I do know this to be fact." He continued to show a dead serious look to the pair of men. His face loosened up after a moment, he then said "May I ask you something personal, my friends?"

They both nodded in agreement.

"Danny, do you believe in God?" Galen asked.

Danny immediately answered "Of course, yes. If not, I would have been dead by now."

"How about you Simon?" he asked.

Simon thought for a moment, before saying "Well, no..."

Galen gave him a confused look "Why?"

Simon took a moment to gather his thoughts. "Well, it's my opinion that if there was a God, then this world would not be so screwed up. If there was a God, then why would he or she allow the evil known as the Supreme Commander and the Council to gain control of this country? Why would he or she allow those horrid bombs to be built? Why would a God allow this planet to be burned to a crisp? Why would he or she allow for all the selective genetic breeding and enhancement by government officials to create the Blessed... although, I still think the slang term Frogspawn still a bit more accurate. With all of these things going on, and this world being such a war-filled mass of hatred, paranoia and discrimination... then throw on the experiments going on here... do I think there is a God? No, absolutely not... I can't... I don't believe there is a God, Galen."

Galen smiled "Let me propose this hypothesis to you then... what if there was a force, such as the Earth Gaia that allowed for man to destroy everything they built so it could be reclaimed later? What if indeed this is a master plan for the end of mankind, and the rebuilding of nature-kind?"

Danny interrupted "Ah, aye! God could be cleanin da planet for da next dina-sar!"

Galen laughed. "Ah, yes Danny... I think you understand! What say you, Simon?" he asked.

Simon digested the conversation then replied "Well, that is definitely some food for thought. I guess it would then be a distinct possibility. Galen, is this the type of stuff you think about now? Perhaps they made a mistake fixing your brain?" he gave Galen an evil grin.

After a moment of the three laughing, Galen replied "Well, yes... it was a thought that occurred to me the other day. I have wanted to ask you ever since I thought about it. Thank you for humoring me... and my thinking."

Simon looked at his friend, and felt his eyes were tearing up. He held back the tears to say "I'm so glad that you made it through the procedure, Galen. You have done so well, and I am so happy."

Galen found he too could not help to stop the tears from swelling. The two men hugged again. They spent the rest of the day relaxing, talking, joking and enjoying each other's company until Stephanie returned to gather her patient.

*   *   *

The pair arrived back at the lab and greeted Derrick who was still working at the main console.

"Hello Doctor Derrick. How is Lisa?" he asked.

"Doctor Wilcox told me you somehow knew about the procedure" he admitted. "So far so good – she has shown no adverse reaction to the process... at least so far. As expected, she has not shown any improvement yet either. Do you understand what I am telling you Galen?"

Galen smiled "I understand everything you said Derrick. I know Lisa will show improvement. Thank you for your candid answer."

Derrick was shocked at his understanding and wondered how much of his brain he was actually using, but not admitting. "Feel free to ask anytime you have a question, okay?"

"Thank you Derrick. You are very kind, and I will never forget what you have done for us."

He turned, and returned to his room. On the way, he stopped at Lisa's room, and looked in. She was sitting up in her chair, resting quietly. The sedation necklace around her neck hissed slightly every few seconds.

"Hurry and let your brain wander Lisa... hurry and become one!"

"Become one?" Stephanie asked upon overhearing him.

"Oh, I just meant become one of the normal people. Like Derrick, you, and me, Steph" he replied.

"There! He called me Steph again! I wonder where that's coming from? Oh no..." She hid her expression from the two men in the room as to not give her thoughts away. She looked at Derrick, no he had not noticed any brief moment of panic.

She made sure Galen was safely inside his observation room, and then secured the door. She then went to her work area, and activated the computer console. She entered the commands to review the recording of the procedure on Galen. She watched the beginning of the procedure, then forwarded the video. She then stopped the fast-forward function, and once again started to watch the image – the image showed her running the selection program. She bit her lip in nervous anticipation. On the monitor, in the playback, the computer was running the random selection of the donor. She watched the replay, and the reality of what she had done hit her like a shooting star – she watched herself as she reached over to the keyboard of the computer that was picking the random DNA sample. On the screen, an unknown face showed as selected donor in the image. Then what she imagined was only a dream, or a fleeting thought became reality – she watched herself enter the commands to change the selection. Moments later, Derrick's face appeared on the monitor. *"My god, I really did it! I deliberately changed the conditions of the experiment. I changed the donor, and used Derrick as Galen's tissue sample!"* She put her head down on the desk in shame as she continued to mentally berate herself *"How could I have been so unprofessional? What was I thinking?"*

"What's wrong Steph?" Derrick's voice shocked her back to reality.

"Oh, nothing Derrick, I'm just tired I think…" She replied as her hand nonchalantly entered the "delete recording" command.

Galen, watching the scene through the clear door of his observation room, smiled.

14

"Okay, let's try again Simon…"

Catherine's face showed how tired she was. She and Simon had put in a very long day of training, and she was about at the end of her energy and mental sharpness. But she knew that Simon was almost there – he was almost about to find his ideal focal point. She just had to keep pressing him a little more. She just had to force him to make the connection with his inner energies.

Simon had been working on learning her techniques for months now. He had been working so hard, and trying to do the best he could. She knew he was putting in all of this hard work just for her. She knew he was trying to please her – and he was. He was doing anything he could to help her succeed. She didn't want to think of the outcome of their success, however.

"Concentrate on a single point of your body. Let all of your thoughts go to that single point. Let the energy flow from all parts of your body to this single location. Concentrate Simon…" she spoke in a soft, comforting voice.

Simon closed his eyes and began to meditate. He did exactly as she instructed and thought of a single point on his body. As he concentrated, he began to feel the energy move within his body. He concentrated even harder.

"Yes, that's it Simon… think of that spot as a single point of light. Move your entire body to that point. You can do it." she had excitement in her voice now. She knew he was so close to discovering his inner potential – to release his focused energies, and then to draw on the energy of the outside world.

She detected a glow, and she felt the energy flowing within him. Simon could feel it too – he continued to concentrate on that single point, that focal point within his soul. Suddenly the energy within his body erupted forth. His mouth opened and a low-pitched hum emitted from his mouth. The hum was loud, and it resonated throughout the room.

Catherine opened her eyes and looked at Simon. Simon's throat was glowing – he had focused his energy to his vocal chords. She smiled as she realized that once again, the smart-ass facet of this complex man was bursting forth. He had picked his throat as his focal point, and had actually succeeded in channeling his inner energies to that single point. Unfortunately, his selection of a focal point provided some problems that he had not thought of, and also had not yet become obvious to Catherine.

The hum became louder and the building began to mildly shake. A few books fell off the shelf, and glasses began to shudder from the shaking caused by the sound. Reality hit Catherine, and the humor of the situation suddenly changed to seriousness. He was using his voice as a focal point – and it was starting to rip the room, and perhaps even the building apart.

"Umm Simon... although I am quite pleased that you have focused your energies, I think you need to try to focus on a different spot... PLEASE!" She pleaded with him as he was tearing the building apart with his voice.

Through the hum, Simon whispered "I am not sure I can do it Catherine, this is the only place I could focus to."

"You must try... think of another part of your body. You can do it."

Simon closed his eyes tighter and concentrated as hard as he could. The energy in the room was now moving and was being pulled into Simon's body. The hum had once again gotten louder. Catherine knew that if he didn't move the focus soon, they might all be killed as the building was shaking violently, and she knew it would eventually crumble.

A few more moments passed, and the hum continued. The computer on her desk suddenly popped – she shrieked as sparks flew out of the computer processing unit and her display terminal. She began her own meditation – hoping to assist Simon to move his concentration. She didn't really want to stop him now, he was so close. But she would break his meditation with her own mental will if necessary to stop the process. She was prepared now – the energy was flowing through both of them. *"One mental shock should do it..."* Suddenly, the room became quiet once again – he had stopped the hum.

She opened her eyes and looked at Simon – his eyes were closed and he was smiling. She looked down and noticed – his hands, they were glowing. He had moved his focal point from his throat to his hands. Between the two of them, life energy was flowing from all parts of the room. The energy was flowing to his hands, and from there the energy flowed to her hair. The energy was swirling around the room in a dance like flames flickering. His mental energy was mixing and dancing with her energy – it was a beautiful sight.

She opened her eyes wide and the soft glow of energy began to emanate from her eyes into the room. To her surprise Simon had also opened his eyes, and a similar soft glow was pulsing from his dark green eyes.

He smiled at her. "Did I finally get it right?"

"Yes... yes! You definitely got it right this time, Simon. I'm so happy" she said with pure delight in her voice.

He looked deep into her eyes, and took in the sight of the energy flowing from her. *"Her eyes are so beautiful!"* As he thought about the pair of eyes in front of him. To his surprise, energy flowed from his eyes to hers.

She gasped as his energy pierced her eyes, and mixed with her own mental energy. She had never felt anything like it. She returned the stare – entered into his eyes with her mind, her energy leaving her body, and flowing into him. She had never had an experience like this with anyone before. His mental energy was so compatible with hers. Their energies melted together and flowed between them. They both moved into a state of total relaxation, they became drawn to each other like they were magnetized.

They continued to stare into each other's eyes, unable to remove their gaze. She was not sure how, but she suddenly felt herself float, and then she felt her body began to drift closer to him. He too had begun to levitate, and had also started to move toward her. As the distance between them closed, the energy became even more intense. They both could not stop the gaze; the force was too strong and they were too close. Catherine trembled inside as they were now even closer. She almost screamed when she felt the vibrations as he moved his glowing hands up to her face.

He touched the soft skin on her face, and energy arced between her hair and his hands. They both moaned quietly as the energy flickered between them. The dancing of their energies was providing such a wonderful feeling. They were both in a state of mental ecstasy. She closed her eyes and he did too. She had totally abandoned herself to him – she knew this state of closeness was wrong, but she could not help herself.

She opened her mouth slightly, ready for what she knew was about to happen. She could feel his lips close to her now – the energy arced and flowed between their lips. "*Yes... please now, Simon...*" Only millimeters separated them, and they both anticipated the lovely kiss that was about to come.

At first, they were not sure what broke their concentration – but when it happened, their floating immediately stopped. Two loud thuds filled the room as they both fell solidly to the floor.

"OWWW" Simon cried out. "What the heck happened?"

The door buzzer rang again. Someone was also pounding on the door. Catherine fussed with her hair for a moment, making sure everything was proper, and then went to the video intercom.

"Yes, what is it?" she asked with a disturbed tone in her voice.

It was her assistant Michael. "Umm, is... is everything... okay in there? There was this horrid noise that almost tore down the building, and then this glow could be seen coming from the office windows. We were a bit worried something was going terribly wrong. Then Zardonagon told me to come investigate. So, here I am."

"Oh, yes..." she replied with embarrassment "We had made great progress tonight. I didn't realize the energy was disrupting the building as bad as it did."

"Well, you made a mess of quite a few of the computers here doctor. Zardonagon was not happy with the expense he said he would have to pay to replace them. What should I tell him?"

"Don't worry about it Michael... I will take care of Zardonagon for you. No need for you to have to deal with him."

"Okay... thank you doctor! Do you need any help... anything I can do? Should I come in?"

"No... everything's fine here. Go back to bed, and I will keep it quiet for the rest of the evening. Good night Michael." She smiled reassuringly at him, and then turned the intercom video off.

She turned to Simon – he had a frustrated and confused look on his face. She giggled and he smiled.

"You did it my dear! I would suggest however, that you not use your throat as a focal point in the future!"

"Well, as much as I would like to, I'm not sure I will be able to prevent it. I was actually thinking of another spot... a spot a bit lower... but then my throat became the focal point" he told her with a mischievous smile on his face.

"Simon, I swear, you are so bad! But nonetheless, I'm very proud of you."

"Well, thank you!" he said with pride. "Umm... what else just happened though?"

Her face turned slightly blush. "Perhaps we should forget about the aftermath of your success?" She now had as serious a look on her face as she could muster. "I think we almost went too far."

"Catherine, we both felt it... I don't think I had ever felt anything like it before."

"It felt wonderful, there must be a total mental compatibility between us. But Simon..."

"No, don't say anything else... let's think about what happened, and remember how it felt. We can discuss it again later. For now, I want to relish in what I felt."

She smiled at him. She so wanted to go to him, and ask him to hold her. Her professionalism was holding her back. She knew she would lose him soon – she had to protect herself, and her heart. She also wanted to protect him as he would be different soon, and they could never be together after that. She had to put her mind back to business. She was now convinced that she could never have him, and they could never be together. The war, and this effort was about to take him from her.

"Simon, I think we need to make some decisions." She seated herself in the chair across from him. "Unfortunately, with your success comes something that is very painful for me to discuss with you. It has been such a wonderful nine months... but I cannot shirk my responsibility to the project. It's my life after..."

"You don't have to explain it to me..." he interrupted "I would never do, or ask you to do anything that would endanger your life. I know if you fail at this, your life would be at risk. I know what I have to do. It's why I have worked so hard to get where I am. You saved me from the death camp, I will make sure you succeed and live... no matter what the cost to me."

Her eyes began to tear as she felt so horrible, and yet so lucky she picked him. He saw the tears drip down her face. He stood up, leaned over to her, and wiped them from her cheeks with his hand. She closed her eyes, and enjoyed the brief moment of his touch to her face.

"I think you want me to pick my fate tonight, don't you Catherine?"

"Yes... let's look through the catalog of available animal samples, and see if there is some DNA that would suit you both mentally and physically. This is your choice... I want it to be just right."

She looked at her computer, and although it looked a little worse for the wear, it appeared to still be functioning.

"Oh umm... sorry about that." he said, his eyes looking down and around the room in embarrassment.

She looked at him, laughed, and activated the console. "Okay Simon, a couple things to know. First, there are a few species that you cannot pick... they are guaranteed failures. For example, they have never had a successful bonding with any avian species. I guess it is something about the bone structure being too fragile for a human frame. Also snakes and most reptilians are out due to the small primitive brains of these species. They found humans lose total mental control after this type of bonding. We want you to have some control after all. Most insects are not good also... hopefully for obvious reasons. I won't stop you from picking those, but you had better know that they more than likely would be choices that will kill you."

He studied the screen – there was a tree of biological genus listed. "Okay, I think I do not want to be aquatic..." he removed that genus from the list. "Land animal definitely..." he announced as he selected that genus. "For sure a mammal, I believe..." he selected that tree and eliminated all other possible species trees.

"Then you could be an Opossum...or an Ocelot" she joked.

He studied the next screen presented to him. There were different classifications of animals listed now. "Catherine, you know I do have one problem here with my selection..."

"What would that be Simon?"

"Well, you know my hatred for war... especially *this*... worthless war. I'm really having a hard time wanting to pick something that could be used to kill others."

"Simon remember however, that if you do not pick something that could have any warfare possibilities, Zardonagon could and very likely will kill you on the spot." She knew Edward was capable of anything, especially when he was in a rage. She worried she would not be able to stop him in that situation.

The images of various types of animals flickered across the screen – the screen changed to a new image every few seconds.

"Okay, I will do my best to pick something that will at least appear like I could be vicious" he said, and then chuckled. "There! This classification I think!" He selected the classification and expanded it on the screen.

"Oh, really?" she said with a snide tone to her voice, and then laughed.

He looked at the list of available animals. Many had already been selected and used in experiments. He knew he was required to pick one that had not been used before. He continued to search the screen, the list continued to flash possible options to him, when suddenly his eyes lit up, and he stopped the selection rotation.

He studied the image before yelling out "There!" as he pressed the button to select. "This one is perfect!"

She looked at his selection. "Really? That one?"

"Yes, this is what I want to become. You can't talk me out of it, so don't even try."

"If that's your choice… I would never dream of talking you out of it" she reassured him. She entered some commands, and locked in the selection. "That is now what you will become. It will be a secret to everyone except you and me."

"It is SO perfect Catherine. It is SO me!"

"You know Simon… I think you're right. It's so you… it's a perfect match!" She then noted the time on her computer. "Oh my, no wonder I'm exhausted… we must call it a night!"

"Oh darn… and we were having so much fun! Very well, it's off to sleep for me then." He stood up, and went to the door. He opened the door, and saw the waiting guard standing vigil outside the opening. He turned to look at her. "Good night Catherine. It was a wonderful evening for me, thank you."

"It was for me also… good night Simon… sleep well."

He turned, and walked out into the hall. "Ah my escort! Living quarters please!" The guard gave a snort, and motioned him down the hall. She laughed as the door slid closed behind him.

Now that she was alone, she could not control her emotions any longer. Tears now flowed freely from her tired eyes. She knew she was about to lose him, and she so wanted to somehow prevent it. She continued to try, but was unable to stop the flow of tears. Mediation was worthless, as she could not concentrate. She just sat on the couch, and cried for hours. Finally, the constant stream of tears wore her down. She finally became so fatigued that she laid her head down on one of the couch pillows, hugged another pillow, and eventually cried herself to sleep.

15

Galen was not sleeping well this night. Whenever he closed his eyes he could swear he heard voices. Voices of people he had met, and also some he had never met before. Voices of both familiar and unfamiliar people – so many voices. He rolled back and forth in the bunk trying to keep the voices out, but he could not. He finally awoke in a sweat, and jumped out of bed. He panted while trying to clear his head. *"Who are these people speaking to me, what were they saying... and why?"*

He walked to the sink to pour a glass of water. *"Perhaps tonight was not a good evening to sleep"* he thought. He instead decided he wanted to browse through the computer – he needed to learn more and discover as much as he could about this world he just had awoken into.

He turned on the computer terminal and started logging onto the web-net. His typing was interrupted by yet another voice. This voice sounded loud and close, not distant like the other voices that awoke him from his slumber.

"Where... where am I?" the voice cried out "Who am I?" The voice was crystal clear to Galen, he thought at first someone was actually in the room speaking to him. It was a female's voice, but one he had never heard before.

"Who am I? Where am I? Why am I here?" the voice cried out again.

Galen put his hands over his ears to stop the voice, but it did not help.

"Why won't anyone answer me? Why won't anyone tell me who I am?" the voice pleaded.

"I do not know who you are, or even where you are" Galen replied speaking "I don't even know where you are speaking from." Galen looked at his computer monitor trying to figure out if perhaps that was the source of the mysterious voice. He waited, but did not get a response.

"Why won't anyone answer me?" she cried out again.

Galen looked frantically for the source of the voice. He then stopped and thought a moment. He covered his ears and waited.

"Is anyone there? Won't anyone help me?"

He heard it again, but his ears were closed to the outside. So, he now knew that the voice was calling to him inside his own head. He let that digest in his brain for a moment, then concentrating as hard as he could he thought *"I am here – I can hear you."*

"Who are you?" the voice cried out "Where are you?"

"I do not know where you are, so it is hard for me to answer" he really did not know exactly what to say to her. *"Can you tell me where you are?"*

"No... I cannot see anything, only a dim light in the distance. I want to stand up and look, but my legs won't move. I feel I am paralyzed!" she sounded panicked.

Galen's eyes suddenly opened wide. The room outside was dark; the only light was the light inside his cell. *"Lisa?"*

"Who... is that who I am? I don't know... I have never known. That name has only a tiny meaning to me... no, not that name!" she said with despair.

"Not *that* name? What name has meaning?"

"I am not sure... but I know Lisa only as a shadow... nothing in the name Lisa brings any memories to me..."

A large smile came to Galen's face. He put a soft tone to his thoughts. *"Stephanie?"*

"Yes, that is familiar. Is that who I am?" she spoke calmly now.

"Well, that is partly who you are ...you are both Lisa and Stephanie. I made sure of who you would be."

"Where are you? Are you near? I feel you... at least I think I do..."

Galen, without thinking, stood up, walked to his cell door, and entered a code into the door lock. The door opened, he walked out, and went right to Lisa's cell. He entered the code again, and the door slid open. He rushed to the dark eyed girl, and looked at her. She was looking at him also.

"Is that... is that you?" she asked.

"Yes. My name is Galen." He said still projecting his thoughts to her.

"That is a nice name, Galen. Why can't I move?"

Galen looked at the collar around her neck. It continued to hiss lightly every few seconds. He thought for a moment then went back to his cell, got onto the computer console, and furiously typed in various searches and commands. He entered a final command and went back into Lisa's cell. The hissing had stopped. A moment later, her eyes started moving around as she looked at her surroundings.

Lisa stood up and stared into Galen's eyes. Her dark eyes pierced into his blue eyes. She stared at him before saying. "You have nice eyes Galen." Her voice was dry and gravelly. It had been years, if ever since she actually spoke, and she was surprised she could even know or could remember how to vocalize words. She smiled at him, and he smiled back.

"Galen, all I remember is anger and hatred. I don't even know why I was angry... just that I was, and it frightened me constantly."

"You are escaping from your hell now Lisa. Your life will soon be much different. I will help you." He spoke to her with a reassuring voice.

"Somehow, I know that... somehow, I knew you were there, and you would help me."

Galen was suddenly filled with a feeling he never felt before. He looked into Lisa's dark eyes and felt so happy. She was filling him with warmth and he did not understand why. He reached up and touched her cheek with his hand. She closed her eyes and enjoyed the hand lightly touching her skin. She had never been touched in such a way ever before. She smiled as he felt her soft skin on his large hand.

Galen's joy was interrupted by a sound outside the lab. *"Someone is coming!"*

"Lisa, I must now go back to my cell. I also must activate your collar which will paralyze you again. Do you understand? It must be done for now." He now spoke with a serious voice – he needed to let her know of the severity of the situation.

"I don't want to lose these feelings, but I guess I understand. I trust you… for some reason." She sat back down in her chair waiting for the poison to flow again. She closed her eyes and said "Promise me I will see you again soon Galen… please, promise me!"

"I promise Lisa… until the next time we meet. I will so look forward to that moment, farewell!" he closed the door behind him and ran back to his cell closing the door behind him. He entered commands into his computer console and the necklace began hissing again. She immediately stiffened as the drugs took effect.

"Oh, Galen… I can't move again… it is so cold…" her voice faded away in his mind.

Galen extinguished the light right as he heard the lab door open. He gave a soft sigh of relief when he realized he barely got everything secured in time. He heard footsteps in the darkness, and then the lab door opened again.

"Derrick, what's wrong? What was so important that we needed to get up at this time of the morning?" the voice Galen now heard was Stephanie's.

Derrick answered her "The security system showed the cell doors had been opened. But everything appears to be secure" he said looking over all of the security controls.

Galen snuck over to his computer console and activated it. He started to enter commands and quietly gasped when he realized his error. "I forgot to cover my tracks! I left a trail of security holes for them to follow." He started typing frantically – looking for traces of logs and security manifests – anywhere his movements might be shown.

"What the…" Derrick called out while reading one of the log reports. "It shows me opening the cell doors. How could that be?"

"Perhaps you were sleepwalking?" Stephanie said jokingly with a giggle.

Derrick continued to study the log until suddenly the entries just faded away as if they never existed.

"Wait, wait... NO!" Derrick shouted as the log entries disappeared one by one. "Well that's it... the logs are gone. What could have happened to them? The strangest things go on around here sometimes. I swear it is Edward doing this to us..."

"C'mon Mister Paranoid. I think you need more sleep!" She grabbed his hand and led him out of the lab. Neither of the two scientists even noticed that Galen was still awake.

Galen, satisfied with his quick work, shut down his computer console and returned to his cot. It only took a few moments before he was once again sound asleep. While he slept, he began to listen to the voices again. So many voices, each voice had a wonderful story to tell him.

16

Edward was sound asleep when the communication device started its shrill alarm, bringing the old doctor out of his sleep. This alarm however, was unique from any other chime and identified the caller to Edward.

He immediately jumped out of bed, quickly put on a robe, and looked in the mirror to straighten his hair. He ran to the device, and activated it. A shadowy figure appeared on the screen. No details were shown of this person, only a grey outline of the caller.

"Edward, do you have some progress to report?" the man said. He spoke with the tone and accent of an old southern United States citizen.

"My mighty Commander…" Edward replied, then paused to gather his thoughts "we have made great strides and I feel that soon…"

"Don't bullshit me minion!" the shadow snapped "Do you think I'm stupid? I have agents everywhere, and I know you are as far from giving me a super warrior as you were four years ago! I'll tell you what… how about I give you another six months to produce some real results in your experiments. If after that time, you have not given me a warrior then I will replace you. You do want to live a long and fruitful life, don't you Edward?"

The old scientist gulped in fear "Of course mighty one…"

"Then it's settled Edward, you will produce results in six months or you will be liquidated and replaced. Have a good evening Edward."

"Thank you… I will have your warrior ready for you in the time you have granted me, my Supreme Commander!" Edward replied as the screen went blank.

He thought a moment then quickly picked up the communication device, and threw it into the wall in a rage.

"Shit, shit, shit, shit!" He paced around the room thinking of what to do. He walked to the bar and poured a large glass of bourbon, and gulped half of it down. After a few moments, his eyes lit up. He went across the room and picked up the semi smashed communication device and placed it on the desk. He entered a code and activated the screen. One of his assistants appeared.

"How many bonding subjects do we have available?" he asked the man "I want to push up the schedule tenfold from now on."

The man on the screen looked at his console to view the list of subjects then replied "We have enough subjects for at least three weeks of experiments before we will need to pick up another batch from the prisons."

"Good, begin scheduling more trials then... plan on getting a new batch of subjects every week from now on" he barked.

The man nodded in agreement, then said "Oh, I just remembered... Doctor Harmony said her subject will be ready for his bonding in a week."

"Good!" he said with delight. "That means that soon, I will finally be rid of that bitch! Schedule her subject for transformation as soon as possible. That is all..." the man nodded again as he disconnected.

He thought for a moment and a smile came to his face. "Speaking of bitch..." he entered another code, and activated the screen again. On the cracked screen was Derrick Swanson.

"Swanson, I have decided to use your technology for the advancement of my project..."

"What?" Derrick replied confused "What do you mean using our technology? What is this about?"

"You will pick a subject, and insert natural genetic materials from my experimental matrix into them... and then monitor the outcome. I will use your successful test subjects to benefit my project!" he ordered while slightly chuckling.

Stephanie shouted into the communication device from behind Derrick "You can't do that. This is not your project. It's not right..."

"I can do whatever I want, bitch. It is my order... mutate a patient within the week or suffer the consequences!" He shut off the device before they could say a single word in rebuttal.

"Yes, I think this just might work..." he smiled and took another sip of his drink.

*   *   *

Derrick just stared at the communication device unable to mutter a word. He was totally caught off guard, and was now confused. Stephanie was fuming – her face red with pure anger.

"How dare he take our findings... and worse, use our successes? I would like to mutate his brain... with a snake! I won't let him... he will not take either Galen or Lisa. I will find a blaster and use it on him if he comes near our patients!"

Derrick had never seen her so angry. "Steph, I don't think we have a choice. He could have us taken out and shot for just saying we won't do what he asks." he said calmly, hoping to reduce her anger.

Her cheeks were still bright red with anger. She stood there just staring at Derrick with rage in her eyes, unable to answer or say a single word. Suddenly her eyes swelled up, and the rage turned to pure sorrow as the salty tears began flowing down her face.

Derrick grabbed her, and hugged her while she cried. Her tears flowed for an hour, constantly mumbling the whole time. She cried until she was totally devoid of emotion. Derrick, his shoulder now completely soaked, took his finger and lifted her chin up so he could look her straight in the eyes. He smiled with a worried look. "Are you feeling better?"

"No, but I am too tired to keep going..." she said with a small but sad smile on her face.

"I know you don't want to do anything to ruin what we have done... or to hurt either Galen or Lisa... but we really don't have a choice." Hearing him say that made her want to cry more, but her eyes were now devoid of moisture. He thought for a moment before telling her "I think we might be able to find something that we could bond with them as to not change them dramatically, or affect them greatly... just enough to satisfy Edward. What do you think, Steph?"

She sniffled a couple times while she tried to compose herself. Finally, she was able to think for a moment about what he said. "Yes, perhaps just a minor mutation would work. But which one? I don't want to hurt either of them."

"I think Lisa would be our best, first test subject. We will have other healing subjects by then and could also continue with them. This would make sure that Galen would not be changed. I know how special he is to you."

"NO!" a voice shouted across the room. This surprised the two scientists, who looked over to the cells to find Galen standing at the door. He had been listening the whole time. "Pick me for the mutation. I can handle it... really. Leave Lisa alone for now!" he pleaded.

"Are you sure Galen? Lisa has not progressed like you have..."

"She has progressed and will continue to improve. I know it does not appear like she has done as well as you have expected, but give her the time... PLEASE!"

"Very well, Galen..." Derrick responded "if that's your wish, I don't know how we could refuse your request to volunteer.

"Thank you Derrick. I will be an excellent test subject... I promise. As a matter of fact, I may have an idea for your mutation. Let's rest now and discuss this more in the morning" he suggested.

"Well... okay Galen..." Stephanie replied, slightly surprised by his willingness to volunteer. She gave him a light smile before admitting "Some sleep will definitely give us clear minds for a proper decision. Good night"

Galen returned to his cot and fell asleep. The two scientists continued to talk quietly for a few minutes. Finally, Stephanie – totally spent from her emotional outburst, called it a night and left the lab. Derrick sat quietly for a moment and stared at the brain activity monitors of the two subjects. Both read 48 percent of total brain capacity.

He continued to study the monitors, then stood up and walked over to Stephanie's work bench. He picked up a hand-held monitor, and walked over to Lisa's cell. Lisa just sat in her chair not moving a muscle. He aimed the device at her through the door. Derrick saw the number 180 flash on the screen before settling at 48 percent. He looked at the device, and curiously tapped it into his palm to shake up the electronics. He then aimed it at the girl again – 48 percent brain capacity. He then realized her cell was totally quiet – he did not hear the sound of the calming necklace. He decided it was not a good idea to check the necklace function alone, and instead assumed that the computer had made adjustments. Thus, the necklace was not emitting its paralyzing drug as quickly now. He decided that it had to be the improvement in her brain capacity that caused the device to determine a lesser dosage. *"Yes, she just must not need as much medication now."*

He then walked over to Galen's cell, and aimed the device at him while he lay in his cot, sound asleep. For a brief moment, it read – 253 percent – then 48 percent. Derrick looked at the device closely trying to figure out why the readings were changing in such a manner. But when he tried again, it simply read 48 percent. He shook his head confused, and finally giving up, turned the device off. He turned, and walked away from the cells.

As Derrick walked away, Galen still lying in bed, smiled. He rolled over in his cot, and returned to the voices in his head. They spoke to him while he drifted back to sleep. While he slept, he listened to sounds of the stories. Stories of people from not only those in the complex, but around the world. There was one voice however, that he would reply to while he listened to all of the others – a voice that he told "Yes Lisa, the cycle is in motion now. Everything is as it should be."

17

The sun that shined through the lab windows woke Galen from his light slumber. The voices had spoken to him all night while he simultaneously had a mental conversation with Lisa. He had shut down her calming necklace the night before so she would no longer have to suffer through the pain of drug induced paralysis. She had been talking to him at a steady pace. They were getting to know each other quite intimately, and had become very close through their mental conversations.

Lisa did not have much of a life prior to her awakening – at least not a life she really remembered. All she remembered prior to a few days ago, was anger. She didn't even know why she was angry, she just felt the anger, and it controlled her.

Derrick and Stephanie were busy at work preparing for today's experiment. Galen was ready to be the Guinea Pig – he had no fear of what was to happen today. He was completely calm and at ease. He thought it was odd that he had no apprehension about the mutation that was going to happen. He told Lisa all about it.

"Are you sure you are going to be alright?" she asked through her thoughts. *"I do not want to have anything happen to you."*

"Yes, fear not... I know that everything will be just fine"

"I hope so, I have become used to you being here for me."

Galen went to the door "Stephanie, have you thought about what to do with me yet?"

"No, not yet Galen..." she sighed while answering him "as a matter of fact, we have no idea" a larger sigh escaped her lips.

"Any thoughts Galen? After all, it will be you who will be affected the most" Derrick asked.

"Actually yes... perhaps you could just do a simple skin bonding? Like me with a plant..."

Stephanie's eyes lit up, and opened wide "Yes! That actually would be the safest and most useful mutation we could initiate. You're brilliant Galen!" She was suddenly excited about what was about to happen.

Derrick shrugged his shoulders since he did not know what would be best – after all, that was Stephanie's expertise. "Hey, you're excited... then so am I." he admitted.

"Good! I'll start working the bonding calculations for the computer matrix." She ran to her work area and began typing furiously on her computer console making the needed computations. "Hmm, how about Aloe?" she mumbled.

It took Stephanie two hours to make the needed computations and to prepare the computer for the mixing of the two types of DNA material. She finally looked up, and told the two "Okay, we're ready."

Derrick unlocked the door to Galen's cell. He calmly walked out into the room, went right over to the table, and laid down in the proper position. "Ready doctors."

Derrick walked up and checked the device and his patient once again. "Okay, this should be a fairly quick and easy bonding, but we will put you in stasis for the process. Hopefully, it will not cause you any discomfort. Should it however, we will be prepared to sedate you. Sound good?"

"Absolutely, thank you Doctor" he returned a smile for his concern.

He began to relax – in doing so, he found that he once again was hearing all of the voices. He allowed many of the voices to tell him stories of their daily events. He picked up on one person in particular, Simon Piccolo. Simon's thoughts told him of his latest meeting with Doctor Catherine Harmony. How close he felt to her and how he had such desires for her, but felt he would never have her. He told him stories of his fear – of the unknown and of the procedure that was going to take place. He told of his fear of the changes that were going to occur, how they were going to occur, the mystery of what he will become, and how he could live with the changes.

Suddenly, his thoughts stopped. He was in a stoppage of time – nothing was occurring, nothing was felt, nothing was happening at all. He could not sense or feel a thing. What seemed like an eternity passed. He was dead, and his brain could not sense or hear anything. His heart did not beat, he could not feel, did not see, and did not hear. He could not move or even determine what was going on. He was aware, and yet not aware.

Then without warning, he was back. His heart was beating, and he was once again breathing. Simon was still thinking of Catherine and his feelings toward her. Lisa was thinking thoughts of worry. She was witnessing what was occurring, and she feared for him.

Galen began to feel different as the viruses multiplied and mutated his body. His skin suddenly felt sensitive. He felt a hunger like he had never felt before. He knew he had eaten, but he was starving. He could not understand why or how he felt. He also felt cold – he wished he had a blanket.

Stephanie's face now hovered above him. "Galen, how are you feeling?" She had a look of concern.

"I am a little cold, and very hungry... but otherwise good... I think."

She smiled "Okay, let's get you up then." She urged him to sit up, and then attempt to stand. He had no problems standing as he felt strong. He stood next to the table for a moment but then felt a tugging by some invisible force on his body. He felt an urge he could not fight. He looked to the lab window. Without saying a word, he walked away from Stephanie who was checking his health, and then dashed to the window in three quick steps. The sun was shining through the glass and the light hit his skin – it felt wonderful. He smiled as the sun bathed his skin and warmed him. He also noticed that his hunger was now fading. "*My skin must be using the sun to feed me. Amazing!*"

Derrick watched him at the window for a moment before asking "Are you doing okay Galen?"

"Absolutely!" Galen shouted "This feels wonderful! Also my hunger... it is gone!"

"Galen, your skin must now be photosynthetic. You must be able to feed yourself with sunlight through your skin... amazing! I have never seen anything like it!"

Galen was smiling now. He felt completely satisfied as he walked from the window back to the two scientists. He stopped as he caught a glimpse of his reflection in the mirror. He stepped back far enough to gaze at himself. His skin had a light green tint – otherwise he looked exactly the same as before. "Wonderful!" he shouted out. He touched his face and looked at his hands as he stared at himself in the mirror.

Suddenly, the communication device sounded and Derrick answered – it was Edward.

"What progress have you made?" he barked.

"We have successfully bonded our subject's DNA with a plant and were able to stimulate a successful mutation" he proudly told his boss. Galen walked up behind Derrick so Edward could view him.

"Is that all?" Edward spouted with repugnance. "Can he be shot with a blaster and live? Can he kill someone with some special talent caused by that green skin? That is worthless! Mutate him again, this time with something useful... NOW!" he yelled, then disconnected the transmission.

"What?" Stephanie shouted "That bastard! I'm going to..."

"No Stephanie, it's alright..." Galen interrupted "I am sure we can come up with something else to mutate into me." He flashed a smile that immediately calmed her anger. "May I look through the web-net for something that might be a good fit?"

"I don't see why not..." Derrick admitted.

"Yes, pick something for yourself Galen. That would be the least we could do" Stephanie told him.

He returned to his cell and began to search for a good match. He typed commands furthering his search when suddenly he stopped typing, and listened. In his head, he heard something different than the thoughts of the others. He no longer heard voices – instead he heard and felt something different. He heard the wind – he felt the wind swirling around his body. He sensed sunshine on his body, but he was not in the sun. He felt himself growing, and thriving. He experienced the living and growing of plants. Those feelings were so beautiful to Galen that it caused tears to roll down his cheeks in total bliss. He wondered where he could find those plants. Where was this spot where the planet was still young and fresh? Where was there a spot on this planet that was not burned to a crisp? He just wanted to immerse himself in those sounds and feelings. Reality set in however, his mind returned to the present, and to his searching. He reminded himself that two friends were depending on him to pick just the right change – and he was not going to let them down. He searched until he found what he thought was the perfect match.

"Steph, Derrick, I have found it!"

The two rushed to his cell and gasped at what was on the screen. Stephanie finally said "Galen, that's an insect – are you sure that's what you want?" Her eyes were wide while she stared at the image on the screen.

"Yes Stephanie, take the shell of this insect... and merge it with my skin. It will provide me with a hard shell. One that should be able to withstand the force of a blaster... at least I hope!"

"If that's what you want Galen... then okay, let's get started" Derrick announced.

They once again spent hours preparing the computations and algorithms for the bonding. Stephanie prepared the retroviruses for transmission of the mutated DNA, and started a growth culture of the manipulated viruses. Finally, Stephanie announced she was ready, and Galen once again placed himself upon the experimental platform.

Hearing Derrick say "Here we go Galen..." was the last thing he was aware of when they started the process. Time once again stopped for him as they put him into stasis. When he came back to reality, he felt pain. He groaned as he felt his skin change, and mutate. Stephanie ran to him with a hypodermic device in her hand.

"No Stephanie, I will be alright..." he told her, while waving her off. "Agggg!" he cried out again as his skin turned into a solid state. He looked to the visions he had before the process – he looked for, then found the plants blowing in the wind. Grasses grew tall in the sun, flowers bloomed and produced pollen for the various visiting birds and insects. Finding the visions again calmed him while his skin mutated and the changes took hold. The pain was still there, but he could now maintain control, and was partially able to tune out the pain. He felt that wind blowing around his body. Even though his skin was stiffening he could still move with the breeze. He imagined the sun shining on his body, feeding him, and bathing him in comforting warmth. He felt an unexpected change in his chest. *"What just happened?"*

As the pain subsided, he found he was able to easily return to the present time and location. He opened his eyes, and sat up albeit, slowly. His skin was stiff everywhere, and felt slightly uncomfortable. He looked at his hand and was amazed with how it looked. The once-green skin was now colored a glowing gold, with a very slight green tinge undertone. He tapped his fist on his chest – it was hard and solid. As a matter of fact, the skin over his entire body was now as hard as stone.

Stephanie and Derrick were staring at Galen in awe. They were not sure what to make of the changes that had occurred. Derrick performed electronic probes and scans on the now-mutated man.

Galen walked over to the mirror again, and was surprised by his new look. He was now covered by this golden, glowing skin. The light green undertone told him he still had the plant inside him, but yet he was so different from just a few short hours ago. His legs and arms were for the most part the same – except he appeared to be much stronger than before – he flexed his muscles in admiration. The one thing that was completely different was his chest – he now seemed to have developed an extra pair of breasts. The nipples on his prior set of breasts were now gone. He had four muscled bumps now covering his upper torso. His lower torso was also muscled, and rock solid with a hard-shell skin. His face looked the same except the golden-greenish glow that surrounded his entire body. His hair was the same – the sandy color was as before, and despite the hard skin on his head, his hair was soft and flowing.

He tapped on his abdominal skin. "Yes, I believe we have achieved what we were working toward." He walked back to the window and stood in the sun. He realized he still photosynthesized the wonderful rays. This told him that the plant part of him was still fully active in his body. "I think you now need to shoot me..."

Stephanie's eyes opened wide in surprise "No, that won't happen!"

"Stephanie, it must..." he pleaded. "If we can't prove I indeed have something valuable to him, then he will want even more."

"He's right Steph..." Derrick interjected. "It would be a good test. Maybe just a thin shot to the arm or something?"

"I don't like it... but I think there will be no stopping you two. But I am certainly not going to watch!"

Derrick laughed. "Ok, ready Galen?" he directed him to the door. He led him to the building exit. Right outside, there was a guard at the door. Derrick instructed the guard to shoot Galen in the arm.

The guard took careful aim, then pulled the trigger. The blaster shot emitted from the gun and hit Galen squarely in the arm – then bounced off his skin, and ricocheted into a wall. The guard was stunned for a moment in amazement. Galen was unscathed and smiling. Derrick then instructed the guard to aim his blaster at Galen's torso.

The guard took careful aim at Galen. He once again pulled the trigger, and fired the beam right at his heart. As before, it ricocheted off of his hard-shell skin and flew into the sky.

They returned to the lab and Stephanie gave a huge sigh of relief upon seeing the return of a smiling Galen.

"You two have done it..." Galen announced. "I feel great by the way. As a matter of fact, I could not feel any better."

Almost like clockwork, the communication device once again rang, announcing Edward's expected call.

"Well, do you have something worthwhile to tell me this time?"

"Yes, we have now mutated Galen so he has a hard-insectoid shell..." Derrick boasted. "His shell will now reflect a blaster shot... and I would assume he would hurt me... if he struck me with his shell hardened fist."

Edward nodded his head. "Now that is progress! Very well, continue with his mutation and report back to me on a regular basis..."

"What?" Stephanie shouted "We were not to continue mutations on Galen!"

Not hearing a word she was saying, he continued. "Oh, and mutate the girl also. As a matter of fact, I will give you more subjects. I expect you to constantly be mutating test subjects. Keep providing me results." He disconnected the communication without asking for any feedback from the two scientists.

"Damn him" Derrick spouted.

"Derrick, Stephanie?" Galen asked "Might I be able to select more mutations for myself? I find this process fascinating and I don't mind helping you... but I would like to have some control of my destiny."

"Of course, Galen" Stephanie answered. "I think you'll be able to make yourself into a fine warrior. Although I don't think that creep deserves any success."

"Thank you, Steph, thank you Derrick. I will need to rest some... then I will begin my research and selection. You have still done so much to make my life better, and I will never forget this." He smiled, nodded his head, and then quietly returned to his cell. He laid down on his cot, and opened his mind again to the visions he had earlier. They were different this time, however. Now, he felt himself as the grass itself, being rubbed against as he ran through it, while at the same time felt his insectoid body was being stroked by the blades of grass, as he ran.

He then experienced scents, tastes and feelings different from anything he ever experienced before. He determined he was now experiencing life in the plant world, and in the insect world. It was a wonderful experience. He also experienced the pain and fulfillment of the eating of plants. He then experienced an animal eating, while at the same time felt the animal tugging and pulling pieces of his own body into his own mouth. It was painful, yet he felt the pleasure of the stimulation of growth that the browsing was creating. He relished in the taste of his own plant body on the animal's palate. He also experienced the feelings an insect experiences while being eaten – it was horrible, yet fascinating. He enjoyed his experience for the longest time until he realized he needed to share his experience.

He then opened his mind to the voices that spoke to him, and related what he felt. He found however that there were now very few minds available to his probing mind. To the ones he could reach out to, he gave them a mental image of everything he had just experienced. After giving all of his experiences to all the minds he could find, he stopped to rest and began to just listen. He started to drift to sleep, when suddenly a loud and distinct voice spoke to him. This voice was not at the institute or anywhere nearby. As a matter of fact, the voice in his head was so far away that Galen could not determine even the direction of the source – but it was as loud as when he spoke to Lisa in the next cell. The voice did not even speak in the same language as Galen, but somehow, he understood every word and thought of this person. Galen sat up in surprise at the voice and its questioning.

"Are you there? Are you now one too? I think it is now time for us to talk and plan my friend."

18

Catherine was told to see Edward in his office right away. She assumed it was because Simon was ready for his transformation as part of project Fury Warrior. She arrived at his office ahead of time and was summoned in as soon as she arrived. Edward was sitting at his desk with his normal scowl on his old face. She assumed the scowl was for her. She knew of his distaste for her and her project.

"Sit down Cat, can I offer you a drink?" he said as his face suddenly turned to a smile.

She couldn't believe he called her that. "Please call me Catherine" she said.

"Oh, I thought you went by Cat..." he questioned.

"Only by my friends" she snapped back.

"Very well, we will dispense with the pleasantries..." he snarled, his mood had now returned back to his normal, hateful self. "Catherine, do you know why I am in charge of this project? It is because I was the head of my class at Sector 14 Technology Center. I was the best... I had a unique understanding of the human genetic sequence and at the same time a complete knowledge of molecular manipulation. I was ideal for this project."

"Didn't hurt that you were Blessed too..." she added.

He continued without a pause. "When the Council found out about my work a few years back they almost begged me to take over this project."

"Begged, why do I have a hard time believing that..." she muttered.

He ignored her insult. "I know I seem a little harsh at times, but it is for the common good of the Alliance" he told her. "The Alliance needs these warriors. This is the only hope for us to win the war... at which time the Supreme Commander can bring peace to the world once and for all. So, for the sake of all of our lives we need these experiments to succeed. So far, they have worked... but not to my desired expectations. So, I am hoping that your experiment will indeed give me the warrior that I can finally control and command."

"Listen, we both know what's at stake. What exactly did you call me here for anyway?" she asked impatiently.

"Fine, I tried to be nice and explain why this is important..." he snapped "but instead, I will just come out and say it. If your experiment does not produce the desired result... that is a controllable sub-human capable of fighting warfare... your life will be over. I will tell the Council you failed me, and your head will be placed on a stake. So, I hope your patient is indeed ready for this, or you will be one dead bitch. Do I make myself clear?"

"Perfectly" she answered. "This will work, and then I will likely be out of your hair. You know however, the opposite could happen and I will be bothering you for the rest of your life?"

"Then prepare your anarchist friend for conversion... tomorrow" he barked, then shooed her away with a double swipe of downturned fingers.

Her eyes opened wide as she realized what was going to happen. *"No, I can't let this... I must... no, I can't stop it..."* the realization hit her brain like a shock wave – Simon's time was up. Without revealing anything, she replied "Very well, he'll be ready. I assume he gets the standard last night?"

"Well, since we stepped up conversion testing we have dispensed with that luxury. However, because I am feeling generous, I will give him his last night in the luxury suite. Now leave me..." he ordered as he once again gestured the brushing of the younger woman out the door with his old hand.

She did her best to keep her composure while she exited his office. But as soon as she was on the opposite side of the now closed door she let out a huge gasp. She almost collapsed against the wall as she fought back the tears that were fighting to burst from her eyes. She stood there for a few minutes until she was able to regain her composure. She was sure the old letch was watching and getting a good chuckle from her fighting her emotions, but she didn't care. What was important was the reality of her situation. This reality hit her full-force – she was about to lose Simon.

She took her communication device from her belt and requested Michael. Her assistant appeared with a soft smile on his face. "Michael, would you get Simon and have him meet me outside in the common area please?"

"Of course, Doctor, we'll meet you there right away" he replied and disconnected.

She stopped by her office, then went downstairs and outside the lab building to the common area. This area was the space between the buildings of the institute complex. There were walkways that connected and guided people between the various buildings. The open area was mostly comprised of crushed lava rock and some old lava flows along the crater sides. Despite the barren appearance, it gave many of the employees a good place to stretch their legs, and provided a place to find some peace. Simon and Michael were waiting for her by the time she arrived.

She smiled with a slightly pained look as she approached Simon. "Hello Simon... thanks Michael, that will be all..." she said as she approached the two men. Michael nodded, said goodbye to Simon, and then went back into the lab building.

"Catherine, is everything okay? You look troubled."

"Yes..." she replied softly "we can talk later. First I would like to get you somewhere more comfortable."

"It's my time isn't it Catherine?"

"Please Simon... let's get out of the common area before we talk please." She was fighting with all she had to keep back the tears. She started walking toward the residential quarters motioning Simon to follow. He obediently followed the quick pace of the doctor.

The pair reached the luxury suite and Catherine swiped her identity bracelet over the door. The opening door revealed a suite with every imaginable comfort. The suite was one of the best supplied quarters in the complex. It was paneled in rare woods. There was a variety of beverages, stimulants, foods, and entertainment options. The furniture was opulent and comfortable. The suite had a sitting room with food processing unit, a bathroom with shower, and a bedroom with a king-sized bed. This suite had every luxury possible.

When Simon walked in, he whistled with amazement. "Wow, take a look at this spread!" Simon gave another whistle as he looked around the lavish quarters. "So, this confirms it... it's my time, isn't it?"

Catherine nodded her head and replied "Tonight is basically your last night. This is a special suite that is reserved for test subjects. It is all set for you tonight... whatever you need or want, I will get for you."

"Will you stay here with me? I could use your company tonight."

"If that is what you want... at least for a little while."

"Yes, it is Catherine... please..."

"Perhaps we could practice your meditation again. I want you to be as prepared as possible."

Simon gave a slightly disappointed look on his face. "Always work, eh? Okay, if you think that's best. Then could we maybe relax and enjoy this place afterwards?"

"Well, maybe we could first relax... then practice." She said giving in to his disappointment.

He looked around the suite like a kid in a candy store, examining every item of luxury. "Wow, I have not seen anything this luxurious in years! Amazing!"

"Glad you like it. Would you like a drink?"

"Please!" Simon answered with excitement in his voice.

She poured them each a glass of synthetic wine, and they sat on the large couch. She raised her glass in toast, and he clinked his glass against hers lightly in reply. They sipped on the wine then looked at each other for a silent moment. Feeling uncomfortable, Catherine looked away then stood up.

"Simon, I think you need to see this. You need to know exactly what is going to happen tomorrow..." she said as she walked over to the computer console. She typed in a command, and an image appeared on the screen. "This man was converted yesterday." The image was of a black man. He was naked, and strapped to a table. Simon immediately recognized him.

"My god, its Danny..."

"You know him?"

"Yes, he was one of the few friends I had made in the living quarters. The other was Galen... and well, you know what happened to him..."

"I'm sorry Simon" She placed her hand in his as they watched the video.

The device began to glow, and after a few minutes Danny's body began to disintegrate into only an outline. This outline remained on the table for quite a while. Catherine forwarded the video ahead until it started reintegration. Danny's body was placed back together piece by piece, molecule by molecule. After a few minutes, he was fully reintegrated.

Then, his body began to change, and he began to scream in pain. It was horrible for Simon to watch, but he knew he had to. Danny's body sprouted fur, his nose became longer, and his face completely changed. His arms and legs appeared to get shorter. His fingers became stumpy and short, with small claws growing at the end of small fingers. His knees bent the opposite direction, and his thighs became large and muscular. Whiskers appeared on his face, and extended out of his nose. A thick tail grew from his back, and hung down from a slot in the table. His ears moved up and forward on his face, and became rounded. His eyes bulged and turned black. The transformation went on until Danny lay motionless on the table totally transformed – into what, Simon was not sure. After a few minutes, they wheeled him out of camera range.

"My god... poor Danny" Simon whispered as he realized his friend was no longer human.

"I thought you would want to know the procedure. I wished I had known that was your friend however. Please forgive me..."

"Of course... it wasn't your fault. I could never blame you for that" he reassured her.

"Thank you. How about we enjoy some more wine?" she asked trying to change the subject.

He refilled the two glasses and gave Catherine her glass. They once again toasted and sipped on the wine. They stared into each other's eyes. She was getting that melting feeling she always got when looking at him. They stared at each other in total quiet until she broke the silence.

"Simon…"

"No, don't say anything Catherine" he interrupted. "I have an idea however. How about we do that meditation practice now, hmm?"

"Well, if that is what you want Simon…" she told him as she stood up, and put two large pillows in the middle of the floor.

They both sat on the pillows and began to concentrate. Catherine's hair began to glow when she was interrupted by the sound of Simon's voice. He had focused on his vocal chords again.

"Simon, you must move your focal point! Remember, the damage…"

After only a few seconds, the glow on his throat vanished and his hands instead started to glow. He smiled at her, and she began her concentration again. She closed her eyes, and let the energy flow in and out of her body.

"Catherine, open your eyes."

She complied with his request and saw him smiling at her. Like before, the energy flowed from her eyes into his. They both entered into the restful, ecstatic state that their two mental energies seemed to cause when combined. She could not help but let out a slight moan as his energy entered her brain. She concentrated on not abandoning her control. He had been mentally courting her for months – she had fought it off by keeping her professional manner and rejecting his advances. But now he was going to be gone and she wanted so badly to let go. Her professional demure was still preventing her from revealing her true feelings. "I don't think we should go any farther…"

"Please don't fight it. I think you know how I feel, and I'm sure you feel the same. Please, just give me my dying wish of one sweet kiss" he pleaded.

"Very well, one kiss... one small kiss. But you have to concentrate and earn it..." she conceded as she allowed the energy to flow freely between them.

She intensified her concentration and felt the mental passion build between them. She felt herself rise off the pillow and float into the air. She felt her heart beat faster and her temperature rise. She felt him close to her now as he too was floating. She fully opened her eyes and let the energy flow between them. He was just inches away from her.

"Just one beautiful kiss..." he said as their lips met, and her defenses crumbled.

Electricity like energy flowed between their lips and tongues as they kissed. Their arms wrapped around each other, and the passion level rose. It was the most beautiful, erotic thing either of them had ever felt, or would ever feel again. They were experiencing something they had never felt before with anyone else, and knew they would never feel again. The pair experienced that one beautiful kiss – a kiss that lasted the rest of the night.

19

Galen had been working constantly at his computer console since that first night – he had been determining each possible combination of nature and man that would be of benefit to him. He knew the choices he would make would forever remain with him – him, and any others that followed. He wanted to be exactly sure in every decision he made. As he studied the aspects of animals and plants he made mental lists of each creature's characteristics, and then determined if the characteristics would be a benefit or detriment to the human body.

He studied the offensive and defensive capabilities of animals, plants and insects. When he discovered an ability, he felt he would have to have, he added it to an electronic list. The list had become bigger and bigger as he found attributes that he felt he would be necessary for survival. After he had exhausted every possible creature and plant with available DNA in the computer storehouse, he stopped and looked at his list. There were thousands of possible abilities he could add. He decided he needed to pick the very best and most valuable attributes of the natural world. Perhaps he could even select some that could be used only when needed. He reworked the list down to only a couple hundred attributes, then down to under a hundred. He looked at the list and reviewed each attribute remaining on the list. Now he felt the list was complete – this was what he was to become.

He studied the list once again, and closely reviewed each ability. From the animal world, he combined speed from the Cheetah's leg muscles, strength from the Elephant, eyesight from a combination of Eagles, Owls, and Cats, and protective hair from the Moth. From the Deer, a digestive system modified to live off of plants instead of meat and claws from the Tiger. From the plant world, he selected the ability to vine, secrete certain fluids, and regenerate injuries. The list was extensive and complete. He realized that if they added every selected attribute, he would really no longer be human – but he would be something better. Indeed, this is what he wanted to become. He was to be the next evolution of humankind.

He walked to the cell door and called to Stephanie. "I am done with my list, do you want to enter it into the computer, or shall I?"

He transferred the list to the computer. Stephanie glanced at the enormous list on her computer screen, then looked at Galen with an astonished look "My goodness, you compiled that list already? It would have taken me days or weeks and you are done in hours. Are you sure your brain capacity readout is correct?" She had a smirk of disbelief on her face.

He shrugged his shoulders. "I don't know why the readout would not be correct Steph."

"I wonder that myself..." Derrick grumbled softly. He was still suspicious of the changing readings he got from the hand held monitor the other night. But since he was unable to get it to reoccur, and like the scientist he was, if it could not be reproduced, then it was not real. He convinced himself once again that it had to be a fluke or an equipment glitch.

Stephanie jumped in to stop that line of talk. "It doesn't matter Galen... what's important is how you've not only exceeded the expectations of our original experiment, but more how you have actually become a kind of member of the team."

Derrick watched the exchange between Stephanie and Galen. He found himself gritting and grinding his teeth in jealous frustration. He looked away and did the best he could to remove the jealous thoughts from his head. After a moment, he was able to go back to his work, while trying to forget his petty emotions. Besides, he was no longer like us – she would never be attracted to what he was about to become. He also realized that after they were finished with him, Zardonagon would steal him away – and then do who-knows-what to him. His jealousy turned to pity – he felt truly sorry for what would probably happen to Galen. The young man had done nothing to deserve what was going to happen to him once in the hands of Edward. This emotion then turned to sorrow as he honestly realized that Galen had become more like a friend to them. He was a good person, and was actually helping them to succeed. His crinkled mouth loosened, and then a smile crossed his face as he returned to his alignment of the bonding device.

Galen was now at Stephanie's computer console working the computations for the next mutation session on his computer. Stephanie sat behind Galen watching him work and was amazed by how he was able to program the computer for this next phase. "I cannot believe how you have learned to use the computer Galen. Your learning capabilities are just amazing!"

Galen's gold skin glowed brighter upon hearing her complement. "You telling me that makes what I have learned even more special! The computer was so natural and easy to learn. It was if I knew how to use it before I ever became aware."

Stephanie turned away for a moment and bit her lip in guilt. She knew why he so easily learned the computer – she knew he obtained that ability from Derrick's DNA. The secret was killing her, but she dared never admit to her indiscretion. "Obviously, it was an ability that was always in you. We just brought it out in you... right Derrick?" Her partner was so involved in his work he just muttered some sound of agreement.

Galen worked for two hours as he entered all of the computations needed to provide the computer the data required for bonding of all the various DNA strands in both his cells and the host cells. In addition, he entered the proper areas to remove cells, determined how many retroviruses would be required for each phase of mutation and programmed the order to insert the viruses and instigate the mutation of the cells. He rechecked all settings to convince him that the computer had been provided with all the information needed for his mutation procedure. He stopped typing and backed away from the computer console rubbing his eyes.

"I have completed the programming needed to perform the next set of mutations. Steph... Derrick... would you mind if I took a brief rest before we proceed? The computer will take a couple hours to load all of the data and materials needed anyway."

"I see no reason why you shouldn't rest... have a nice nap." Derrick replied.

Galen walked back to his cell. On the way, he stopped at Lisa's cell and looked into the room. She was sitting there, still not moving. The paralysis drug had been stopped days ago by Galen but she continued to act as if she was not aware. She had found that lately it had become harder and harder to communicate with Galen. It worried her but she continued to act as if the necklace still functioned. Galen looked at Lisa and smiled while at the same time the glow of his skin intensified and almost lit up her dark room. She looked at him with her dark eyes and gave him a very small smile.

He moved from her cell door, and returned to his cell. He closed the door behind him and jumped onto the cot. He closed his eyes and started to live his life outside. Outside, in those places that were untouched by the bombs, wherever those places existed. He lived the lives of nature -- the plants and animals he was hoping to merge with soon. He opened his thoughts to Lisa. She could slightly feel his presence – but could not hear his voice. She did feel the same sensations through the visions he was sending exclusively to her. What she could see and feel was the most wonderful thing she had ever experienced. She wanted to join him on his journey and hoped that he would suggest it soon. She would not refuse any offer to join him and she found she was becoming impatient. She wanted to be with him and wanted to live exactly like him – she would do whatever it took to be with him.

Two hours passed quickly for Galen, especially when he was in a state of mental connectivity with nature. However, his internal clock told him it was time – he stood up, and poured a glass of water. He sipped on the liquid and pondered what his life would soon be like. He was excited to feel all the different abilities that would be inside him.

When Galen left his cell, and joined Derrick and Stephanie, he found them staring at a single computer display. The pair had determined that this many mutations would be too much of a strain on Galen's body. But as they continued to study the mutation patterns that Galen himself devised, they were amazed to see he had combined all DNA modifications in one fell swoop. He would do a total mutation with only one cycle of bonding and reintroduction.

"Galen, are you sure you can take this many changes at one time? I'm very worried..." Stephanie asked. She was furrowing her forehead in concern

"Absolutely! I have calculated all bonding and mutation factors, and I have estimated that it will take approximately fifteen minutes for the computer to do the calculations, twenty minutes to combine the DNA in the bonding matrix, eighteen minutes to inject the DNA into the retroviruses, twenty-nine minutes to mutate enough viruses for injection and forty-nine seconds to reintegrate the modified cells and start the mutation process." He had genuine excitement in his voice.

"Wow, I guess you have it all figured out." Derrick said, slightly skeptical.

"I know Derrick... you cannot believe I could calculate the timing to that degree. You will see..." he said laughing, as he walked over, laid down on the table, and waited for the pair to begin the process.

"Sedative this time Galen? This is a big change" Stephanie suggested.

"Actually... I think this time I will take one, thank you" he said in agreement.

Stephanie had a hard time finding a spot on his hard-shell skin where she could administer the sedative. After using the electron scanner on him, she finally found a very small spot on his arm pit where the hard-shell skin was slightly thinner than the rest of his body.

"Ah, you found my Achilles heel I see!" he said as she administered the sedative. He immediately fell unconscious.

She turned from table and saw Derrick pointing the hand scanner at Galen. "Why are you scanning him Derrick? What's wrong?" she was slightly disgusted over his skepticism.

"I got a strange brain activity scan the other night. I just wanted to see if I could get that reading again." As before, the scanner read only 48 percent of brain capacity being used. "I just don't get it... how could he do all those calculations with only 48 percent? It just doesn't add up."

"Perhaps his 48 percent is in a different area of the brain, thus allowing him to perform the math?" She knew deep inside that Galen possessed Derrick's knowledge of the process, and was probably using those skills. She didn't dare admit to her partner however, as it was a selfish lapse of an unprofessional moment.

Derrick finally gave up, let out a big sigh and put the scanner down so they could perform the mutation. The computer gathered the samples and started its calculations. Fifteen minutes had passed when the computer indicated it had finished its calculations.

"Well, I'll be... he got it right on the calculations" Derrick admitted to his surprise.

They initiated the bonding sequence, which took exactly twenty minutes. The DNA was injected into the retroviruses, the viruses were put into the culture, and the cultures were allowed to reproduce to a sufficient number of cells. The timing was eighteen minutes to inject the DNA into the retroviruses, twenty-nine minutes to mutate enough viruses for injection – exactly as Galen predicted.

"Well, let's see if he got the mutation process correct. I hope for his sake he's right in his timing on this one..." Derrick said as he activated the bonding device.

"Activating stasis field" Stephanie announced.

The bonding device was activated, and the retroviruses were inserted into Galen's waiting body. The two scientists then waited nervously for the bonding to be complete, forty seconds passed – and nothing.

"I'm worried now..." Stephanie admitted.

"Me too..." Derrick was cut off by the computer message indicating that bonding was complete. "Ah, there we go... kill the stasis."

Stephanie immediately shut down the stasis field as Galen began to show signs of the mutation process beginning. She looked at Derrick who was once again pointing the hand scanner at their subject.

"Derrick, really!" she yelled with disgust.

"Just want to monitor this... that's all" he said trying to weasel out of his suspicious curiosity.

Galen's body started to pulsate in variations and brightness of gold light. His skin bulged and buckled as it began to change. His hair fell out almost instantly, and as quickly began to be replaced with bright purple fibrous strands. His leg muscles begin to flex and pulse as they developed – the flexing of his muscles ripped his clothing apart, the shredded material fell to the floor leaving him naked on the table. He convulsed and shook as his bone structure changed to accommodate his new form. His legs and arms got longer and his back extended to match his larger form. Lumps and bulges formed then disappeared as his internal organs rearranged and modified. His stomach and intestines made horrid gastric noises as they mutated and realigned. His ears lengthened and enlarged to increase his hearing. His teeth fell out and were immediately replaced by a set of sharper, stronger, and thicker teeth. Stephanie ran over and picked the discarded teeth out of his open mouth with forceps so he would not choke. His hands were developing claws that once formed, receded into his fingertips.

For fifteen minutes, the process went on and on. Then without warning, the changes stopped as quickly as they had started. Galen woke almost immediately after the process finished. He was stiff, but found he could sit up without any problems. He looked at his new hands – extended a claw, admired it, then retracted it. He looked at his legs and noticed the new muscular structure. He rubbed his legs to feel the stiff taught muscles.

He slowly stood up and walked to the mirror, but paused after only one step. To the scientists, it appeared that he moved too fast, and almost lost control of his locomotion. He thought about his movement before he began to take small, single steps. For a few moments, he had to work to prevent himself from taking off in a run.

He cleared his voice a couple times before speaking. "I guess I am going to need to practice walking slowly..." He now spoke with a slight resonation in his voice.

He took some more small steps until he reached the mirror. He stared at himself and admired his body. He ran his fingers through his bright purple, fern-like hair. Then he looked down at his pubic hair – it was the same fern-like consistency and color as his head. He noted his sexual organ was no longer the way it was before, as it was simply – different. Both sets of hair seemed to wave back and forth as if they had a life of their own. They acted like were searching the air for food and water. His face still had the same features as it did before, with the exception of a stronger looking set of cheeks. His skin still had the golden glow with the slight green tinge under the surface, and his outer epidermal was still as hard as stone. His eyes had the warm golden tone as before the process.

"I am pleased. What do you two think?"

"Ummm, well... I could better answer if you would put on some clothes" Stephanie said, her cheeks bright red with embarrassment.

Galen laughed while Derrick tossed him a jumpsuit. "Well Galen, you were wrong by the way" Galen looked at him with a puzzled glance. "It took fifty-four seconds to perform the bonding. You were a bit off there..." he chuckled, and then smiled at him.

Galen thought about it a moment, then gave a hearty laugh. "You got me there, Derrick! I'll have to determine what went wrong" he said in a joking manner.

"Well if you are done admiring yourself Galen, I would like to do an examination" Stephanie pointed him back to the table.

"Stephanie, would you mind if we did that after a nap? It seems that the process really sapped my strength. I guess you could examine me while I sleep if that would be okay?"

"Well, I guess I could do most of the tests while you sleep. Sure, go ahead and lie down, I'll be there in a few minutes."

Galen took small, stiff steps back to his cell, laid down on the stiff cot, and immediately fell asleep. He mentally expressed his experience with all who were listening. It was even quieter to his mind than it was before.

Stephanie gathered her medical scanning devices. Derrick walked up to her with the hand scanner.

"Haven't you given up on that yet?" she asked him in a scolding tone.

"Yes, I think I no longer need to try" he told her as he held the scanner display toward her.

Her disgruntled face turned to a look of shock when she saw the display. "How could this be? How has it been reading 48 percent, when all this time when this was the real measurement?"

"I don't know, but I think he's been mutating the whole time, while somehow keeping the readings from us... at least that is what I think has been happening. It appears he is no longer concerned with being discovered." He shook his head while he once again examined the reading: "398 percent brain capacity used."

20

Simon woke from his sleep, looked next to him, and remembered that Catherine had left hours ago. He sat up, got onto his feet, and slowly walked to the window. The sun was starting to rise and he could see the orange, reds, and golds peek through the window of the luxury suite given to experiment victims on their last night. He wished Catherine was here with him to view what might be the last sunrise of his life.

He was nervous, but despite that, he realized he had actually slept really well. He seemed to remember his dreams as being very relaxing. He kept seeing his friend Galen in the dreams. He remembered seeing and hearing the sights and sounds of living with nature. He, or for that matter, not anyone in the northern hemisphere had ever actually experienced living in the natural word. The natural world in this hemisphere was gone. He wondered if there was anywhere in the world where real nature might be found. He found the vision exciting, yet so relaxing. He wondered about the meaning of these dreams.

He realized that soon they would be calling for him. "Today I will die..." he said to himself with sarcasm in his voice. He chuckled lightly, but deep down knew this to be a semi-truth. He knew after today he would either be dead, or at least as good as dead. Today, they were going to experiment on him.

He wondered how this could have happened to him. It was only a little over two years ago, he was living free and happy. Life was full, and he had a world to save. He never would have realized that his ambition would be his undoing. It all began when he started to dig a little too deep, and uncovered too many lies. He discovered how back then, long ago, the United States President had deceived the people. That is when he started speaking out about the lies told by the Supreme Commander and the Council – he became too cocky. That was when he became the last straw for the Council. He had become a threat to the Council, and thus was placed on their list. It had only been days after he spoke out, that Jared, the Blessed secret service officer had arrived at his door. He arrested him, put him on trial, and sent him to his death in prison. That moment, when he decided he was invincible, that was when his life took this downward spiral.

Prison, then this – this facility. This was to be his way out of the death camp. Only through this experimental program was he able to escape an eventual violent and painful death. However, was this to be a better death for him?

His mind wandered to Catherine. She was assigned to him to make this process easier, and it was expected that this work would make the experiment successful. She trained him in techniques that would help him mentally survive the change that was going to occur. She had prepared him for what surely was to come. But she did more than even she expected, as she taught him true love. He knew she felt the same, even if she never admitted it. Last night gave her away. Gave away her true thoughts and feelings. He now knew she loved him – if only she had told him, but she never said it. But they had formed the ultimate bond – all without the aid of a machine, thus it was totally illegal – but for some reason allowed.

He knew there was no denying what feelings were beneath the professional attitude – not after last night. But she had left to prepare for today. He knew having to subject him to this was breaking her heart. He knew she had finally found love and was about to lose it to this horrid experiment.

Yes, today he would either die, or become a monster. He had hoped his pick for the genetic splicing and injection would help him to survive and perhaps help him to keep his mind. Thanks to Catherine's intervention and recommendation to the Council, he would be subjected to a new way of performing the splicing. He would be the first to select his nature bond, his joining animal. Not even Doctor Zardonagon knew of his choice. He hoped his choice would be good enough. He knew that if the experiment failed to satisfy the doctor he would likely be destroyed to appease his anger and the frustration of failure.

He had heard of Edward Zardonagon's "finger injector". With this device, he would ensure that he would die slowly and painfully if it pleased him. Zardonagon did not care about the pain that any failed subject would experience. If the rumors were true, any thought of a failed experiment would throw him into a rage. His rage would end up in the destruction of the test subject, most likely to give him a way to cover his failure.

However, if the experiment went well today, he would be changed but might still have his mental state and abilities. He was a smart man, perhaps he had made some common-sense mistakes, but he knew he was intelligent. He knew he had a very high IQ. He knew this intelligence would help him, and he would survive this. He would become the hybrid of two species, and could be a warrior if he desired.

He would not become the soldier they wanted however, and he would not help to kill others for their petty dispute of a war. No matter what he became, the one thing he knew, was he would not fight for the Council in their endless war. This stupid war – the war that had destroyed most of this planet and most of its population. This war, that for only a very few of the high-ranking government elites, provided satisfaction. If anything, he would use his abilities to end this war – provided he survived today.

His thoughts were interrupted by the communication screen chime. It rang three times before it finally broke his deep thought. He walked to the wall and answered it. He felt overjoyed when he saw it was Catherine.

"Good morning, I hope you slept well after I left."

He studied her face on the view screen. She had a smile on her face, but that smile was tense. He could tell she was upset, but he also knew there was a good reason for her feelings. It was sweet of her to try to hide her tension he thought. "I slept very well surprisingly. I had pleasant thoughts to guide my sleep."

She gave him another warm smile, but her eyes were giving her feelings away, and those eyes showed she was frightened. "There is a special breakfast prepared for you... with real bacon and eggs!" she said that proudly as if she bagged the biggest animal of the hunt. "It's a rare find without a government job!" The smile on her face was sincere, and then that giggle escaped her lips. That funny sound warmed him inside.

He just smiled and let out a chuckle.

"What?" she asked.

"Oh, it's nothing... It was very sweet of you to do this for me." he answered.

"Well, your last meal as a total human should be speci..." She stopped mid-sentence when she realized where she was going with her statement. "Dammit, I did it again!"

He saw her uneasiness and said with a smile "It's okay... it WILL be my last meal as a total human being." He hoped his words would let her recover from her verbal stumble.

He thought for a moment and realized that for the first time ever, he did not feel like eating. "Anyway, as wonderful as the meal sounds, I'm really not feeling very hungry... but thanks anyway." He kept that pleasant smile on his face for her.

Her face however, looked pained. She attempted as best as possible to try to smile as she spoke "I can definitely understand that."

He put an evil grin on his face and then said "Besides, I had the best last meal any man could have had last night."

She smiled, blushed, and let that giggle slip out again.

"That's right... smile for me Catherine, SMILE! Makes it all worth it to me..." he said this in an almost a singing tone.

"Very well, it's in the food dispenser for you if you change your mind. If you eat it, please enjoy it. I will be by at 8 AM to take you to the lab for the process. Simon, I hope you understand if there was any way I could stop this..."

"Please, this is not your doing. You have done more than I could ever ask. You have trained me to hopefully survive. You have also made me happy in ways I could have never had imagined. If this is the end, I have no complaints."

She reached for the control switch "I'm glad I could do what I could to help you. I'm sure you'll survive this! I'll see you afterwards and we'll laugh and talk! I know it. See you soon." The screen turned blank as she flipped the switch.

He saw a tear form in the corner of her eye right before the screen went dark. He felt worse for her than himself. This had to had been torture for her. He knew the only thing he could do to help her was to get through this successfully and survive.

"*Man, bacon and eggs...*" The thought of that delicious food gave him a brief moment of hope and thoughts of devouring that food – but then decided against it. *"No, I don't think I want food in me when they do this. I don't want to throw up on a lab tech!"* He laughed to himself as that thought went through his mind. *"Humm, better yet I should eat it, and then throw it up on Zardonagon!"* Now he bellowed out loud over that thought. After laughing for a few moments, he sighed and returned to his window gazing. "Today could be the first day of my NEW life." He had a new goal to achieve today – he was determined now to do it.

He went to the food dispenser and typed in the instructions for a glass of water. He drank a sip of the water, set the glass down, and then once again returned to the window. The sun was now casting a bright orange glow across the crater walls that held the institute. He looked over the buildings that housed the giant super computers that would do all the computations and manipulations on him at a molecular level.

After a few minutes of window gazing, he realized he was only slightly hungry, but totally parched. He returned to the food dispenser, drank the glass of water, then summoned another. As he took the glass out of the device, the video screen once again began ringing. "Not even a few minutes of quiet for the condemned man, eh?"

He let out a large sigh, put down the water, and walked to the communication device. He smiled thinking it was once again Catherine. He walked to the display and activated it. It was not who he thought, as a matter of fact it was the one person he did not want to see at all today – Doctor Edward Zardonagon.

"Ah Piccolo, good to see you are up and about, ready for an exciting day?" He was smiling as if he was the snake that was about to strike at a big rat for dinner.

"Yes Zardonagon, I'm ready for this, as ready as I will ever be..." his reply was cold and somber.

"Well, I can understand you are nervous, but I am certain that the experiment will be a complete success today." Edward had a phony tone to his voice. "However, I would like you to take a prescription tonic at this time please. This tonic will relax you, and help you with the transformation process. Just go to the food dispenser, and it will be dispensed for you.

"Very well" he replied and walked to the dispenser. A glass of clear, but slightly murky liquid was sitting in the machine waiting for him. He picked up the glass and was about to drink it.

"NO!" a female voice shouted. It sounded to Simon like the voice was inside his head.

Confused, he thought about the term "little voices in the head". He always associated that term with the little voices of common sense but never an actual loud voice yelling. Once again, he looked at the glass in his hand and began to put it to his lips.

"NO!" This time the voice was so loud it hurt. He sat the glass down on the table for a moment, and rubbed his forehead. He then looked around for who might be screaming at him.

"Is there a problem Simon?" Edward queried trying to look around him to see what he was doing as Simon had his back to the monitor.

"No, no problem at all, just a brief headache. I'm sure it is just the stress of what will be happening soon" he explained.

"The tonic will help with that headache. Now drink down the liquid from the glass that was dispensed for you." He spoke in a staccato and deliberate cadence and tone.

He picked up the glass from the table, then drank the contents of the glass. A crusty smile came across Edward's face as he saw the contents of the glass go down Simon's throat.

"Very good, you will feel better... and you will be relaxed in just a few minutes Simon. See you in an hour." The monitor went dark.

Simon put the glass on the table. "Sure, I'll be relaxed alright." He wondered what was in that glass, and why there was a truly audible voice in his head telling him not to drink it. He wondered why the voice ordered him not to drink the tonic. He was very confused by what just happened.

He returned to the window, and stared at the fading sunrise transforming into blazing daytime. When satisfied with his viewing, he went to the closet and took out the outfit he was to wear for the procedure, and started to put it on.

It was a tight-fitting jumpsuit made of a thin paper. He could tell by looking at the construction and materials it was designed to only be temporary. It was meant to only provide him with some privacy between this room and the molecular chamber. "Too bad it does not come in navy blue with stars..." He said to himself with a slight chuckle as he put the jumpsuit on. He pulled it over his shoulders and then kept it from flying open by sticking the bonding strips together. His fashion review was interrupted by the door chime. He answered it to find Catherine and a couple lab interns – it was time.

She looked absolutely striking to him. She was wearing a purple skirt outfit that clung to her tightly. Her lab coat was open, and he was able to scan the curves of her body through the dress. *"She wore that for me, I'm sure!"* He noted her hair was done differently today. Her white skunk stripes were pulled into single strands and wrapped around her head, and then tied in the back. Her long dark brown hair was bundled into a pony tail with a professional looking ribbon holding it together. She was a wonderful sight, he thought. His examination of her looks must not had been very subtle.

She looked at him and seemed to know what he was thinking as she blushed at his gazing of her body. "Hello Simon..." She did a similar scan of his body up and down. "That outfit looks... interesting..." she giggled.

He grumbled something totally unintelligible.

She now forced a smile for just a brief second, then said "Ready to do this?"

"Well, even if I said no, it wouldn't matter... so let's do it." he said with a slight smirk on his face.

"Very well, if you will follow me... we will head to the chamber." She directed him down the hall. She thought he was very brave. She knew he was being this gallant just for her. She wondered why fate was forcing his life in this direction. She blamed herself for his predicament, but also knew if she had not selected him he would by now be quite dead.

It was a very short walk to the molecular chamber. Not a word was said while they made the walk. He wanted to speak, but found himself too nervous and scared to say anything.

She was also nervous. She was thinking the whole time about her fear of losing him. She wanted to tell him, but couldn't. They arrived at the chamber door. She swiped her identification bracelet past the scanner, and after a moment the door opened.

The chamber was fairly small. There was a stainless-steel table in the middle of the room with steel straps to secure his arms, legs, head and torso. *"Were those metal bands really necessary?"* he wondered.

To the right was a large wall filled with super computer interface equipment. It was glowing, blinking, beeping and chirping. Computations were being updated and displayed constantly on the various terminals.

Above the table was the molecular disintegrator/reintegration array that would tear his molecules apart, rearrange them, and then reassemble them back to hopefully some form of his former self. Behind the table was a partially round steel wall – he assumed it was some form of protective barrier for the operators.

On the left was a window where the control chamber was housed. Inside that room, he saw his nemesis – Edward Zardonagon.

How Simon had grown to hate him. *"Someday, you will be repaid for your evilness."* He had hoped his thoughts did not show on his face. The man disgusted him, but he also had the strings to his life or death. He could decide to make the manipulation fail, and then kill him if he desired. He wondered how many of his enemies had suffered that same fate in the past. Even more important however, was his grasp of Catherine's fate. He knew this would surely kill her if the experiment failed.

His thoughts were interrupted by Jason Baines, one of the lab technicians. "Mr. Piccolo, we will need you to disrobe, and lie down on the table."

Simon blushed thinking that he would once again be naked in front of Catherine. "Well, if I have to…" he said quietly as he sheepishly looked at Catherine – she now had a small smirk on her face.

He removed his jumpsuit and jumped onto the table. "This table is freezing!" he yelped. He became accustomed to the table temperature, then settled down onto the hard surface. As soon as he was fully settled, all of the steel straps automatically moved into position and snapped around his body, he was totally immobilized.

Catherine looked at him with a serious face. "Simon, we must all be in the control room during the process." She leaned close to his ear and whispered "I know you will make it through this... also, I love you."

His eyes opened wide as he heard the words, he wanted to return the words but his thoughts of her were interrupted by a sting in his neck. They were giving him an injection, his body started to instantly go numb. The numbness was spreading from the injection site to his arms and legs. His mouth could barely move and was not mobile enough to return any words of love to her.

"That injection will completely numb you for the process..." Edward said over the speaker system. "Don't worry, you won't feel a thing." He was smiling while he said that – a lie. In any case, he partially closed his eyes in acknowledgement as his neck and face were almost totally numb.

The room darkened and the metal shield slid from behind him and formed a circle around him. All he could see now was the metal wall and the molecular array above him.

Edward spoke on the speaker once again "Prepare for your amazing transformation Mister Piccolo!"

Simon was now frightened. *"Here we go, I wonder what death is like? I might just find out today... maybe that would be for the best?"* he thought to himself. Despite being on the cold steel table, he was nervous enough that sweat formed and rolled down his forehead.

In the control room Edward sat in front of a large computer console. "Begin phase 1 A, molecular decomposition... activating the array." He activated virtual switches and typed onto the computer console. A loud hum filled the room as the reactor began the process of energizing the molecular disintegration array. In the monitor, they could see the array light up in bright colors that illuminated Simon's naked body.

Edward announced "Phase 1 B, obtain DNA sample for computer analysis." He flipped some different switches and entered commands into his computer console. The disintegration array lit up slightly, the hum intensified, and then returned to its previous state.

"Phase 1 complete...beginning phase 2, obtain DNA sample of bonding animal" he announced.

Without any additional noise or effort, the computer located the sample in the enormous repository located in another building, and removed a sample set of cells. The computer indicated that a successful sample had been obtained.

A display on the main console illuminated and showed the computer representation of the subject's DNA and other information of his genetic makeup. On a second screen a display of the bonding animal's DNA and genetic makeup was displayed.

"Catherine, your friend's DNA donor is listed but not shown on my screen. I hope you two picked wisely... for his and your sake" he said with disgust in his voice.

His words sent a shiver up her spine, she now had goose bumps across her entire body. "I'm sure he will be successful due to this choice. He will use this donor to his best advantage" she replied.

He smiled as he said softly "That's good... I would hate to have to destroy your lover. And please don't deny it. We have cameras in that room and I saw your activities last night." An evil chuckle escaped his lips. "I really enjoyed the show... especially since you didn't use the Pleasure-Matic. You know you can be sent to prison for that... Well, for both your sakes...you had better hope this works."

"You bastard! How dare you!" She was livid with rage but at the same time she dared not provoke him at this stage of the process.

"You should have remembered that every room in this complex is monitored" he cautioned her. "I would have thought you would have been more professional. However, that is a discussion for another time... I have more important things going on right now. Besides, if this does not go well... it won't matter..." He returned his attention to his computer console. "Ah, the computer has determined the best splices and bonds; we are ready for phase 3."

"Begin phase 3" Edward announced a moment later as he flipped more switches and entered the commands to begin the sequence that will reduce his subject to individual molecules. The light intensified in the array and began to break apart Simon's body. Small bubble-like spheres of light bounced off of his body and were lifted into the array. His eyes opened wide as he was able to feel his body being torn apart. A tear rolled down her cheek as molecule by molecule his body was broken apart and moved into the joining matrix of the computer. Within seconds there was only a light outline of the body left on the table.

On the main computer screen, a display of the progress of the bonding process was shown. When it was working at full capacity as it was now, a loud hum was heard everywhere. In the control room, this was no exception as the loud hum and vibrations were both heard and felt. The entire supercomputer complex was fully dedicated to the splicing and bonding process it controlled inside the matrix.

Sixty percent complete, she noted on the main console. Sweat was dripping down her forehead and onto her cheeks. She felt the sweat but ignored it and instead focused on the computer monitor as if her constant stare would help him to survive this ordeal.

"Seventy-five percent and so far, so good" Edward commented, pleased with the progress to this point.

The process continued for what seemed like hours to her, but was actually only a single minute. Without warning, the loud hum of the computer stopped. "What happened?" she gasped.

Edward laughed at her fear, then reassured her "The bonding process is complete and successful. Begin Phase 4, reintegration."

The computer complex churned to life once again, this time the machine gave off an even louder hum. The array in the chamber once again lit up – a bright red color emanated from the emitters. A loud, high pitched noise began as the array started its work. A light outline of a human body appeared on the table, red bubbles of light floated out of the array emitters and down onto the outline. Bright red beams of light bounced across the outline of his body as molecules were brought down and placed back in the proper position in his now reappearing body.

His face had the same facial expression as when the disintegration process started – his eyes wide open and almost popping out of his head. It was obvious he had not only felt what was happening, but was almost in a state of shock from the process. The beams of light continued to dance across his body, as he became more and more whole. After a few minutes, the lights stopped and the array darkened. The high pitch whine quieted and the computer hum went silent.

"Process complete and if my readings are correct, he lived." Edward said, pleased with himself. "Now, to see what we end up with."

He spun around in his chair and looked at her with a smile on his face. "This is the part where the real magic occurs…" he told her. "I hope we get a good bonding and your training actually does some good."

She did not care about what he was saying and really was not listening. She was too concerned with the man in the other room. She watched and waited for any changes. "Perhaps the bonding did not hold, maybe he would not change?" She said to herself almost hoping for a failure in Edward's process.

Suddenly, his body began to convulse – still being held down by the restraints, he flailed like a fish out of water. The room was filled with the sound of his body pushing up and then slamming down on the stainless steel. Moments later, the noises of his body flailing on the table stopped. The quiet only lasted a second before the room was filled with the sound of his screaming. The screaming caused by the pain he felt in his body as it began to change.

His legs began to lengthen and his bone structure began to change. His arms were changing proportionately, and his fingers began to get shorter. His chest became round and tubular shaped. His face began to contort and distort. He continued to scream in agony, while his teeth grew and formed into sharp pointed fangs. His mouth contorted as his canines also changed into fangs in his now stretching mouth. His nose melted into his mouth, and formed a snout. The snout became longer and more pronounced. His ears moved up to the top of his head and became pointed.

He constantly screamed in pain as the process continued. After a few minutes, even his scream had changed, and was now a high-pitched wail. The sound was so loud, and so high pitched that it started to interfere with the equipment. Computer command modules began shorting out, sparks flew from the equipment.

"What is that noise he is making... and what is it doing to my equipment?" Edward yelled.

Simon continued his high-pitched wail, hardly stopping to even take a breath. The pain was just too intense. After a moment of pure worry, Catherine looked at him, and a smile formed on her previously worried face – she noticed his throat – it was glowing. He was trying to control the pain. His mouth was only slightly open, but the sound emitting from it was intense.

His body continued to change and manipulate according to his new DNA pattern. Fur sprouted from all parts of his body, his spine expanded and grew. The spine popped through his skin at the base of his pelvis, and grew until it was almost touching the floor. A new layer of flesh began to cover the new boney extension of his spine.

Edward was panicked at this point – he had never experienced a subject that had a voice that could destroy all of the equipment. "Quickly, activate the molecular neutralizer and destroy him!" he shouted to his assistant.

"What? NO!" Catherine replied.

"He is destroying this complex, and must be stopped. He drank a chemical compound that when we activate a special subsonic signal will cause his currently weakened bonded molecules to unbind and destroy him." He shouted over the loud wail.

"No, you can't do it... I won't let you!" she demanded.

Jason Baines behind her shouted as apologetic as he could in the noisy room "Sorry Doctor Harmony, the breakdown process has already started."

She looked with horror out into the chamber and saw a bright blue light emit from the array. "No, no, no... you can't!" she cried.

After a minute, her face changed to a smile when she realized something else had gone wrong, he was not being molecularly torn apart – he was still alive.

"Why has he not dissolved?" Edward growled to Jason.

"I don't know doctor, are you sure he drank the compound?" the assistant queried.

Before Jason completed his question, Edward was reviewing the surveillance video of his call with Simon. Simon had a glass in his hand; he sat it down on the table and grabbed his forehead. Then he took a glass of liquid from the table and drank it, but it was not the dispensed liquid!

"He fooled me... he did not drink the compound!" Edward snarled, his nostrils were flared and his face was flush red with anger. "Shut down the activator and any other equipment you can. Let's try to save what we can from that siren out there."

The wailing continued from Simon's now long snouted mouth. His spine had stopped growing and now was covered with a thin layer of fresh skin. Fur began to cover the skin as it hardened. The rest of his body was now completely covered in a thin layer of white fur.

Simon was in excruciating pain during the entire transformation. His mind was active and he could feel everything that was happening, but could not do a thing about it – except suffer. He tried as best as he could to use his meditation to control, and alleviate the intense pain. He wished he could just die and be done with it.

As he suffered, he began to hear a voice in his head once again – this time it was a male voice. "Simon, concentrate on my voice. I can now speak with you my friend" the little voice in his head whispered. "Simon, listen to the melody and relax. You are becoming one with nature. Let nature calm and soothe you through this change. Let nature remove your pain."

As the voice attempted to calm him, Simon realized that he indeed could hear music in his mind. The music was nothing he had ever heard before. The melody was of trees blowing in the wind, the sound of crickets and frogs singing in the night, birds announcing their presence to the morning world, elephants holding their long trunks in the air and trumpeting calls to their kind, insects buzzing through the air in search of warmth and food, the ocean waves crashing against a cliff.

So many sounds, most he had never heard before. He could not distinctly identify any of them, and yet he could hear and feel each and every sound in the melody. It was the most beautiful thing he had ever heard in his life. His mind became one with the melody of the music. It relaxed him, and disengaged his mind. He no longer felt any pain, no longer ever realized that he was still changing. His voice suddenly stopped, the silence in the room was now deafening.

"He stopped..." Edward noted, of the obvious.

The control room was dead quiet now. They all gazed at the monitor. Simon was still laying on the table, his body was still changing, but he now was completely quiet.

"Could he be in a state of shock?" Catherine wondered. She looked at the monitors showing his vital signs, nothing indicated shock. When she closely looked at him in the monitor, she was surprised to find that he was actually the opposite – he was in a state of mind from the moment before the process. He was now totally at ease –and now his hands were glowing. She smiled knowing he was still with her.

The white fur that covered his body was in some spots darkening – his hands, feet and face were turning a dark, almost a black shade. His eyes were now changed from green to a bright, sapphire blue. Whiskers appeared from his nose and extended out to almost the width of his shoulders.

"What the hell is that?" Edward shouted as he began to see the final product of his work.

"You are now one of us, so let go" the voice in Simon's head told him. "Enjoy your new-found awareness and abilities... we will speak again my friend... I am so glad you are with us." Simon could tell the voice was now gone, and he was alone once again.

The music had stopped, but it didn't matter because the pain had also stopped. He also found he could no longer meditate. The glow had faded from his hands without his realizing.

He had closed his eyes but now slowly opened them. His vision was completely different – he no longer saw all of the colors he used to see, but what he did see was so crisp and sharp.

He could hear voices – did he hear Catherine? He smelled a putrid odor, probably from the process but at the same time he could lightly smell Catherine but her scent appeared to be in the distance.

His mouth and tongue were dry and parched – he wished he could drink some water. He felt cold lying on the table despite his new layer of fur. He noticed his heart was beating faster than it used to, but it did not actually feel unusual. His skin was itchy, and felt dirty but he could not move to scratch it. For the moment, he would have to endure with the irritation. His fingers and toes felt different, he thought he could actually extend his fingernails.

"I survived this and I appear to be able to think!" he thought to himself. He was pleased thinking that he and Catherine would soon be having more wonderful conversations in the future.

The table he was strapped onto was raised up at an angle, and the wall around him opened and moved away. The door to the room opened and Catherine and Edward entered.

"Simon, can you hear me?" Catherine asked as she ran into the room.

Simon answered her "Yes, I can Catherine!"

Catherine saw Simon open his mouth, but she never expected to hear what came out of his mouth.

She gave a pained look when she heard his mutated voice utter "Waaaa mawaaaa".

Catherine pleaded "Oh please Simon, tell me you can understand me!"

"Muuwaaaa Mewooow" is all that came out of his mouth. Simon saw the tears and wondered why she did not understand what he was saying. He did not realize that his language was totally alien to her.

"Catherine, Catherine why are you crying? Listen to what I am telling you, I am fine! I made it!" He pleaded, thinking she could understand him.

"Muawaa Muuaaaa...Mewuuu Waa Waa" was all that Catherine heard from Simon.

Edward was now totally disgusted. "What a total waste of time and resources! I think this charade has gone far enough, I do not want to answer for this failure."

Catherine turned to him to find he had taken his finger injector out of his pocket and placed it onto his index finger. "No! You cannot terminate him. This is still my project... my experiment. I have the full backing from the Council, and I now need to study him to find out what went wrong. I have to see if I can somehow find his human part. I will get that human part to come out. You will NOT use that on him!" She had fury and rage in her eyes – how dare he even consider destroying him now. Without thinking she pulled a small blaster out from under her lab coat and pointed it at the old grisly scientist. "You will NOT touch him" she reiterated.

A slight smile appeared on his face, a smile she knew was fake. "Very well, you may have all responsibility for this experiment. I will be happy to testify at your punishment hearing in front of the Council. Now get out of my sight before I change my mind... and take that pussycat you... you, stupid bitch!" He looked at Simon with disgust "What a waste, not even a creature that could be worth anything in battle...what a waste!" He turned and stormed out of the chamber.

She looked at Simon and gave a pained but truly happy smile. "Well Simon, unfortunately you have to now stay in one of the cells built for experiments. But I got you one of the better cells... I had it set up with comfortable bedding and plenty of supplies" she told him with some pride while fighting back her tears.

She looked at what he had become – she thought he was a fine-looking hybrid. His fur was a light oatmeal color across his body, and his arms and legs were a dark, almost black fur. His face was covered in the same dark, black fur, and his nose and mouth were now combined into a long-pointed snout. His eyes were large and the most beautiful color of glowing blue she had ever seen. His pupils were still human, round and currently open wide. He had large ears that now were more on top of his head than on the side.

For the most part, she felt he had lost most of his human traits. But somehow, he still looked like Simon. She felt compelled to touch him, to pet him. He was confined, she was not afraid. She walked over to him and reached out to slowly stroke his ear. Her hand caressed his ear and worked to behind the ear. As she continued to stroke his ear she noticed he was closing his eyes. *"Could he understand that she was comforting him?"*

Jason Baines interrupted her thoughts "Oh I need to enter his hybrid name into the system for identification. What did he want to be called?"

She looked at him lying on the table, and said without looking up "Simonese, his hybrid name is Simonese."

"Very well" he replied and entered the name into the computer "I think we need to get him to his cell before the doctor changes his mind." She noticed Jason had a concerned look on his face.

"Yes, let's go now" she said to him. As they loosened the table and extended the wheels, she gave him one last scratch behind his ear and whispered to him "You are one good looking Siamese cat, Simon." Her heart stopped for a moment when she thought she heard... a purr?

*   *   *

Simon was given the best cell available in the post-experimentation living quarters. It was on one of the upper levels and was larger than many of the other cells. Catherine had a large purple velvet foam bead bed made so Simon would have a comfortable place to sleep – as opposed to the mounds of hay given to the other sub-humans.

He was on the bed, curled into a ball napping, still exhausted from his transformation. After a couple hours, he finally woke up from sleeping, sat up, and looked at his new surroundings. The cell was all white except for his bed. There was a water trough, a feeding station – he was not sure what food would be dispensed, and a box with sand – his litter box?

Seeing the litter box gave him a bit of a depressing shock of what his new reality was all about. He let a sigh escape out of his mouth, although it would not appear as a sigh to any human. Also on the wall was a mirror. Upon noticing the mirror, he got up on all fours; stretched his back, reached his front legs out as far as he could and stretched them, then a long stretch of his back legs. Now that he felt fully stretched and relaxed, he walked to the mirror and gazed at himself. *"Yep, I am definitely a cat now"* he thought. He admired himself in the mirror. He thought he actually made a decent looking animal, and for a moment felt proud of himself. He turned his head to the left, and then to the right admiring himself. He noticed the light oatmeal colored fur on his body. His arms, legs, tail, ears, and face were a dark black color. He liked the color points that he was given, he thought. He flicked his tail back and forth in the air looking at this strange new part of his body. He then noticed he was wearing pants. The pants went around his hind quarters – there were holes for his tail and legs, and a slot in the rear. He guessed that even if he was no longer completely human, Catherine felt he should still be presentable and not have his genitals on display.

He chuckled to himself when he noticed that these pants were made in the style of one of his old shirts. *"Thanks Catherine... my old standby... blue with stars!"* he thought as he admired her handiwork. She had them made of the same material that was used to make the undergarments worn in the prisons. The pants would open and close as needed as to facilitate him using his box.

He then realized that perhaps he needed to test out the new garment. He walked into his box and squatted – the pants worked perfectly as they automatically opened, and he was able to do his job. Somehow, he knew exactly what to do, and to cover his job with the sand when done. While pushing the sand around he looked up and noticed the camera in the corner.

"Great, they're watching me using the john. I'll have to remember that camera is there" he told himself.

He walked out of the box, went to his bed, and sat down. A beam flashed down into the box to immediately clean the mess. As he sat there, he realized he felt really dirty. The built in feline instinct took over, and he began to lick his hand to clean himself. The shock of his instinctive reaction to clean hit him, and he stopped. The human side of him thought *"How can I do this? It's disgusting!"* However, the feeling of dirtiness overcame his human repulsion, and he went back to his bathing. Licking his arms, then his hands, and wiping the spittle to his face. He continued licking with abandon – cleaning his chest and belly. After a while he had cleaned most of his body. He stopped for a moment pondering the one spot he has not yet cleaned. *"Hmm, this could prove to be very interesting..."* he thought as he started to lift his leg for the final cleaning. Before he started however, his memory flashed to the camera in the corner of the room. He decided to leave this cleaning for some other time.

He rested some more, until his stomach told him it was time to get up. He walked over to the food dispenser – as he approached a few golden, round nuggets were automatically dispensed. They sat in the bowl that was attached to the dispenser that hung on the wall. Simon examined the food in the bowl below his face. He sniffed the food – the human side was repulsed by the smell, but his feline side told him it was something nutritious and more than likely, delicious. After a few minutes of staring at the nuggets he finally gave into his hunger, reached in with his snout, and grabbed one of the nuggets with his mouth. His strong teeth and powerful jaws made quick work of the crunchy nugget, as he chewed and chomped on the food. To his surprise, it tasted very good. It had a slight flavor of fish and chicken. Simon thought it was not as bad – and actually better tasting than some of the synthesized meat food products slung at some of the local haunts near his old apartment.

After his meal, he walked to the water trough and moved his face in for a drink. His eyes opened wide as he moved his face too close, and his long snout dunked into the water with a splash. *"Owwww, I am going to have to watch this big nose now"* he thought. He once again tried to drink by slowly inching his snout close to the water while lapping with his tongue. He determined he would be quite busy adapting to his new way of life. He was going to have to relearn everything.

After his drink, he went back to his bed and once again curled up to relax. The silence was interrupted by a voice that seemed either next to him or in his head.

"Simon, can you hear me?" the voice asked.

"Meooow-aa-wow-wow" Simon replied vocally.

"No Simon, use your thoughts to speak to me" he requested.

Simon concentrated for a moment. "Can you understand me now?" he asked.

"Yes! That is perfect Simon. I am so glad you are okay my friend. This is Galen."

"Galen, is it really you? How... how are you communicating with me?" he asked.

"Once you obtained your nature part, I found I was able to communicate with you. Do you remember me speaking to you during your transformation? I gave you the nature song to soothe your transition" he replied.

"That was you that gave me those wonderful feelings Galen?" Simon asked.

"Yes, that was the nature song. Eventually, you will be able to listen to it whenever you want. It is the most beautiful and relaxing thing one could experience. It is something that only someone special like you and me can experience. But something that you could not experience until you achieved your transformation. Also, I was unable to communicate with you until you had achieved your full hybrid state."

"So..." Simon thought for a moment "if you were unable to communicate with me, then who warned me of the tonic?"

Galen laughed. "That would be Lisa, you have not met her... at least in person, but you have in dreams" he told him.

"Hello Simon" Lisa interrupted "I'm so glad you're safe and are now one of us. We are so lucky to have a friend such as you. So strong and powerful."

Simon was surprised by yet another voice in his head – could he take all these people in his little skull, he wondered. "Hi Lisa, thanks for saving me. I might have been a puddle of jelly if you hadn't warned me of the danger."

"You're quite welcome Simon" she acknowledged. "I'll let you two boys talk now…" Simon felt her presence dissipate almost as if she had physically left.

"Simon, there is something I must ask of you. Whatever you do… don't let any human know of your awareness. It is imperative that you let no one know that you actually have rational thought. We must keep the lower-humans in the dark of our awareness…"

"Wait…" Simon interrupted "did you just say lower-humans? I thought I was the subhuman here?"

Galen laughed "Simon, you may not realize it yet… but you are so far above a normal human being now. You will come to realize both sides of your hybrid form soon. You will realize how powerful and advanced you are, compared to the weak and average human being" he told his friend.

"Wow, I would have never guessed" he said as he pondered his new situation. "But why mustn't I reveal my intelligence? If we're advanced, shouldn't we tell them?"

"No" Galen replied. "There is a master plan now in play. The fate of the human race is in peril and only they can help themselves. If we tell them of our advancement, then we would become involved in their fate. That is not our destiny, and living in this crater is also not our destiny. Thus, we will need to leave. To leave, we need our new abilities. If they discover that you have rational thought, they would surely entrap us even more securely, and we would never escape. Worse, I fear that if Zardonagon discovers exactly what he has created, he would abuse and torture us to get what he wants. That cannot happen. So please Simon, do not speak in human voice to any lower-human…not even Catherine."

Simon's heart sunk with those words. "Galen, I'm not sure I can do that. I think I could trust her, we could trust her. Please…" he pleaded.

"I know you want to tell her Simon. But do not, at least not now. She is a good person, and eventually you will be able to reveal yourself to her. Trust me when I say this… Okay?"

A sigh escaped out of his black feline lips. "Very well, I won't reveal myself to her at this time… but it's going to be hard to hold back."

"I know you will be able to do this my friend. All will be revealed to her in time. Besides, until you relearn human speak… she will not be able to understand you anyway" he chuckled.

"Oh… that's right" Simon admitted with a mental laugh.

"If you ever need me, just open your mind to me. From now on, I will not enter your brain without permission. Until we speak again, good night my friend." Then, as quickly as he entered his mind, he left it. Simon felt the void in his brain from his missing friend. Simon put his head down as he once again curled into a tight ball. He started to fall asleep – the lights began to automatically dim as they sensed his drifting into a slumber.

The morning brought Simon to be woken with a start. Large, stainless steel, hardened bars dropped from the ceiling to the floor in front of him. These bars blocked his ability to move to, or near the door. Loud clicks then filled the room as steel pins moved, and unlocked the main steel door. The door slid open, and Catherine walked in. The keeper was behind her, and brought in a chair that she promptly sat down onto.

"That will be all, thank you" she told the keeper who checked the bars then returned to the hallway, and closed the door behind him.

"Hello Simon, how are you feeling?" Catherine asked him.

Simon sat up, and looked at her before saying. "Maaaaw-a-wooow."

He realized he might be seen as replying to her question. So he turned his back to her, and walked over to the feeding station. He began eating some of the golden kibble nuggets that dropped out of the chute.

"Simon, I know you can hear me and understand me. Please tell me you know what I am saying… please at least show me you recognize me…" she pleaded.

Simon's heart sunk to the floor. He so wanted to turn, and somehow show her he knew not only who she was, but how much he loved her – but he dared not. Instead he turned, looked at her,

217

and then returned to his meal of golden kibbles. He crunched on a few more of the delicacies, then returned to his bed, sat down on his hind legs, and stretched his front feet long in front of him. He sat like a porcelain statue, and looked at her with his almond shaped sapphire eyes.

A tear came to Catherine's eyes as she realized he perhaps did not know who she was. After a moment, she regained her composure enough that she could speak. "Well Simon, I'm sure you're bored just sitting here... soon you will be able to venture into the open plaza. But for now, I have a couple things to keep you occupied... I just need to know which item you want to play with."

She stood, turned, and brought a large bag out from behind the chair. She began to search in the bag, while saying "So, which do you prefer..." she removed a large ball of red yarn. This ball was about a foot and a half in diameter. She pressed a button on the wall and a small opening appeared in the bar barrier. She rolled the ball to him. "This ball of yarn..." she then reached in the bag, and removed a small computer laptop console. She also slid it through the opening "Or, would you prefer this laptop with the past four days of the Sector 1 Times crossword puzzles?"

"Oh man, she is so sneaky!" he thought as he wantonly looked at the laptop computer. She knew exactly what he loved to do to fill his time. After a moment, he reached over and batted at the ball of yarn. He ran across the small portion of his room, and grabbed the red ball with the claws on his hand. He then threw the yarn across the room – following it as fast as he could. He grabbed the ball again, tossed it into the air, and followed it wherever it went.

Tears dripped down Catherine's cheeks. She stood up with a look of surrender on her face. "Okay Simon, I will check on you later..." She pressed the call button, and once the door opened, walked out without turning to look back.

The door closed and Simon immediately stopped playing with the yarn – allowing it to bounce off his back – it rolled across the room as the bars rose back into the ceiling. An audible sigh escaped from his small mouth, and a tear came to his feline eyes. He began to lick his hands, then washed his face, removing the tears.

He felt something in his brain as if someone was knocking on a door inside his head. He thought of opening the door, and he heard "Simon, I know that was the hardest thing you could have done." It was Galen, once again he spoke to him telepathically. "Trust me, it was the best for you... and her."

"Why for her?" he asked.

"If she knew about your awareness, she would be in grave danger" he replied. "Now, there is something important I need to discuss with you. I think it will help take your mind off your current situation. You need to start training... to learn how to shift between your forms."

"Between my forms?" he inquired.

"Yes, you will soon find that you will be able to shift from human to cat abilities at-will" he explained "Thus, you will utilize the best of both forms. You will become unstoppable and powerful. I will teach you, and while you learn, I will disable the camera above you. They will never know how strong you have become. Are you ready to start?"

"Sure, why not? Nothing else to do... except play with this lovely ball of yarn" he answered with a laugh while he stared at his true desire – the crossword puzzle computer.

"Excellent! Let's start with your vision then" he told him. "Did you know that you can shift between human and feline vision? You will be able to use the feline vision for sharpness and night vision. The human vision will provide you will depth and color detail. It is quite easy to shift between them... want to try?"

"Absolutely!" Simon answered.

"Very well, all you have to do is readjust your eyes with your mind. Think human and concentrate on how your vision used to appear to you" he instructed.

Simon looked around. He noticed that everything was sharp and crisp, but he could not determine any colors. He knew his bed was some other color, but he could not tell what. The laptop had a color he knew – but it appeared gray. The only thing with color was the ball of yarn. The red color in the yarn was bright and vibrant to him. He started to think about what things looked like before the other day.

He pictured colors and sights in his mind. He concentrated as hard as he could, and suddenly his eyes started to change. It felt like they were going to pop out of his skull, but he maintained his concentration. The feline pupils in his eyes started to shift and change. The long thin pupils started to widen, and the points on the top and bottoms flattened out. After a second, the pupils appeared round like a human. His vision changed and he noticed that the colors in the room were becoming rich and vibrant. The purple in his bed was beautiful to Simon as he now realized the loss of colors he had experienced of late. He saw the blues and greens in the laptop, and the ball of yarn was still red, but not quite as bright. He also noticed that all of the details of the items in the room were not quite as sharp.

"Wow, amazing!"

"Very good Simon, not that hard, is it?" he asked. "Now, think about your cat vision, and cause it to return to feline form.

He did as Galen asked and concentrated. After a moment, his eyes indeed did change back to cat form. The colors faded, and sharpness increased.

"Excellent Simon!" Galen praised his student. "Now, with practice you will find it easier and easier to change when needed. Let us continue to practice on changing your vision. We will work on you learning other abilities later."

After an hour of training with Galen, Simon did notice he was once again quite tired. He rested his body down on his purple velvet bed, and closed his eyes. He wondered how Galen came to learn this knowledge, was able to train himself, and got good enough that he could train him and perhaps even the other hybrid humans. A few moments of thinking, and Simon fell fast asleep – a slight, high pitched snore was emanating from his small mouth.

After a few hours of rest, the lights illuminated and the bars came closing down around his bed. This once again awoke Simon. He opened his eyes, and then sat up quickly and alertly. The door opened, and a man walked in. Simon recognized this man as Clancy Yates, the zookeeper. He was accompanied by two other keepers. He walked over to Simon, now behind the bars, and looked at him with distain. Simon felt very uncomfortable from Clancy's stare.

"What a disgusting creature – I've always hated cats!" he said to his two companions. He took a stick out of his belt, and started moving it in and out of the cage, barely missing Simon's face.

"Bah, bah, bah!" he said as he taunted Simon. Simon did his best to not flinch from the stick that almost touched him over and over.

"So, you don't find this, or me fearful, little kitten? How about now?" he asked as he jabbed Simon in the chest with the stick. The stick immediately discharged a massive plasma bolt into Simon's body, which sent him flying into the wall. Simon was stunned by the force of his head hitting the wall behind him. His nervous system was disrupted by the force of the plasma bolt. All Simon could now do was lay on the floor and watch, as Clancy laughed at his limp body.

"Maybe now you'll be afraid, stupid kitty" he told Simon with a serious tone to his voice.

The two men with Clancy laughed as they continued to clean the equipment in the room. They restocked the food processor with needed minerals, and ran a cleaning laser around the walls and floor of the room. After a few minutes, they finished their chores, and left the room with Clancy following up in the rear. He stopped and looked at Simon, still stunned in the corner – he had a look of repulsion.

"Until you meet my stun wand the next time cat. Have a nice day!" he said, and followed up with an insane laugh as he left the room. The door closed and locked behind him, and the bars automatically rose back into the ceiling.

Simon did not move from the floor for hours, suffering from pain and numbness. Unable to move, all he could do was try to think the pain away while trying to bring life back to his dead legs and arms. Eventually, the feeling did come back to him – which caused him to hurt even more. He stayed there the rest of the day, with a tear of sorrow in his eyes and a plot in his brain – a plot to somehow get back at Clancy for his evil ways.

21

Galen sat back into his bunk, tired from the mental workout he just endured. He had just saved his friend Simon from losing his mind during his transformation, and thus was exhausted. As he laid on the cot, he stared at the ceiling.

"Galen, did you succeed?" Lisa spoke to him through their minds. Galen's mind woke up to hear her mental voice.

"Yes Lisa, we did it... and he lived. I would not have succeeded if you had not intervened and told him not to drink the formula that would allow Zardonagon to break down his molecules."

They had discovered that in their current forms, Lisa was able to mentally communicate with some of the human population – whereas Galen was not. Galen found he was able to communicate with the Hybrids, Lisa, and the other mutated Humans. It was almost by design, Galen thought – as Lisa was able to easily send a telepathic message to Simon while he was Human. During Simon's transformation, Galen was able to take over and send messages. He found he could even send the "song of nature" to Simon to help him through the transformation process. He wondered if his training with Catherine had made him more susceptible to mental communications than other humans. In any case, whatever made it possible, was a good thing, they were able to save him.

"I was happy to help..." she told her companion. "Galen, do you think I will be able to join you soon? Why do they wait to progress me to the next level?"

"Don't worry my dear... I will see that they allow your advancement to occur..." he had great confidence in his voice.

His confidence made her smile, and he could sense that smile in her thoughts. "I know you will... I have nothing but the upmost faith in you fulfilling your promises!"

Lisa heard something and opened her eyes. She was shocked to see Stephanie standing at her doorway looking at her. She had forgotten that she had her eyes closed and had a very large smile on her face. A smile that was so large that Stephanie could see it from the doorway.

Stephanie called out. "Come over here Derrick – I need to go into Lisa's cell."

He came to the cell, shock wand in hand. Lisa had been docile of late, but he remembered what she was capable of doing based on her past actions. Stephanie opened the cell door and walked in – Derrick close behind her. She examined the calming necklace, and then looked at the computer console. She poked around the controls, and examined the log files of the calming necklace. She was shocked to see the device was out of medication, and had been empty for quite a while.

"Derrick, this device has not worked for weeks!" she exclaimed, and then looked at Lisa. "Lisa, can you hear me?"

Galen sent thoughts to her "Go ahead Lisa, tell them you are fine."

Lisa looked at the two scientists "Yes Stephanie, I can hear you…" Her voice was raspy and gritty from lack of use over the years.

Now Stephanie had a shocked look on her face, but then began to smile as she realized Lisa was better off than she previously thought. "Lisa, have you been acting subdued this whole time since your healing?"

"Yes, I was scared… so I acted like I was still under the drugs" she lied somewhat, but hoped it would alleviate some of their questioning.

"Oh, you poor dear!" Stephanie smiled at her. "There was no reason to fear us, but now that you're with us… do you want to try to stand, and come out into the lab? Would you like something to eat… I bet it's been quite a long time since you've ate anything but tube food."

Lisa realized she had not actually tasted food for as long as she could remember. "Well, I guess I could try some food…"

Derrick interrupted "Just a small amount however… your system will definitely not be used to food."

"Oh yes, that's true dear…" Stephanie added "perhaps just a very small nibble?"

They released her binding straps, and helped her to her feet. Derrick took a slight step back when Lisa rose from the metal chair – he chuckled slightly at his apprehension. The trio came out into the lab, and Stephanie called up a small simulated salad from the food processor. Lisa took small bites and found she really liked the flavor of the food. Galen came out of his cell and joined the three. He looked at Lisa and they passed a smile to each other.

Derrick had returned to continue his furious work on his computer console. After a minute, he stopped and turned to Galen with a disgusted look on his face. "Ok, I think I know why the necklace malfunctioned... Did you sabotage the device Galen?" he asked.

"Well, I cannot lie... I did find a fault in the device's software and took advantage of the weakness to drain it of its medication, and then shut it down. So, yes I guess I did and I am truly sorry Derrick. It was for the good of Lisa."

"You know, if she was still in her old state she could have hurt or killed us!" he scolded him.

"The unit did not malfunction until after you healed her, doctor. She was no longer a threat to anyone. I knew this."

Stephanie interjected "Well, in any case... we're glad you're doing better... even though you had to fake that you were not for such a long time. We're glad you are with us dear." She put her hand on Lisa's hand. Lisa returned her kindness with a smile. When they touched, they both felt a connection – somehow, they felt a similarity. Stephanie was confused from the feelings that entered her mind upon touching her.

"So, will Lisa be in ready for her next phase of mutation doctors?" Galen asked with some excitement to his voice.

Derrick responded "Well Lisa, do you feel up to the mutation process? I guess we could plan on proceeding tomorrow."

A large smile flashed on Lisa's face. "Oh yes! I'm so ready. Please can we do it tomorrow?" she begged.

"I don't see why not..." Derrick replied. "Edward wants us to start upping our experimentations now that Galen was such a success. I have at least another five hundred additional subjects coming next week. If all goes well, I'll be building some more bonding devices so we can perform even more mutations. So, I guess tomorrow would be as good of a time as any to do another experiment. Let me submit the process into the logs then." He got up and looked at the trio. Lisa and Galen were smiling at each other.

"I will no longer be the only one" Galen announced. "I'm so happy!"

Lisa looked at Galen, smiled, and then turned to Derrick. "Thank you Derrick, I really appreciate this!"

"Don't thank me yet... we have not gotten you through it. Also, if Edward catches wind of this experiment he may try to interject his own thoughts and ideas."

"He won't..." Galen said with confidence.

Derrick gave him a puzzled look, then silently turned and walked away to begin making preparations.

After finishing the small amount of food – Lisa found her stomach to be slightly upset. She excused herself, and Galen followed suit. The pair of mutants quietly returned to their respective cells.

Galen activated the computer console and began to enter commands. After a moment, he found himself in the experimental database for the complex. He searched with stealth until he found the project files. He was shocked to see an entry for Lisa's upcoming mutation. The entry was from Edward Zardonagon.

"Premise of mutation has been overridden. The original blending and mutations have been modified to meet my needs for Project Fury Warrior. The following mutations will occur on the subject "Lisa": Claws from the crab for cutting damage, Gills for underwater warfare operations, feathers for warmth in cold climates..." The list went on and on – but it was nothing like the original plan of mutation.

Galen slammed his fist down on the computer console, almost breaking the unit. He regained his composure, and mentally placed his mind into a state of meditation to calm his anger. After a moment, he opened his eyes again and stared at the mutation algorithms. "Fine, we'll see about that..." he said as he started modifying the computer mutation bonding patterns. He worked on the pattern until he was satisfied with the changes. He then shifted his attention to the bonding program itself, and began to make modifications. When he finished his work, he opened the security logs, and made fake entries – thus covering his tracks.

With his work completed, he smiled as he now realized that no matter what they do tomorrow, Lisa will mutate based on the designed plan – his designed plan. She will be mutated like him. He laid on the cot, closed his eyes and slowly drifted to sleep, all while connecting his mind to the wilds of nature – somewhere.

The next morning, Lisa was prepped, and guided to lie on the bonding table. She was not afraid, but instead was in total anticipation of her changes. Stephanie smiled at her excitement as she checked the bonding program on her hand-held computer. Once all was ready, she administered the sedative. She returned to her console and continued to read the program. She noticed the modifications made by Edward, her anger turned her face flush red.

"Derrick have you seen what that bastard has done to our work... again?" she asked.

Derrick with a confused look, walked over to her console, and examined the bonding sequence. "My god, he's done it again!" He cried out with anger. He immediately started entering commands into the program console but then got a look of despair on his face. "He's locked the program out so we can't modify his selections of mutations... That bastard!"

"What can we do Derrick? I don't want to do this to her!"

"Nothing we can do. He holds all the cards." He let out a huge sigh.

She looked at him and said "But Derrick..."

"No..." he interrupted "there is nothing... absolutely nothing we can do. You know what he'll do if we don't follow his experiment plan to the letter?"

She shook her head in agreement, then pounded her fists on the desk. Tears welled in her eyes and ran down her cheeks.

From his cell, Galen called out to the pair. "May I see the plan? Can I be of help?"

Stephanie released the door lock, Galen approached the two, and then looked at the plan. He looked thoughtfully at the plan only saying "Hmmm..." After a minute, more of inspecting the plan he announced "Nope, it won't work. His combinations will not bind... the body will reject them and ignore them. I'm sure of it!" He then smiled "Go ahead and try... she'll be fine."

Stephanie dried her eyes, and then shrugged her shoulders. "Well okay, if you're not worried then why should I worry?" she started the sequence for the computers to begin the bonding calculations. She was surprised by his lack of concern, and his confident demeanor.

The pair of scientists put Lisa through the bonding process. When the mutation began they waited and to their surprise, Lisa did go through her mutation. As Galen predicted however, the mutation modifications that Edward changed or inserted did not occur. Instead, Lisa ended up looking exactly like Galen with the one exception – still having with female human-like breasts – four of them. She also had different sexual organs. Her fern like hair was long and flowing down her back in a bright shade of purplish pink. It moved as if it was in the wind, or was in the ocean collecting plankton. Her arms and legs were muscular and long. Her eyes had golden irises with cat like pupils. Her skin was also golden with that greenish tint of color that indicated she too was photosynthetic. She sat up and smiled at the trio admiring her.

Derrick scratched his head in frustration. "It's as if we didn't even try to use the bonding plan..." he had a slight tone of relief in his voice. "Edward is NOT going to be happy. I'm sure he will accuse us of changing the plan to go against his wishes."

Galen smiled at Derrick with a sympathetic look. "Don't worry Derrick. Just tell him the plan was too radical for a proper bonding, and the body just did what it felt was natural instead. He should be able to understand that." He spoke in a comforting manner.

"Why don't I feel it will be that easy?" Derrick asked with a grimace on his face.

Galen had already returned his attention to Lisa. He softly smiled at her, and through his thoughts told her "You are beautiful. And now we are one in the same with nature. All is as it should be now."

"Yes, I see it all now. What is now, and what is to be in the future. It's beautiful Galen..."

He walked over and hugged her while he told her "Things would be changing very soon, they will not interfere with our evolution much longer. Also, I found something very interesting in their computers today..."

22

"Sorry sir, but we ran the program exactly as you programmed. The mutation just did not hold." Derrick had a worried look on his face, as he knew the reaction this news would cause.

Edward popped a berry into his mouth and chewed it thoughtfully. His lips were bright pink, almost as if he was wearing lipstick. He held up a pink berry to the communication device to show Derrick. "Have you ever had one of these? They are called bora berries... they only grow down south. They have underground gardens where... somehow... they get these to grow. I suspect they grow them from genetic samples in the same manner we use our samples for our experiments."

"Ummm, no I can't say I ever eaten one of them."

"Too bad... they're very tasty. Here's another property of this berry... they have a slight narcotic effect. They tend to make you a little loopy, or at least... happy. Fortunately for you, I am feeling slightly... happy..."

"Well, that's good then..." Derrick said sheepishly.

"That doesn't necessarily let you off the hook, it just means I will not have you executed this time. Be prepared to build more bonding devices. I want and expect your team to start doing mutations at the rate of at least a hundred a day. I'll be sending many new patients for you, and I will be programming special enhancements for each patient you cure." He immediately disconnected the device before Derrick had a chance to reply.

Edward sighed, and turned away from the monitor. He then admired himself in a mirror on his desk. His pink lips formed a happy smile on his face – a smile that hardly ever appeared. He really only smiled during times like this – when he was eating bora berries. His berry stained smile resembled a circus clown, but he thought it actually made him look handsome. When he finished admiring himself, he turned back to his computer monitor.

"Now, to see what that bumbler did to my experiment..." he said to himself.

He read the logs and was surprised to see that the computer executed the program exactly as he expected. He wondered *"if that was the case, and it ran perfectly… then why didn't the mutations hold?"* He determined that it must have been too radical of a change. He would try his desired mutations again but not quite so many in one shot. Maybe smaller changes would prevent the body from rejecting them.

He looked at his chronograph, and then shut down his computer. Once again, he stared at his reflection in the mirror, and adjusted his hair while he admired himself. After a few more minutes of fussing, he ate another berry, and then seated himself as straight as possible in his chair – looking straight at the door. A moment later the door chime sounded. He pressed a button on his desk to open the door – it was Catherine. He looked at her with a scrutinizing look. He noted that despite his previous attitude toward her, she was dressed quite provocatively. She wore a tight purple skirt with a white blouse and matching purple lab coat. He admired the amount of leg he could see – at least up to her knees. He wished he could see more of those shapely legs. He knew however, she would never give into him voluntarily, and that made him angry. But the berries made him feel good enough to ignore his inward hatred and anger for her. He stared at her another moment before finally saying "Come in Doctor, and have a seat. Can I offer you a drink?"

"No, thank you…" she said coldly as she sat down at the chair in front of the desk. She used her lab coat as a shield against his peering eyes.

"Very well, suit yourself. You don't mind if I have one, do you?" he queried with a smirk on his pink lips.

"Please, help yourself…" she replied. She pondered over the director. He was wearing a dark blue suit with a small dark blue metallic tie against a white shirt. His skin was pale, with a bluish tone of gray – a little more so than normal. His deeply inset eyes were as gray as his skin tone – the dark bags under the deep sockets showing how tired he truly was. The skin on his face was overall saggy, and he looked to be in worse health than normal. Then there were those pink lips – she wanted to chuckle at the clown-like appearance it added. She feared it would not be to her advantage to laugh at him right now – he seemed to actually be in a good mood.

He poured himself a drink then returned to the chair behind his large desk. "I have called you here to listen to your progress on your subject... the cat. Has he come around yet? Can I try to make him a warrior?"

"No doctor, not quite yet. He has still not fully recovered from the bonding. I think he has some adjustments to make before he will be ready."

"So, has he made any progress? Has he tried to speak? Has he shown you he recognizes you? Anything?" he interrogated.

"No, unfortunately nothing yet. But I am sure..."

"So, you basically have wasted my, and the Institute's time and money on a worthless experiment. Is that what I should take from this?"

"No... I'm sure he's going to come around. He will become aware of his human side and his intelligence will emerge" she stressed.

He focused his gray eyes into hers, and said calmly "And how long am I expected to wait for your pussycat to come around? Or should I just have him incinerated right now, and be done with it?"

"You... you wouldn't do that, would you? Not after everything I have done to get him to this point! He will come around... I promise you... It will just take some time. I'll continue to jog his memory until he realizes who he is. So, leave him be. I'm sure the Council would like me to have the time..."

"The Council has also lost patience with your experiment. They told me today I could do what I wish..." he said knowing she would not see through his lie. "Perhaps you could convince me of your sincerity for this project?" He gave her an evil grin from his pink lipped mouth.

She attempted to hide the repulsion that swelled in her mind, and was attempting to streak across her face. She almost wretched from the thought of his old gnarled fingers touching her. She swallowed deeply before saying "Perhaps another time doctor..." she was barely able to gulp that rejection out. Thinking quickly, she said "I need to go work with Simon now. If you will excuse me..."

Without being excused she stood up and ran out the door. Edward continued to smile as she left. He watched, and relished the moving curves of her slim backside – he found it gave him a pleasant show. He then grabbed another berry, and threw it into his mouth while laughing with a maniacal tone. The narcotics of the berry flowed from under his tongue directly into his brain and he began to laugh and spin around and around in his chair – all while he chuckled uncontrollably.

Catherine ran down the hallway with tears running down her face. Only when she was well away from his office did she finally stop, and calm herself. She was more worried for Simon than herself. After a moment of drying her eyes, she spent another moment in light meditation. She knew she needed to regain her composure. Recovered from her emotions, she walked over to the patient living quarters, and found the keeper who would escort her to Simon's cell.

Clancy Yates was working this evening. He was a short man with a wrinkled face. It was obvious he had worked in the radiation and sun much too long in his younger years. He had large cauliflower ears and a bulbous nose to match. He was very muscular however – and those large muscles were strong enough to punish and torture the poor experiments in their cages. She knew of some of the atrocities he had performed on some of the converted patients – there was nothing she could do about it however. Clancy was the overlord of the patient kingdom. When she walked into the room she caught his eye. Surprising her as he jumped out of his chair, and came to a state of attention.

"Hello Clancy, I need to see Simon Piccolo right away..." she asked of the keeper.

"Very well. This way." he grabbed his stun stick from the rack on the wall and motioned for her to walk down the hallway to Simon's cell. He made sure to walk behind her most of the way. He enjoyed the show of her moving hips in her tight purple skirt as she walked. When they arrived at the cell, he jumped in front of her almost causing her to run into him – which he hoped would had happened, but didn't. He was always hoping for a cheap thrill in this manner. She stopped herself fast enough to prevent the collision with the short man, causing him to frown at her avoidance before entering the door code. The bars in the cell lowered into protective mode, which was followed by the large steel main door opening.

Simon was lying in his bed as the two entered. He sat up and saw Catherine, then saw Clancy next to her.

He immediately bristled the fur on his back, and stood up on all fours in a defensive position. He was not about to let him touch him with that stick again. He began to growl at the pair while looking at Clancy. "Grrrrrrrrraaaaaaaaaaaaaawwwwwwwwwwww" Simon snarled. He then let out a loud hiss.

Catherine was taken by surprise from his actions when they entered the room. She feared that perhaps instead of coming back to his human self he was in actuality falling deeper into the mind of the cat. She decided she needed to take drastic action.

"Clancy, leave us alone will you?" she asked of the keeper.

"Well, okay... but it's your head if you get too close and I'm not here to protect you" he said with apprehension in his voice. He did not want to be responsible for her if something happened.

"Don't worry..." she said as she typed some authorizations into her portable computer. "I have relieved you of responsibility for me while I'm in this cell. Thank you, Clancy."

He grumbled something unintelligible, then turned and closed the cell door behind him. Only after Simon was sure he had locked the door did he stop his growling. A moment later, he relaxed his posture.

Catherine noticed his change of behavior and had a slight pang of hope. She thought for a moment, then looked at Simon. "Okay Simon, I'm going to take a chance that you're still in there" she told him as she entered some commands on her personal computer. The bars slid up removing any protection she might have from the Human/Feline hybrid. If he was not in control of himself, she might be killed.

Simon sat down on his hind quarters, and straightened his front legs stiffly making him look like a statue. He stared her as she moved toward him one slow step at a time. She took a step, then after a moment she stepped forward toward him again. He cocked his head at her for a moment, and then relaxed his front legs to lie down in front of her while folding his front legs under his chest. She was now directly in front of him. He stared up at her.

"So, it was Clancy that riled you up, eh?" She looked at him and he was looking up at her, staring her straight in the eye – or was he? "Simon, are you looking up my dress?" she asked with a slight chuckle in her voice, and smile on her face.

He immediately changed his gaze to her face – then sat up, and looked her straight in the eyes.

"Simon, you're in there, aren't you?" she told him, hoping he would give her a sign. She reached up and stroked the top of his head. He closed his eyes, and enjoyed the feel of her touch. After a minute, he realized he was giving in, and might reveal his awareness to her by accident. Upon this thought, he turned and walked to his bed, then curled down and settled into the hay. She followed and sat next to him.

"Why do I feel you're in there... but for some reason not telling me? Are you upset that I did this to you? Do you hate me for this?" She scratched his head more while trying to figure out his reason for hiding from her. He continued to lie there and not give away anything despite his desires.

She sat there for an hour, trying to get him to come out of his cat shell. Despite his feelings and her attempts, he resisted. After a while, he found he was starting to fall slightly into a napping state. She let out a large sigh as she finally gave up on her attempts.

"Okay Simon. For whatever reason, you're not going to let me know you're in there today. I'll come by tomorrow and perhaps you'll have forgiven me enough to let me know you are there. And I DO know you are in there!" She stood up and started to walk to the door. She stopped, and turned to spy the crossword computer lying in the corner of the room. She had brought it for him, hoping it would bring out his human side. From the way it was lying on the floor however, it appeared to her that he had just batted it around. All he had done was to use it as a cat toy. "Guess you won't need this for now..." she told him as she picked up the device, and took it with her. The bars once again came down to keep Simon in the back of the cell while the door was open. The door opened and she walked out, stopping at the doorway to tell him lovingly "Good night, Simon." She turned, walked out into the hallway as the door closed behind her, and the bars returned to the ceiling.

"*Good night Catherine...*" He knew that she would be thinking that she had failed. He felt horrible for having to deceive her in this way. His thoughts changed right away as he felt a presence announcing itself, hoping for him to allow access to enter his mind. He allowed the intrusion.

As he expected, it was Galen. "Simon, are you alright my friend?" he asked with a worried tone to his voice.

"Yes..." he replied "but doing this to her is killing me however."

"I know. Please be patient. She will know soon enough, I promise..." he reassured him. "Have you been adjusting to your new configuration? Are you able to shift abilities?" he asked.

"Yes..." Simon answered. "I have found I can change my configuration based on my needs. If I needed to... I can change my leg configuration to biped... if I need better senses, I shift to them to feline. Why?"

"It's the reason I am contacting you tonight. I need to speak with you regarding something very important. I will soon have a task for you. This task requires a hybrid with your abilities, your intelligence, and your ability to adlib when needed. It will also require some memorization which I would like to get started this evening. Are you up to it?"

"Of course... what do I need to learn and how do I do it?"

"It's simple... get ready..." he answered, and suddenly a rush of maps and schematics began entering Simon's head – flooding his mind with a mass of information.

He felt woozy from all of the information that had just flowed into his brain. He felt as if his head was going to explode from the massive rush of data. Then more data flowed into his head. Within a few minutes the flow stopped, causing him to flop down in exhaustion. He mentally started to review, and inspect the information placed into his brain. "Galen, these are maps of the complex... and you have also given me schematics of the security system. What's going on?"

"For now, just study what I have provided. You will be very important to all of the hybrids, and also to us mutations of nature. Simon, may I ask you something? I found a reference to something in the historical documents that I am unfamiliar with, and cannot find any information about... at least not yet. Have you ever heard of anything with the initials P-A-W?"

Simon eyes lit up. "Ah yes! The People Against War. They were a radical group... labeled terrorists by the Council a few years ago. They reportedly attempted to destroy a few military bases, but were stopped and killed. They found many fragments of the group and squashed it. They weren't terrorists however. At least not terrorists against the common person... they were only trying to save mankind from what the Alliance was becoming. I know this as fact... as my parents were members. Some say they are still around, that they still exist in the shadows. Why do you ask?"

"Oh, just some information I found the other day that had references to those initials. I was just wondering what that stood for. I thought your knowledge of history would provide some insight... and I was right." He paused for a moment, then asked "Simon, have you ever heard of the PAW Paradigm?"

"The PAW Paradigm? No... in all of my studies, I have never come across that term. Never heard or read anything from my parents with that term either. I'm actually surprised you were able to find anything about that group. The Council is usually pretty good at cleaning the data of anything they don't want known." He was impressed with Galen's recently acquired ability to find anything on the World-Net.

"Well, I don't think even the Council knows of these references. They were pretty well hidden..." he revealed. "I think I have kept you awake long enough my friend. Get some rest."

Simon felt the loneliness in his brain return. The fatigue set in quickly, as he started to fall asleep. While he slept, visions of maps and schematics filled his head.

*   *   *

Catherine had just finished checking in with Clancy Yates at the front office and was returning to her quarters. His communication device rang, and upon seeing the name Clancy answered it quickly – it was Edward.

"Is she gone now?" the old man asked.

"Yes, for now. She said she would return later though." Clancy replied.

"No matter..." Edward disregarded his comment. "I would like you to set up something tomorrow. And I would like Simon Piccolo to participate. I have a little game in mind... I believe we have someone that knows him quite well. Let's get them back together again, shall we?" He spent the next few minutes telling him his plan.

After Edward told him of the complete plan, Clancy acknowledged "Well... of course, doctor. I can arrange that easily. It will occur exactly as you instructed. It will prove to be most entertaining..."

23

Simon awoke from his sleep with a start due to the arrival of Clancy Yates. The lights were activated on high intensity, and the bars slammed down from the ceiling with a bang as Clancy entered the cell. In his hand was his plasma stun stick. Simon upon seeing him sprang to his feet in defensive posture—his back arched and ready to leap, the fur on his back standing on end, and his teeth showing in a vicious manner.

"GrrrrrrrrrroooooaaaaAAAAAaaawwwwwwwwwww" Simon growled hoping to put some fear into the nasty zookeeper.

"Shut up cat! Maybe you would like a taste of my stun stick?" he threatened as he waved the stick at the captured human-animal hybrid.

"GrrrrrrrrrrooooOOoooaaaAAAaaawwwwwwwwwwww..." Simon continued growling at his captor.

"Listen, I only came in here to bring you good cheer. You get to go out into the exercise plaza. You should be thanking me" he told him.

Simon continued to growl and hiss.

"Bah!" Clancy spat out at Simon while activating the door on the back wall, exposing the tunnel to the center plaza. "Now get out of here before I change my mind!" He waved the stun stick at Simon to force him into the tunnel.

Simon cautiously entered the tunnel and watched the door close behind him. He thought he heard Clancy laugh as he entered the tunnel – "*what's he up to?*"

He hoped that this complex was the same as the complex for non-converted humans. He walked down the tunnel and another door opened, exposing the center exercise plaza. He walked out into the plaza – the tunnel door slid closed behind him.

This plaza was laid out exactly the same as in the human habitation complex. There were trees, rocks, and patches of grass laid out around the circular area. Missing however were all of the furniture and decorative items that made the human plaza so comfortable. What Simon also noticed that was different – the lack of cleaning in the plaza. There were dung piles everywhere. In addition, this plaza was not clean smelling like the other habitation quarters. As a matter of fact, it smelled like an animal house in the zoo. He found his sensitive nose to not enjoy any of the odors. As a matter of fact, the smells made him sneeze. He would smell the air, and it disgusted him to the point that he let out a verbal grunt of repulsion to the odor.

He wished his cell tunnel would reopen so he could leave. To take his mind off the smell, he decided to walk around and look at the other hybrids in the plaza. There were all sorts of various combinations of human and animal here. He saw hybrids of Hyena, Orangutan, Horse, Tiger and Greyhound to name a few. There were at least 40 different animal hybrids in the plaza, not one of them was of the same combination of species.

To his surprise, he was actually able to recognize the human parts of the hybrids that he had previously met as a human – he could see in their faces that they recognized him also. None of them spoke a word to each other however, which he thought was strange. He assumed they all had some form of communication, or that they had all learned to speak by now. He wondered if Galen was only helping him learn these abilities – or was it possible that they all knew not to speak.

One other thing he noticed – there was only ONE of each type. There might be a female or a male of a single variety, but never a pair. He found that odd. He wondered if they were just keeping mating pairs apart, or perhaps they could not merge the same animal twice, or did they just not desire any two sexes of a single animal hybrid. It would be a good way to maintain control he thought.

As he wandered around the plaza, he noted that the cell entrance tunnels were all opening and lighting up with various colors to indicate who should be entering. As a tunnel opened and the colored light activated, the particular hybrid would obediently walk to the tunnel and enter – the door automatically closing behind them. Simon wondered how much torture was required to make the hybrids so obedient and trained to react in this manner. After a few minutes however, Simon noticed that all of the hybrids were leaving except him – his tunnel was not being activated.

He felt Galen's presence approach, and request to enter his mind. "Simon, there is something wrong... I'm not sure exactly what it is however..." he told him. "I'm going to get some help for you down there. Do the best you can to hold out until help arrives." He felt him leave again.

In the corner of his eye he noticed a tunnel open, and a large, lumbering creature came walking out, the door closing behind him. This hybrid was huge – with a large bull-like face, enormous set of horns, giant chest, and strong muscular arms and legs. He was covered in a dark, short-haired hide. He snorted as he walked.

The large beast continued to slowly walk closer to Simon. As he approached Simon got a horrid feeling as he thought he recognized the face of this hybrid creature. "*My god, is that who I think it is? No, it couldn't be!*" His fears were confirmed when he noticed the tattoo on his head. Even in his new hybrid state, the tattoo remained and was visible like a brand – the skull with snakes coming out of the eyes.

As the creature with the hybrid name of Oxbow approached, he came to the realization that he had been setup. He was alone in this plaza with the one person who would have a grudge against him – Orville Bronsky.

He hoped that perhaps Orville would not recognize him in his new hybrid state. Then again, he also knew that Orville would kill him just for fun – assuming he still had the same Orville personality he had come to know and fear.

He walked up to Simon, and then walked around him in a slow circle, looking him up and down. He finally stopped in front of the now tense cat, and put his large face up to Simon's – his nose touching Simon's small nose bridge. Drops of mucus dripped from his nose onto Simon's once clean snout. Spittle dripped out of his mouth as he let hot breath exhaust onto Simon's face. He snorted, and said very softly so that only the two of them could hear "Piccolo... I am going to kill you..."

Up in the keeper control center, Clancy sat at the window chuckling. "Before we converted him he told us about how the cat killed his brother. Now watch this. Oxbow is going to make cat guts out of that kitten!" he told the group of keepers as they gathered to watch the show. They all laughed and started making bets as to how long Simon would last.

Immediately Orville swung his large fist down, but Simon's reflexes kicked in, and he jumped back landing on all fours a few feet away. His back was now flexed and his muscles tense awaiting the next attack. It came quickly, as Orville charged Simon on all fours – his horns aimed at his midsection. Simon shifted and jumped again flying over the large swiftly moving juggernaut.

It took a few feet for Orville to stop, but as soon as he was capable, he immediately turned and charged again. Simon jumped out of the way again – but this time while jumping he extended a handful of his long sharp claws, and ran them across the top of his head as he charged by. Blood shot out of the four long slashes but, the damage did not even phase the rampaging ox-bull.

Orville stopped and saw the blood drip down his face. He stuck out his tongue, and licked at the dripping blood. He laughed as he tasted the blood, while a death lust generated in his soul.

He turned and charged again. Simon this time jumped out of the way and landed on Orville's back – he extended his claws and left more deep gashes. But to Simon's surprise, Orville stopped, and then bucked his rear as hard as he could – sending Simon flying nearly twenty feet away. As he passed, Orville swung his large fist knocking into the side of Simon's body as he flew by. He was somehow able to land on all fours, but as soon as his feet touched the ground, he reeled in pain from the attack. *"Okay, I need to be more careful!"*

Simon was forced to recover from his strike quickly as the large Oxbow charged again. He again leaped out of the way. This time however, Orville was prepared, and as Simon leaped over his body he stopped and turned his head just enough for one of his long horns to strike him in the arm as he flew by. Pain jolted into his arm and into his mind. He became disoriented for a moment while he tried to land on his feet – but instead was barely able to stay upright on three feet.

Orville saw Simon wobble as he landed. He charged again, running at full speed toward the woozy cat-human. "I have you now Piccolo!" he thought as he was now only a few mere feet away from his prey.

Simon's act did exactly what he hoped for. He had fooled Orville into charging him at this particular spot. Right before the large head and horns could pierce and squash the smaller framed Simon, he leaped out of the way. His leap exposed Orville's charging head to the tree directly behind Simon's former resting spot. He hit the tree with such a force that it broke in half sending the top half of the tree crashing to the floor of the plaza. Orville tried to turn to charge again but he could not move as one of his horns was stuck in the trunk of the tree. Branches of the fallen tree pinned him to the artificial turf.

Simon took advantage of the situation, ran up, leaped, then broadcast a swarm of flying paws and claws into the face of the stuck Ox hybrid. His face was shredded by Simon's quick moves and sharp claws. One of his eyes was now cut and he could not keep it open and focused. Simon sent another flurry of paws and claws to the now weakened Orville. He struck his head and neck, doing even more damage.

He was caught off guard when Orville actually broke his horn to propel another attack. He sent him flying once again across the plaza with a pounding fist from his swinging arm. He somehow managed to land on his feet, but this time he actually was stunned. Fortunately, he had enough of his wits about him to spot the tree branch above him – he managed to jump and climb to the safety of the high branch just as Orville's charge went zooming by.

He tried to relax on the branch to rest and regain his mental state, but the cobwebs in his head were thick. He started to worry when he felt the mighty Ox hybrid bash his head into the trunk of the tree – he smashed into it over and over in an attempt to topple him from the branch. Orville finally did what he wanted to accomplish as Simon suddenly slipped, and fell out of the tree. He was now once again exposed to the rampaging beast.

He felt Galen's presence. "Simon, you must get up. I am trying to use the nature song to calm him but he is ignoring it. I have never seen a hybrid ignore the beautiful music. I have help about to arrive. I do have one other thing I can try if needed. But you have to hang on!"

"I AM trying... but I am dizzy, so dizzy..." he told his friend.

The nature song distracted Orville just long enough for Simon to get enough strength and awareness to leap away, and run across the plaza. He was hoping this would give him enough time to recover as best as possible. Unfortunately, he saw the large bull set his sights on him again. The bull was charging him again – Simon was not ready to jump; his muscles were too sore and tired. The gash on his arm was bleeding and hurting badly. He knew this could possibly be the end. He did not have the ability to get up and fight back.

He thought his brain was playing tricks on him when he saw the streaking brown creature zoom by him. He struck Oxbow in the side of his body, which knocked him across the room. He could have sworn he heard the snapping of ribs on the large beast. Orville rolled on the ground in an attempt to catch his breath as the brown streak ran up to him, and sunk a mouth full of sharp-fanged teeth into his ear – tearing it in half. Oxbow screamed in pain as the streak ran around him and once again struck him again with a powerful head butt. The attack once again sent him flying across the room.

* * *

In the control room, boos and shouts of complaints were being thrown down into the melee below. The keepers were mad that Simon had help – after all, it had ruined the betting odds. Clancy began to activate the defensive lasers. "I'll take care of that bastard intruder. That piece of crap will not wreck my fight event!" He shouted, as he began to set the laser sights upon the streaking creature. He reached for the firing button.

"NO! Fire that, and you die with him, Yates!" shouted a voice behind him. He turned to see Catherine standing at the door with a blaster in her hand. "Turn off the defense system, and call off the hybrid, NOW!" she demanded.

"Sorry, no-can-do on calling him off. All I can do is open his tunnel, and if your cat is lucky... Oxbow will obey."

"Hope for your sake he follows his training..." she threatened as she watched the fight below, while at the same time maintaining control over the keepers in the room.

Simon noticed the tunnel open, and the red light come on to light up the opening. Orville turned and noticed the light, but then turned his attention back to Simon. He was about to charge when the brown streak once again slammed the side of the bull's ribs again – which again sent him flying a third time. Oxbow fell to the ground, his legs shuddered from the pain.

The brown streak ran to Simon, and came to a stop in front of him. The creature had a long face, long nose, and whiskers. It had rounded ears, a rounded body, and was covered in brownish-tan colored fur. He had short arms and legs but they were quite muscular, and were equipped with long, sharp claws. His tail was round, it started thick in the back then angled to a fine point on the end. Although he walked on all fours, Simon could tell he was quite tall when he was a human. The hybrid smiled at Simon and he noticed a mouthful of sharp pointed teeth and fangs. He certainly did not want to be bitten by this animal!

Then Simon recognized the human side of this hybrid. He smiled as best he could with the pain wracking his body.

"Aye mon, I have to save you I see!" The furry creature said to Simon softly as he gave him a toothy smile and a wink of his dark eye.

"Danny, that… is you… isn't it?" he asked.

"Aye, mon" he replied. "You recognized me. I be touched! But I'm now known by the lower humans as Mondrake. You are sure a cute kitten there Mister Piccolo!" he whispered then laughed softly.

Their reunion was cut short by the sound of Oxbow as he regained the feeling in his legs. He stood up and once again set his sights on the two hybrids. He started to run, slowly at first, but gradually picked up speed.

"Oh, oh mon. Looks like we are no done yet." Danny said with a worried tone in his voice.

Suddenly, Orville stopped in his tracks, and fell to the ground. He grasped his head with his hoofs. He let out a gigantic wail as if he was in horrid pain. The two friends just stood there and watched as the creature rolled around in pain and suffering. After a minute, the wail suddenly stopped. Orville stood up, looked at the two hybrids, but instead of attacking, turned and walked into his tunnel. As before, the door closed automatically behind him.

"Whew, that was close. The question is... what just happened? I thought we were done for..." Simon pondered.

Galen requested then entered their minds. "It was the agony of the animal. He forced me to use it, although I did not want to."

"Agony of the animal? What be dat Galen?" Danny asked.

"It's a song of all of the suffering that all animals go through... both past and present. It is quite unpleasant to listen to, and will clearly cause a hybrid to stop in his tracks" he replied. "It pains me just to have to transfer it to one of our family. But it was the only way to get him to stop his bloodlust. I hope I won't need to ever use it again."

"Well, thank you once again, Galen" Simon praised his friend. "By the way, how did you get here Danny?"

"I did that Simon" Galen responded. "I was able to override the door system so Danny could get out there and assist you. I also think you will have help from upstairs with getting your cell tunnels open. I will leave you now my friends." The two felt his presence fade.

"Well me friend...I think I had best be going meself. See you mon!" He waved his nose up into the air in a type of wave. As Danny started walking away, two hatchways opened and were lit with two different colored lights. Danny's was a light shade of green, and Simon noticed that his tunnel was lit in purple.

"Purple... Catherine?" he thought as he looked up into the control room. He could not see Catherine standing up there, blaster in hand making sure he safely got back to his cell. Nonetheless, he knew she had some hand in him surviving this ordeal. He hoped to repay her someday.

He arrived at his cell, sat down, and started cleaning around his wound. He removed all of the blood on his fur by licking and bathing himself clean.

Catherine came running into his cell, not even activating the protective bars. She had a first aid kit in her hand. She sat down next to Simon, and started nursing his wounds. Simon laid his head in her lap as she worked on his damaged arm.

After a while, he realized his arm felt better. In repayment to her nursing skills, he began to purr. She smiled at him, then stroked his head lightly with her hand, relaxing him even further. After a few minutes of this treatment, he found himself sound asleep in her protective arms.

*   *   *

Oxbow arrived back to his cell a physical and mental wreck. The song he heard was so horrible that it had completely immobilized him. It also had removed every remaining tidbit of hatred from his mind. He was still very angry nonetheless. He entered his cell and saw the bars were down keeping him confined to a very small area. Standing in the doorway was Clancy Yates and an assistant.

"What a waste of animal you are, Oxbow!" Clancy spouted to Orville. "Why we waste time on pitiful creatures like you I'll never understand." Clancy was feeling pretty smug about this hybrid's predicament. He knew that he was behind the steel bars and could do nothing about his taunting and torturing. He had decided that Oxbow was not the kind of warrior the Council wanted – so he was going to teach him a lesson. He turned to Oxbow and jabbed him with his stun stick, which sent the bull flying into the wall. He laughed at the large Oxbow lying on the ground – his muscles convulsed in spasms across his body.

"What do you think of that, cow?" he taunted Orville. "I have plenty more where that came from too. You lost me a lot of money, and I'm going to make you pay."

"Sir, are you sure you should be doing that to the hybrids?" his assistant Jackson Miles, the thin mousy looking caretaker asked while standing a good distance behind him.

Clancy turned and waved his stick at Jackson. "Listen, if I want to teach these pitiful creatures a lesson, then I can, and will..."

Clancy's voice was cut off by his vocal chords being squeezed and crushed. He could not move as his feet left the ground, and he was being pulled tightly against the bars. He looked into the mirror that was directly in front of him on the wall. Somehow Oxbow had bent the hardened steel bars, and now had him in his cold, large hands. As Oxbow squeezed his neck shut, he noticed the creature was smiling.

Jackson shrieked, backed up, and closed the door leaving Clancy all alone with the hate-filled creature. He pulled the emergency alarm causing beeping wails to be broadcast through the speaker system, alerting the staff of the emergency.

"Now, for a lesson from me..." was the last thing Clancy Yates heard when the creature actually spoke to him. Clancy felt a hot feeling on his neck as his skin started to tear. His brain stayed alive just long enough to see his head being pulled from the rest of his body – part of his spinal cord came with his skull. It dangled and wiggled as Oxbow shook the dying keeper's head. The large Oxbow chuckled, and then smiled as he let go of his body, allowing it to drop to the floor. The headless corpse continued to squirm and spasm while nerves fired their remaining electrical energies into the muscles. Blood shot out of the open gash where his head was previously connected. He then looked at the disconnected head, shook it again, laughed, and tossed it next to the flopping body on the floor. Clancy Yates could see his disconnected body right before his brain finally died – at the moment his head hit the floor.

24

Edward personally checked security lockdown procedures tonight. Since Clancy Yates had been murdered by the sub-human Oxbow, he had decided to crack down on all captives and tighten all security. Humans were no longer allowed to roam in the patient living quarters without advance permission and escort. He was not going to allow any other human – especially Blessed – to be killed by the creatures he had created. He wondered why the creature would kill a keeper, and yet had shown to be worthless during battle exercises. He wondered if it was all an act.

He watched the various security monitors throughout the complex – switching from room to room. He constantly changed the cameras, from one area one moment, to a totally different area the next. As soon as he decided there was nothing of interest, he would change to another area of the complex.

He switched to the lab where the mutation experiments took place. The lab had been expanded in size – walls had been torn down to make the room much larger than before. The room now housed 60 of the bonding devices used to make the cellular mutations that were starting to prove to be the best solution for the Councils need of a "super soldier".

Edward was perplexed however as to why whenever he would design a new mutation scheme it would not take hold. He sometimes wondered if perhaps Derrick or Stephanie were plotting against him, and subversively changing the DNA sequencing programs of his design during the bonding process. He would have to keep his eye on them – especially Stephanie – for more than one reason. He was attracted to Stephanie, but she refused all of his advances – he would keep trying nonetheless. He could not understand however, why she would not want someone of his authority – and a Blessed to boot.

He panned the camera around the lab, he saw nothing unusual. He switched to Galen Wood's cell and – he was not there. His cell door was closed, and security indicators showed it to be locked, but he indeed was missing. "*How did he get out, and more importantly... where did he go?*" he wondered. He considered sounding the alarm and letting security find him, but instead he started switching cameras hoping to locate him personally.

His searching finally paid off as he found him in Lisa's cell. Edward was shocked to find them in bed, having sex. A bright glow emitted from the pair – and the illumination rose at the same level as their passion. Edward zoomed in and rotated so he could get a better view. He moved the camera angles in different ways so he could observe everything that was happening. He found he had become very excited from the spectacle displayed on the screen. He subconsciously began to masturbate to the almost-alien lovemaking displayed on the monitor. The pair of mutated humans lasted much longer than Edward did. After they were done they lay together in each other's arms. After another hour, Galen returned to his cell, opening the doors using the keypads. This made Edward wonder who had granted him that access.

After cleaning up after himself, he turned off the camera monitor, and switched to the security computer. It showed no log entries for Galen either leaving his cell, or entering Lisa's cell. He decided to lock out any computer access to Galen's cell from now on. He also locked out all but three people to the mutation patient cells; himself, Derrick and Stephanie. Edward thought that this would prevent any of Galen's operatives from providing him with a way to get out without his knowing about it. He also activated the steel doors, preventing them from using the ports in the plastic doors to their advantage.

After locking out Galen's access, he thought for a moment then contacted the injection lab. A lab technician answered. "I want you to prepare for an injection experiment in an hour" he barked at the technician.

"Very well sir, who is going to be the subject" he asked.

"Tonight, we are going to try something different... we are going to integrate a mutated human with an animal" he announced. "Should be quite interesting!"

The technician nodded, and Edward closed the communication. He thought for a moment, and then activated his communication device again. This time a large security officer answered.

"Meet me at the mutation lab. I may need your assistance with a patient. Oh, and bring lots of backup..." he suggested and disconnected.

Edward arrived at the lab and the officer was already there – he had done as he had been instructed. He was waiting along with ten other officers – he had indeed brought plenty of backup. The security force noticed that Edward was carrying a canister. Upon Edward's command, they entered the lab. Edward directed them to Lisa's cell.

"Okay, you will open the door and I will throw this canister in... close the door immediately after I throw it in" he directed.

Edward waited at the door while the officer activated the door lock. The door started to slowly slide open. Edward activated the canister and threw it in. The officer reversed the door as soon as Edward's hand was clear. The door clicked shut and Edward ran over to the monitor to watch – all while inwardly he hoped that his plan would actually work.

Lisa began to stir as the gas filled the small cell. She awoke and started to choke. She ran to the door, and started to pound on it. The door began to dent as her strong hands banged on the steel.

Edward then heard a code being entered on the keypad in Galen's cell. He started to sweat knowing that the other mutant was aware of her distress, and was attempting to get out to help. He began to pound on the door, trying in vain to get out. The steel door on his cell also began to bend, but for the moment, it held. They could hear him scream her name, while at the same time, she finally passed out on the floor.

Edward purged the air in the cell and opened the door. Lisa was lying on the ground, unconscious. He took out a hypodermic, and lifted her underarm. Sticking the needle into the one soft spot on her mutated stony skin, he injected her with an even stronger sedative – he was going to guarantee she would not be waking up for quite a long while.

They loaded her onto a gurney and rolled her to the injection chamber. She was put onto the table below the array, and Edward started the computer on its process of transformation. In the control room Edward looked at the girl and thought. *"I wonder if her new body structure could handle something a normal human could not handle?"* He then activated the virtual switches, initiating the disintegration process.

Still unconscious, Lisa's cellular substance was moved into the integration matrix of the giant super computer. Edward looked at the list of animals at his disposal for bonding. He wanted to pick just the right one for this special person.

"Yes, this one I think..." he announced.

A lab technician looked at his selection. "Really? I thought that never worked?" he stated.

"This girl is special... she can handle it" he replied as he awaited the computers notification of a completed bonding sequence. Once notified by the computer that the process was complete, he activated the reintegration process. "We will know for sure in just a few minutes."

After she had been reintegrated, the process of change started quickly as Edward expected. He went out into the lab and hovered over his latest experiment. She mutated quickly and to Edward's surprise, painlessly. "Perfect! Give her a few minutes rest, and roll her back to her cell" he ordered. He returned to the control center to complete his final experimentation logs.

Behind him Edward heard the door open, and footsteps approaching from behind. He spun around in his chair to find a lesser scientist standing behind him. This was a scientist from a different part of the institute. In his hand was a plastic canister with a small device inside. The device was a small, stainless-steel, barrel-looking device – two inches long, and an inch in diameter. There were numerous miniature wires coming out of the ends. Edward eyed the canister and the device, and then looked at the scientist. "Is that it? Are you telling me it is finally done?"

"Yes" replied the scientist. "The mind control device is finally complete. To use it however, you will need a test subject who has a history of suggestibility... Someone who would be a perfect subject for hypnosis."

Edward snatched the canister from the grasp of the scientist. "I will find... someone. Now go. I have no further need of you at this time. If this works, I will need you to start mass producing these."

The scientist, shocked by Edward simply "stealing" his invention, stared at him with fire in his eyes.

"What are you waiting for?" Edward barked "now go... shoo, shoo" he waved the man off. With a whipped-puppy look on his face, the scientist reluctantly turned and left the room.

"Yes, I will make excellent use of this device... Project Fury Warrior will be a complete success now. Either with injected mutants... or with controllable sub-humans." He chuckled to himself as he stared at his new-found toy. Finally, he placed it into his pants pocket. He returned his attention back to Lisa, who had fully accepted her genetic injection and was now fully changed. "Yes, I WILL be a success after all..."

*   *   *

Galen was still lying on the floor of his cell, against the door when Stephanie released the door lock, and opened the cell. He rolled out onto the floor.

"Galen, what's wrong, why are you sleeping on the floor? Are you ill?" she asked.

"Please, I must get to Lisa. Something has happened... I'm certain..." he pleaded.

They walked over to the next cell, and Stephanie entered her key code to open the door. It slid open, and before Stephanie could stop him, Galen ran in. When he saw Lisa he screamed – his booming voice shook the entire building. A couple of windows cracked due to the vibrations of his scream.

Lisa was lying on her bed, and just starting to stir. She however was completely different than when she went to sleep. She still has her flowing purple-pink hair, but her mouth had been transformed into a soft beak. In addition, much of her body was now covered in soft feathers. Her feet sported sharp talons, and on her back, was a large set of – wings.

Galen ran to her side. "What have you done to her?" he screamed at Stephanie.

"Galen, I swear… Derrick and I had nothing to do with this!" she assured him. "Let me check the logs…" She ran off to see who might have done this – although she really did not need to look. She knew who she would find in the logs.

Galen stroked Lisa's pink hair, as tears flowed out of his large eyes. Lisa looked at him – her beak turned up in a light smile. She reached up, and lightly stroked his hair. She struggled for a moment, and then spoke in a rough voice.

"My darling, I'm so sorry. What they've done to me must repulse you…" she began to sob softly.

"No, that's not true. No matter what… my love for you will never fade…" he told her with a teary smile. "Besides, the feathers are kind of cute…"

She appreciated his attempt to humor her, and returned the smile. "Galen, I do have a surprise for you. There is something under the bed that you helped create before this happened. I want you to take it, and care for it in the event I cannot. I was hoping to surprise you today… but well… things are not the same now."

Confused, he looked under the bed and discovered a golden, glowing egg. He picked it up and looked at it with wonder in his eyes. "Is this… ours?"

Her beak turned up in a smile. "Yes, darling. It is the first of a new race of beings. A new start of life and awareness."

Galen placed the egg back under the bed. "I think you will be in good enough shape to care for our child" he reassured her.

She sat up and the wings on her back sprung apart – they filled the small cell, and almost knocked Galen over. She looked at them fully extended, then folded them in. "They might even work…" she said.

Galen stood and took her hands in his. "No matter what… I am committed to you my love. No matter what they have done to you, I will always be by your side until I am dead" he promised.

Stephanie appeared at the door and looked at Galen. She had fury in her eyes. "It was Edward… I knew it was him, but I had hoped he actually would not stoop to this level…"

Galen began to brightly glow. Stephanie could tell it was not a glow of happiness. She could see that his eyes were filled with hatred, and a want for revenge.

"This moment is when things change..." he announced. "He will pay for his behavior. Many will suffer due to his actions." He kissed Lisa on the cheek, stood up, and returned to his cell without saying another word.

After the door of his cell closed, he contacted Simon. "My friend, do you still have that information memorized? It's about time to put it to use..."

25

Cora Lee was both scared and excited when the technicians came to claim her for the experiment. She had high hopes that she would be soon be a sub-human, and would then be reunited with her Danny. She knew however, that she would never see him until she was in the transformed patient's living quarters. No one lived in the human quarters after experimentation – and thus she had gone for so long without seeing her love. She knew that soon she would be reunited with Danny.

She was first taken to a room where she was prepped and dressed in a thin paper gown. Once prepped, she was taken to an operating room. Waiting for her was a surgeon and an operating team. She was confused, and then she became scared – she started to fight them, trying to prevent them from getting her onto the operating table.

Edward entered the room, looked her up and down, and then smiled. "Don't be afraid my dear, we're going to try an extra step in your transformation. An extra step that I think will guarantee a complete success..." he reassured her. "You have nothing to fear, just a short operation and then off to the transformation chamber... alright?"

She just nodded her head – she was too scared to speak. The operating room nurse helped her sit on the cold steel table, and then got her situated with her face resting in a hole in the table. An anesthesiologist along with the nurse gave her a shot to relax her, then inserted an IV into her hand. A few minutes after that, she was unconscious.

Edward's smile turned into a snarl as she blacked out. "Get this over with, I want her in the transformation chamber as soon as possible!" he barked, then set the canister with the mind control device on the table in front of the surgeon.

The surgery proceeded without a problem. The device was inserted into the occipital lobe of her brain, the micro-circuit wires were guided into her temporal lobe, then into the parietal and frontal lobes. Her brain was now completely wired – the incision was sealed and hair regrown where it had been removed. While she was still unconscious, the device was activated and tested. Everything in the device and her brain appeared to be working properly.

The sedative was cut off, and within minutes she was awake and looking around. Edward approached her once again smiling. "Now, that was not so bad, was it?" he asked her.

"No, I guess not... I don't appear to be hurting or anything" she replied.

"Good, then let's get you to the transformation chamber, shall we?"

A pair of aids got her onto the gurney, and wheeled her to the transformation chamber. She was placed onto the table below the disintegration/reintegration array. All preparations were made, and then she was given the numbing solution.

"I will be with you soon Danny..." she mumbled as the numbing injection started to do its work.

In the control room Edward viewed possible animals to use in the binding process. There were multiple panes on the computer screen, displaying the changing available animal choices flashing at a steady pace. He studied the screen intently. "Hmm... what would be good to test out the device? Something that we could never do without it in her head..." he pondered. His eyes lit up and he pressed a switch, which enlarged one of the images to a full screen display. He smiled and said "It is almost poetic..."

His assistant looked at the screen, and the image caused his eyes to open wide in shock. "You... you... aren't going to turn her into THAT are you? It has never worked, doctor..."

He cut him off. "That was before this device... what a better way to test it, then to use it on a bonding with a creature that would actually modify her normal brain function? Yes, this will be a perfect test."

The process was completed, and Edward accomplished his transformation plan perfectly. Cora Lee's DNA was broken down and merged with Edwards's selection, she was then reintegrated, and was now transforming just as he expected.

Edward smiled with evil satisfaction. "Perfect!" he proclaimed. "Now, to turn the device to full power..."

He activated the brain control device, and through the computer increased the power to full. He flipped some switches and an image appeared on one of the screens. The image was fuzzy and shifted, but it was definitely what Edward expected. The staff all looked at the image on the screen. It was a shifting view of the disintegration/reintegration array from Cora Lee's point of view.

"Why is her vision so bad?" one of the technicians asked.

"Imbecile! Did you learn anything in school? She now uses her other senses to see properly. Her vision is minor now" he snapped. "Take her to the arena chamber... then find someone in the experimentation pool, and bring them there also."

He grabbed a hand-held computer, and started the brain control program. He transferred control to the smaller computer. Edward and the staff all left the transformation chamber, and headed for the arena chamber. This room was specifically constructed to test the abilities of the sub-humans. It was composed of a simple, round, concrete floor, surrounded by tall concrete walls, and above the walls were bleachers for the staff to sit and observe. Built into the wall, was a single closed-in room with darkened windows – this was the executive observation room. There have been rumors that the keepers had used the room for staging gambling battles. Edward never bothered to look into the rumors, or for that matter really didn't care if they had staged the matches in the past. Edward entered the observation room and sat in the comfortable leather chair in the center of the room.

Cora Lee was wheeled into the room on her gurney. The technician raised the table so she could easily drop down to the floor in the event the restraints were removed. He started to leave when Edward interrupted his exit with the arena door closing. A panicked look came across the young technician's face.

Edward peered down into the arena from the observation area above. He changed the darkness of the window so the technician could see him looking down at him. He activated the PA system and spoke into the room at the scared young man. "Now don't worry... if this works... as it should... you will be fine..." he said coldly to the technician. He then flipped a switch, which removed the shackles from the gurney, and Cora Lee slid down onto the floor.

She raised up fully, exposing how truly hideous she had become. Her body was covered with scales on the front, her breasts were still human, and were fully exposed on her front or underside. Her arms were still human as was her straw-like blonde hair. Everything else however was now completely different.

Her body was now that of a snake. Her legs, now worthless, simply hung from each side of her body. A long tail extended for 25 feet behind her. She had a rounded head, and a hood that started at the base of her now-long neck, and extended up to the top of her head where her blonde hair started and flowed to the back of her head.

Her eyes were now a green color with diamond shaped pupils. Her nose had flattened into her face, a set of small-slit nostrils took the place of the nose. Her mouth had sharp fangs showing, and as she stood, she smiled. Her smile showed total evil, and was purely hideous. A hiss escaped her smiling mouth as she noticed the hapless technician panicking across the room.

"May I introduce you to my latest creation..." Edward announced to the group in the arena. "I have named her Cora-bra." He laughed with a cackle as he humored himself with his wit.

The human-snake started to slowly slither across the room to the fearful technician. The man lost his bladder on the floor from fear of the grotesque creature quickly gliding in to attack.

"Cora-bra, do not attack that man!" Edward commanded into the control computer. The creature immediately stopped, and turned around. With a slight look of disappointment, she returned to the gurney on the other side of the room.

The door opened, and another man was thrown in. It was one of the patients who had been living in the human habitation quarters, awaiting his transformation. He looked around confused. He looked at the technician who was now in a state of shock. The technician just stared at the patient without moving a muscle.

"Now, we will see if this control device really works as they told me it would..." Edward announced. "Cora-bra, attack the man in the blue jumpsuit, but do not touch the technician in the white coat... Now, kill the patient!"

That hideous smile once again flashed on Cora Lee's face as she spied the patient who was now at the door, pounding and pleading for mercy. The technician was frozen with fear, still standing in the same spot, and not moving or twitching a muscle.

She quickly slithered to the patient, and grabbed him with one of her now-strong hands, and spun him around to face her. He tried to pull away, but to stop him, she sprayed a mist of venom into his face. He screamed as the venom burned his face and eyes. She let loose of her grip on him, and he started to wander aimlessly around the room. She just stood, and smiled while watching him. After watching him a moment, she moved in and slithered circles around the man. She watched and enjoyed the confusion in his new blindness. Like a kitten with a mouse, she played with her prey, not wanting to kill him yet.

She finally became bored with her game, and zoomed around to the front of the wandering man – his arms out-stretched trying to find his way in the darkness. His fumbling hands ran right into her breasts. He reached out and grabbed them. Realizing what he was touching, he screamed and turned the other direction. Now done playing with her prey, in a flash, she lurched out and struck the man with her mouth – her sharp hypodermic fangs sunk into his neck. Massive amounts of poison were injected into him. His neck puffed up immediately, and his breathing became erratic and tight. He stumbled as the poison entered his head, which caused it to puff up like a balloon. She struck him again, this time in the chest. His torso became instantly bloated with fluid. He fell down, and immediately died.

Cora Lee then turned and slithered to the technician who was still in shock, and was still standing in exactly the same spot. She put her scaly face right up to his, and smiled. She was close enough to him that her flicking, forked tongue was getting his face wet with her slimy spittle. After a moment of causing even more fear in the man, she turned and returned to the gurney. She now waited for her next instruction. The door opened behind the technician.

"Get him out of there. I told him not to worry, didn't I?" he asked of his staff. They all nodded in sheepish agreement.

He looked at the snake-woman, now waiting for her next instruction in the large room below. "Hmm... I think we should just leave her in there for now... that is until I find a good place for her to stay. As a matter of fact, no one is to speak of this experiment to anyone. If you do, you will be her next victim! I want to keep her as my ace-in-the-hole. You never know when you will need a secret weapon."

"What about that dead patient?" an assistant asked.

He picked up the controller and gave a suggestion to Cora Lee "If you are hungry Cora-bra, why don't you feast on your prey?"

He chuckled as Cora Lee slithered to the dead man, and wrapped her body around his dead carcass. Her mouth opened wide, and she surrounded the dead man's head, sliding him down her throat – her strong arms shoving his dead body into her now-huge maw.

Edward turned and left the room with a huge smile upon his face. He softly was heard saying "She's the perfect secret weapon..."

26

It had been a few days since Simon's sortie with Orville, the now-deadly Oxbow. He had since had plenty of time to rest, as the keeper staff had done a total lock down of the facility since the death of Clancy Yates. So, he had used this quiet time to rest and recuperate. Since Catherine had used the healing beam on his arm, he found that it was now completely healed.

As he sat on his bed of straw, he heard activity outside his door. He wondered what all the running around was about. After a few minutes, he got his answer. The bars came down, and the cell door opened. Catherine walked in with a keeper and a guard.

"Simon, they wanted me to get you and take you out into crater." She had a worried look on her face. "I'm not sure what's going on, but I have to say... I am a little worried." There were small pools of tears just floating inside her lower eyelid. He knew this had to be bad – she was desperately worried.

The keeper stepped up to the feline/human with a leash in his hand. Simon became defensive, and stood on all fours with his fur ruffled and back arched. He growled softly at the man. Catherine stepped in front of the keeper, and took the leash from him.

"Simon, we have been ordered to take you outside. Please let me put this on you... " she pleaded.

He stopped his posturing and sat his hind quarters onto the ground. He tilted his head down so she could put the leash on him. She smiled at his obedience and gave him a short scratch under his chin. His heart warmed at her touch, and he let out a slight purr.

"Come on my kitty cat. Let's go see what Edward has up his sleeve now."

Escorted by the keeper and the guard, the pair navigated through the protective exit maze of the patient quarters – following the exact path as described by the guard's portable computer. They twisted and turned, avoiding all of the deadly traps that were set for any creature that might escape their cell and attempt to exit through this winding passage. As they exited the maze a loud buzzer sounded attracting Simon's attention. He turned to see a force field had activated in front of the exit portal. He then heard the sounds of the massive walls inside the maze shifting and rearranging. A few moments passed, the buzzer sounded again to announce the removal of the force field and the activation of the maze's deadly traps. The maze was now in a new configuration, its traps all in different spots within the maze. He felt a light tugging on the leash attached to the collar around his neck.

"Come on Simon... we need to get out there, and we had better not make Edward wait."

They exited the building, and walked out into the courtyard. They boarded a waiting hover hopper and were transported to the far eastern side of the crater. Edward was waiting there along with a number of soldiers, and Galen. Galen was bound by a super strong set of electronic shackles. Nearby, a man sat in a protective polymer booth. He recognized this man as Councilman Jared Helman – he wondered if he was the project sponsor. *"Jared... he has to be the father of the bastard who put him here... "* Every Blessed parent had a special way to name their children – this one named all his male children Jared.

Edward had a disgusted look on his face when Simon and Catherine arrived. "About time... alright, let's get this started. Galen, in a moment you will be tested to see how good of a killing machine you really are."

"Perhaps I should start with you?" Galen said with total indifference. The muscles in Galen's face showed how angry he was.

Simon noticed this change in Galen. He had never seen him with such a desire to kill anyone – and as a matter of fact, he had never seen him so angry, ever. He wondered what had happened to bring out such rage in the normally mild-mannered mutant.

Edward walked over to the gold skinned mutant, looked him up and down, and then smiled. "I suppose you would like that. However, I will just warn you that any move against me will activate a capsule of poison gas that is attached to the air vents of your beloved Lisa's cell. If it activates, the ventilation will be sealed shut and the gas released. She will die, I promise you. Now, is that what you really want?"

Galen snorted, but then began to relax his muscles. Edward noticed this change in his stance. "Yes... I thought you might see my point of view on this. Very well, now for the test. Galen, you will wander out into the test area of the crater where you will be attacked by a squad of some very elite Secret Service soldiers. When you are attacked you will defend, and counter attack appropriately. In this test, you will either succeed... or you will die. If you die, then the experiment will be considered a failure and all mutants will be destroyed to prepare for the next hypothesis of mutation transformations. All mutants will be destroyed... except for Lisa... I have a feeling we are on the right track with her. That is... unless you show me the current mutations are capable of being a super warrior. Now, proceed with the test."

Edward stepped back and waved his hand, which activated a massive force field behind Galen. Then he pressed a button on his wrist controller, and disabled the shackles. "Now run in, and kill or be killed, mutant!"

Galen entered the test area slowly. From behind a rock, a sniper fired a blaster beam at the mutant. The beam hit him squarely in the head, but instead of killing him, ricocheted into the open sky. He turned and with his enhanced vision, saw the glistening of the sniper scope up high on the wall of the crater. He took a slow step, then with a sudden burst of speed ran up the wall, and stopped immediately in front of his attacker. He grabbed the rifle from his grasp, which tore the man's trigger finger off in the process. He bent the blaster rifle in half, then grabbed the helpless soldier, and twisted his body until his spine snapped.

In the distance, he heard the sound of a trigger moving. He turned and with his superior eyesight saw the outline of yet another soldier firing on him. With his quick movements, he avoided the oncoming blaster beam and ran to this attacker. The soldier pulled out a heat knife, and waved it in his face. The knife glowed causing heat waves to distort the air in front of Galen's eyes in a threatening manner. He wondered if this knife even posed a threat – he had not tested himself against this type of weapon. He now wondered how heat resistant his skin had become with the mutations.

He decided he would take no chances. He made a quick move to step behind his attacker. He then grabbed the man's arm and shoulder, and with a single quick stroke, pulled the arm off. The man screamed in pain as the mutant quickly put him out of his misery by twisting his head off of his body. He removed the knife from the detached hand and looked at it for a moment.

Galen looked around and saw two more soldiers in hiding. He realized they did not want to attack – for good reason he surmised. He was not going to give them a chance to change their minds however as he rushed across the crater wall to the closest human. The attackers became the prey as he quickly took down the first man with a swift flick of his wrist, sending the heat knife he was holding squarely into the soldier's forehead.

He then used his fast speed to run to the last soldier. The helpless soldier tried in vain to hit the quickly moving mutant with blaster beam after blaster beam. When he realized he had no chance, he turned, and began to run. Galen quickly caught up to the human, and quickly took the final soldier down with a series of motions – the first one broke the man's legs, the second broke his back, and finally the third pulled his head off his body.

The mutant threw the man's head with such force it flew hundreds of yards, landing right in front of Edward's feet. A moment later the gold skin mutant also appeared to the scientist.

"There, is that what you wanted? I hope you are satisfied now!" The anger had returned to the mutant.

Edward reactivated the shackles and deactivated the force field. Immediately after his shackles slammed his wrists together, his communicator activated. He stepped away from Galen, and looked at the Councilman in the booth. A moment later he disconnected, and returned to the mutant. "Yes, quite satisfied... you might actually do. You impressed the Councilman... and he pays the bills here."

He now turned to Catherine and Simon. "So, you saw what this experiment accomplished. It is time for your pussycat to put up or shut up... permanently. He will do the same test. He will kill, or die."

Catherine was shaking. Simon saw the fear in her eyes when he looked at her. Her head was shaking ever so slightly as she fought the feelings preventing her from releasing Simon into the test.

Simon felt Galen pressing to communicate. He opened his mind. "Simon, I am not sure about this. It may be too much without armored skin."

"I don't have a choice... " He replied. "And, to be honest... I'm not sure I can kill. I have never even come close to that level of violence... Perhaps I could just incapacitate them?"

"No, you will have to kill them. They will not stay down if you only try to maim them."

"I'm not sure I can do that..." Simon lightly retorted.

"You have to... put all of your animal instincts to the forefront of your brain... Let the human take a back seat. In this way, fight-or-flight will take over."

I'll try... For Catherine... And, like you said, what choice do I have?" He looked at Catherine – she was still holding tightly to his leash. "She needs to release me so I can at least try... or she will die."

Galen looked at Catherine, and nodded to her. She seemed to understand what Galen was suggesting she was to do – and with a tear in her eye, she bent over, and disconnected the leash from Simon's collar. "Please be careful. Avoid things like you did against the Ox... " she pleaded.

He looked into her eyes and let her hear a slight meow. She gave him a slight push to urge him into the testing area. Edward activated the force field. "Let the test begin. Soldiers, fire at will..."

Simon slowly walked into the area. He turned every sense he had into feline form. He heard the sound of movement to the left of him. His sharp eyesight caught the movement of one of the snipers on the hill. He jumped into a fast run before the sniper could get a bead on his position. He bounced between one rock and then another, hiding each time before he would move to the next position. He finally ended up behind a large rock just a few yards away from the sniper. He saw the sniper looking desperately for him down on the crater floor – his movements had fooled him.

He lowered his body and snuck in so quietly that the soldier never realized how close the feline was. With a quick motion, he pounced on the man, opened his mouth and sunk his teeth squarely around the man's neck. He squeezed his jaw, and felt the man's neck start to crush. With an instinctive motion, he then shook the man's head back and forth with violent motions. The motion snapped his neck with ease, and he went limp in his mouth. He found the taste of blood gave him a bit of killing lust – he also found he enjoyed it slightly, but was sure he would regret everything he would have to do at this moment later on.

His sharp vision caught the motion of another soldier aiming his blaster at him. He dropped the dead man to the ground, and jumped to the side avoiding the incoming beam. He ran to the attacker, seeing the flexes of his trigger finger with his sharp vision. He was able to judge when he was squeezing the trigger, and this allowed him to bounce into a different direction, thus avoiding each deadly bolt.

As he reached the soldier, he jumped, and with multiple swipes of his extended claws he ripped the man's face to shreds. One final swipe of his claws across the man's neck took out his Jugular vein, sending him to the ground to die – blood spurted up into the air.

The sound of an incoming blaster beam was barely heard in time for Simon to jump, and dodge. The bolt grazed his fur, making a horrible smell in his nose. He ran behind a large rock and licked the burning hair – he did not want smoke to give him away. He heard another sound behind him, it was another soldier.

He slunk around to see one of the soldiers trying to sneak up on his previous position. Being as quiet as possible he came up behind the man and pounced again. This time he slashed and clawed at the man's lower back – cutting through tough armor and muscle within a matter of seconds. He did not stop until he had exposed all of his entrails. The soldier never knew what hit him.

He climbed up to a high ridge on the crater wall, and ran around looking for the last two soldiers. He finally located them – one just a small distance from the other. He decided he needed a little bit of human strategy for this attack. He began slinking down toward the closest soldier – when he finally reached him, he jumped to the side of the waiting attacker, and with a quick hand grabbed the barrel of the blaster rifle. He pushed on the rifle, and with his precise vision was able to point the weapon at the other soldier right as the soldier instinctively pulled the trigger. The soldier in the distance quickly fell to the ground.

With that threat out of the way, he extended two sharp claws, poked them into the man's eyes, which blinded him and caused him to scream. He then extended all of his razor-sharp claws, and slashed the throat of the helpless man in two swift motions. He took the man's life quickly and easily. He dropped the dangling head, which caused the corpse to hit the jagged lava rock with a thud. He started licking the blood off of his soiled paw, and found he enjoyed the flavor. After a minute, he finished his cleaning and looked around, but saw no other threats.

"I did it! Wow... " He began to proudly walk down the slope to rejoin the group. *"I guess this might give my true awareness away. Well, maybe now I can actually let Catherine know..."*

He was too deep into his own thoughts. He had lost his concentration, and had totally forgotten the sights and sounds of the battlefield. He was about half way down the slope when he finally heard the noise – it was the flexing of a finger on the trigger of a blaster. He suddenly realized he was being fired upon, so he attempted to jump out of the way. The pain he felt in his leg told him he had not jumped in time. He turned and saw the soldier he thought was dead – he was barely alive, and was somehow able to have gotten a shot off. Simon found that instinctively, he was still able to run. He quickly turned, and ran back to the man to make quick work out of him.

He looked at his back leg – blood flowed from the site where the beam had punctured his body. He let out a slight moan, then trotted down the hill to the waiting group. Edward turned off the force field, and Simon approached Catherine. He looked up at her – then things got woozy – his head began to spin, and he fell over. Catherine dropped to her knees, took off her lab coat, and used it to apply pressure to the wound.

"Get me a wound healer!" She cried out.

Edward's communicator sounded again, and once again he stepped away to speak with the Councilman. After he disconnected, he returned to the wounded feline hybrid, and stared at him lying on the ground. He shook his head. "What a waste... all that time, work and money for what... he did not even make it through the first test. This form of sub-human is not worth the effort... we need to start testing with making sub-humans from mutants instead. I think that is a much better route to take for future warriors"

He turned, walked a few feet away from Simon and Catherine, and then stopped at a group of soldiers. He pointed at Simon, and coldly said "Soldier, kill that pitiful creature. Kill the troublemaking bitch too."

The soldier did as he was commanded, and raised his rifle toward Simon. Before he fired however, he heard a scuffle behind him. He turned to find that Galen was no longer in sight.

Edward also heard the scuffle, and also turned to find Galen missing. "Where the hell did that freak go?" he pondered out loud.

"Right here..." he said over the area PA system. Edward looked up to find Galen in the observation booth, with the councilman. He somehow had broken his electronic shackles, and now had Councilman Helman by the neck. His powerful hands ready to squeeze the life out of the dangling, thin, Blessed man. "That creature is valuable... " he announced. "He may have gotten injured, but he killed every one of your soldiers. I think that is not a bad outcome... considering he went out there with no weapons or protective armor... only his natural abilities." He looked at the Councilman and said "Wouldn't you agree?"

Jared Helman nodded in agreement, then leaned into the microphone. "Yes, he passed the test... release him and get him to medical... let her live too."

Galen turned off the PA, and whispered in his ear "Do not think you can change your mind and reverse your decision... if you do, I will find you... and I will... and then you will die. These binders will not stop me... and I will be able to both find you... and kill you should you go back on your word. This institute, and the dead zone outside will not stop me... I will succeed if I need to. Do you understand?"

Jared gave a disgusted look "I am a Councilman of the Order... I will NOT go back on my words or my orders, Mutant."

He released Jared, and took a step back. "That was what I wanted to hear... " he raised his arms and allowed the shackles to click back together, re-binding his hands. The guards ran into the booth and began striking Galen with their stun sticks. He just stood there and smiled at Jared. "I will be counting on you... and your word... " Finally, he rolled into a ball and fell to the floor. Jared could tell he was faking it – the stun sticks had no effect on him or his system. But Galen wanted to give the guards some feeling of accomplishment – that they could stop him if needed.

The guards picked up Galen, and dragged him out of the booth. Jared stood in both fear and amazement at the large mutant being taken away. Sweat dripped down his forehead as he watched them take him away.

Now being safe, he silently walked out of the booth, and across the complex to his awaiting Hovercar. He silently got in, and right before the vehicle sped away he messaged Edward "Your project appears to be successful... carry on with the work that you, and Doctor Harmony have been doing... Take no further action against the mutant. However, you may want to continue your work on mind control... "

Edward cringed as he heard the words. The realization of having to spare Catherine repulsed him. He now faced the reality that he would have to continue to put up with her. "Take that cat back to his cell. Return to your work Doctor... " he said as he turned and walked away from the pair. He raised his hand and waved it in dismissal as he walked away.

She called over the orderlies to bring a stretcher. They all worked to get Simon on the stretcher, then transported him to his cell in the living quarters. She tended his wounds, and sat with him for the remainder of the day. She found he showed quick progress in healing – he would be fine.

Finally, she left Simon, and returned to her quarters. She plopped herself onto the couch, meditated to calmness, and then spent the rest of the evening just thinking – thinking of a way to get both her and Simon out and away from both the institute, and the plans of Edward.

27

"As you may know, recently the Starlight Space Ark left our Solar System to find a new planet that could be made a home for our illustrious Blessed. In monitoring their flight, when they passed through the asteroid belt, they somehow knocked asteroid M-543 out of its orbit. Astronomers have been curiously watching the now moving asteroid, and they have made an amazing discovery. It has somehow been attracted to the gravitational force of Haley's Comet, and is now following it on its journey around the Solar System. Yes, Haley's will come in close proximity to Earth on its journey... but Alliance astronomers say not to worry... M-543 will continue to follow the comet, and will pose no threat to any part of our amazing Hemispheric Order. This is Connie Dahlia, reporting from the Alliance Astronomical Research Facility."

He turned off the news, shook his head, smiled, and then let out a slight chuckle. Edward was feeling very pleased with himself tonight – news of his Blessed brethren always gave him new hope. He had been looking over the progress reports for the numerous projects around the institute and everything was going forward nicely – he had a lot to be hopeful about.

He had a very successful test with the mutant, and even Piccolo managed to take out the soldiers in his test – although he really wanted to terminate him and Catherine. Nonetheless, it still ended up well. He was finally having some major breakthroughs with Project Fury Warrior. With the successful transformation of Cora Lee, and the mind control device now keeping her a willing semi-intelligent slave, he felt this project now had real direction.

The progress he had made utilizing the discoveries from Project Mutated Healing was stupendous. By modifying the mutations, he had been able to make what he felt was a superior warrior – almost as good as the warrior created by his Fury Warrior project. As a matter of fact, he had Derrick and Stephanie create even more bonding devices. There were now one hundred devices, transforming hundreds of people a day – curing them, and then turning them into exquisite warriors. He could then manipulate them as needed by using Project Fury Warrior – rearranging genetic material as needed to create a specific soldier for a specific purpose.

His only concern was control – he knew he did not have proper control over them in their mutated state. Yes, they appeared to do exactly what he told them, they appeared to train hard, and were becoming ready for battle with the south. But there was just something bothering him about them. Maybe it was something about the way Galen had both escaped, gotten to the Councilman, then was subdued so quickly and easily that bothered him.

Then there was the matter of their mutations. On a consistent basis, he had programmed changes into the mutation algorithms – changes where he had hoped to improve the fighting power of the mutants. But every time he implemented a change, nothing happened. The computer validated that his changes to the DNA were made, but he never saw the results. Stephanie insisted they were just too radical of changes, and thus the body was refusing to allow those radical changes to take hold. But Edward was not so sure this was the case – but he had nothing to back up his suspicions.

Then there was his success with the transformation of a mutant. Injecting the bird DNA into Lisa was a stroke of genius, Edward thought. She accepted the bond completely, and her mutated body transformed perfectly. She had her mind intact, and took all of the changes he desired. He would like to monitor her closely, to guarantee there were no side effects from the process. But Galen so far had prevented him from getting close enough to Lisa to examine her. He personally felt threatened whenever he tried to approach her. Galen eventually would have to be taken care of – perhaps a mind control device would be in order.

That thought gave him a laugh. *"Yes, that might just be the ticket..."* he said to himself. The thought of Galen under his complete control made him feel good.

That brought up another concern regarding the mutants. Since he had performed the successful transformation of Lisa, the other mutants had started to develop wings. He wondered if there was some genetic code being passed between them that was causing the whole of the mutant population to change when a single member changed. He had not had time to check all of the mutants, but in any case, mutants having wings could only be of benefit to them on the battlefield.

He popped another bora berry into his mouth. He considered his next move regarding the transformation schedule for the mutants. He had prepared a schedule to transform a mutant a day into a creature of his choosing – more for fun, than anything else. He wished he had constructed more disintegration/reintegration arrays. He could quickly make an army of mutant Fury Warriors for the Council. He would be seen as the savior of the north. He wondered if the transformations would continue to spread throughout the population. *"Now THAT would be an interesting combination of creatures!"* he thought.

Then there was the matter of Catherine and Piccolo. He really knew deep inside that the demonstration was a success. However outwardly, he made it very clear he felt the project was a complete failure. He really felt that he had done more good mixing the projects, as she had done with a single subject. As a matter of fact, due to all the other recent successes, he really no longer needed those two. It was definitely time for them to go. He needed a way to countermand the Councilman's directive.

He popped yet another bora berry in his mouth, and just thought about the situation. Then, with a smile on his face, he reached across his desk and activated his communication device – after a moment, Catherine answered.

"Yes Doctor, what do you need?" she asked with annoyance in her voice.

"Catherine, I have decided that your project is officially a failure..." he said with a huge smile across his pink-lipped mouth.

"What? But wait Edward – "

"No, you've had plenty of time... Your subject... Piccolo has not come around. As a matter of fact, he seems about as stupid and ignorant as my earliest attempts! Despite his partial success in the demonstration, he really is just a stupid animal going on instincts. No, he and you are failures. I have decided to shut down your experiment. You are now dismissed from service here. I want you to leave the Institute first thing tomorrow."

"But what about Simon?" she asked.

"He is of no value to me. I'm going to have him destroyed... very likely in the most slow and painful way I can come up with... Because... well... just because he's annoyed me greatly. Perhaps

I'll just bake him in the oven… " he laughed knowing that was precisely what he had decided to do with this annoyance.

"Now wait Edward, you can't do that!" she demanded.

"Oh yes I can… and will. There's nothing you can do about it. I'm going to pop him in the oven first thing tomorrow… " he said with total seriousness, then disconnected the communication.

He suddenly felt even better. *"Perhaps some more bora berries to celebrate… "*

*   *   *

After Edward's call, Catherine was in shock. She knew he eventually would have gotten the nerve to remove her – but not to destroy Simon. This whole experiment had just been an emotional disaster to her. She had found herself not able to concentrate recently – her mind was just too occupied with, and worried for Simon. And now this – he was going to bake her Simon.

Tears began to swell in her eyes – she had to control them, she needed to be able to think. Somehow, she needed to figure out a way to save him. She looked around the room for something to take her mind off her sadness, but she could not do it. The tears started rolling down her soft white cheeks. She softly sobbed, because she felt unable to do anything to change the future.

"Why Simon, why didn't you come around? You were so smart and intelligent, and I could have sworn you were really there with me. WHY?" she cried out.

Trying once again to maintain control she looked down at the coffee table. On the table was the portable computer with the crossword puzzle program that she had given to Simon. She picked up the device, and just stared at it. *"Oh Simon, I could have sworn this would have brought you out… but it didn't."*

Trying to control herself, she turned on the device. She thought that by doing one of the puzzles, it would allow her to gain control of her mental state, and then she might be able to come up with an idea. The first puzzle displayed on the screen. To her surprise, this puzzle was already completed. She distinctly remembered putting clean puzzles on this computer. She requested the next puzzle – it was also completed. She went to the third of the four puzzles on the computer, and once again it had been completed.

She then switched to the fourth puzzle, and her eyes opened wide as she saw nine words that had been entered on the final puzzle. The words were not correct puzzle answers, and were indicated in flashing red letters by the program:

"I am still here do not tell anyone rebellion"

Her face now showed a large smile, and she also now had a look of pure determination. *"My god Simon, you were somehow able to do these without anyone finding out!"* She turned off the computer, and headed for the door. She then stopped, and ran to the closet. She put on her lab coat, and attached her id badge. Then, she walked over to a wall cabinet, and pulled out two weapons – a blaster, and a stun gun. She hoped she would only require the latter. Then she headed out the door – she was going to find Simon, and do whatever it took to help him escape.

She stopped right as she stepped into the hallway, looked back at the crossword computer, and said questioningly "Rebellion?"

The end of book 3 – The Civilization of Nature: Alterations and Mutations